An excerpt from *Fever Dream*

A stagehand wove past him with two vases of roses and Petra gestured him to the table beside her vanity where the pink ones already lay. One of the vases overflowed with white roses and the other, significantly larger, with red. He knew the white ones were from Liam and Ashleigh.

Rubio had ordered the red.

He had second guesses now. Was that the expression? Second thoughts? The flowers seemed too garish in her cramped dressing room. Five dozen roses was probably too much. He would have left the room with the stagehand and Yves, but she'd already grabbed the card. *Muitos abraços*, he'd written. *Many hugs*, in Portuguese. He had signed it "R." He had not written *I think you're marvelous*, or *You smell like vanilla and sugar*, or even *I wish you were a horny, cowering, deeply masochistic submissive*, and he was glad for that now.

She read the two handwritten words aloud with an awful accent. He repeated it to her the right way.

"What does it mean?" she asked. "It's from you, right? These are from you?"

Before he could answer she buried her face in the bouquet, taking a deep breath. It was the same thing he wanted to do to her hair. "My goodness," she said. "They're so beautiful." She turned and threw her arms around him. They touched all the time but this felt heightened. Different.

"It means many hugs," he said against her hair. He smelled it furtively. Someday he would ask what shampoo she used. "It's a usual Portuguese greeting or whatever, to be nice."

"But you're only being nice because this was our first time dancing together, huh?"

"Yes," he said. He thought he might be blushing. It wasn't good.

Fever Dream

by

Annabel Joseph

Other erotic romance by Annabel Joseph

Mercy
Cait and the Devil
Firebird
Deep in the Woods
Fortune
Owning Wednesday
Lily Mine
Comfort Object
Caressa's Knees
Odalisque
Command Performance
Cirque de Minuit
Burn For You
Disciplining the Duchess
The Edge of the Earth (as Molly Joseph)
Waking Kiss

Erotica by Annabel Joseph

Club Mephisto
Molly's Lips: Club Mephisto Retold

For Maryara
Muitos abraços
(many hugs)

Chapter One:
Disgusting

Fernando Rubio vaulted up the steps of the grand white town house, his stormy Brazilian temper in full effect. He drew back a fist and banged it on his friends' front door.

"Liam. Ashleigh! *Ash-lee!* I know you're in there. Open up."

The door swung wide and a slight, elderly man peered out. "Mr. Rubio. What a pleasure to see you."

He pushed past Mem and stalked into the house. "Where are they?"

"They are downstairs. They undoubtedly"—Mem slipped around the front of him—"undoubtedly wish for privacy at the moment."

Rubio waved a hand, heading for the Wilders' BDSM-equipped basement. "Whatever they're doing, it's nothing I haven't seen before."

"If you would be so kind as to wait in the living room—"

Ruby ignored Mem's polite but pointed protests and continued through the luxurious home to the lower floor. He stopped halfway down the stairs, scanning the play room until he located the naked couple. *Oh, God.* "That's disgusting!"

At his barked exclamation, Liam turned to search for him with a frown. "Do you mind? Very bad timing, my friend."

"You are both disgusting."

The tall, long-haired man wrapped his arms more tightly around his petite partner. "Why, disgusting? I'm kissing my wife."

"Exactly. You have this entire den of depravity, sex toys and BDSM furniture," he said, waving a hand around the dimly-lit basement, "and you are standing there kissing her."

"Not only that—we just made love," Liam said. "Tender, sappy, emotional, gaze-into-each-other's-eyes kind of love."

"With lots and lots of whispered endearments," Ashleigh added.

"Ugh." Ruby spun and started back the way he'd come. "I'll wait upstairs. You're both..." He searched his mind for an adequate insult. "You're both completely disgusting." He wagged a finger at Ashleigh. "And you! I am furious with you."

He turned his back on her apologetic expression and took the stairs two at a time. There was nothing she could say to excuse her behavior, nothing he wanted to listen to, anyway.

Mem greeted him back in the living room. "Would you care for some refreshment, Mr. Rubio? Coffee? Tea?" He took in Ruby's dour expression. "Something stronger?"

"I don't want anything," he snapped, "except to unsee what I just saw." Oh, and for Ashleigh to not leave City Ballet. He wanted that more than anything.

He collapsed onto one of the living room's deep leather sofas and put his head in his hands. He and Ash had been partners for four years now, achieving new heights of artistry with each ballet. How could she leave him now, after all they'd created together? After all the work they'd done?

A few moments later Ashleigh appeared from below, clad in Liam's black tee. At least he assumed it was Liam's since it hung to her knees. She hugged the shirt around her waist and crossed to sit next to Rubio on the couch.

"Well?" he said. "I'm waiting for your explanation. Why are you leaving?"

"I'm not leaving. I mean, I'm not leaving London." She leaned forward, rubbing her knees. "I'm just taking a break from dancing."

He felt unreasonable anger at her offhand tone. "A break? No. You're quitting the company. That's what Yves told me after class. Why didn't you warn me? You didn't tell me nothing until today. Then, boom."

She lowered her head, her black locks falling across her cheeks. "I was afraid to tell you, so I let Yves do it."

"Well, I almost punched him in the face. That would have been your fault. And how do you think he feels?" Yves Thibault was City Ballet's director-in-chief, and he'd seemed almost as upset as Rubio by the news.

She touched his hand on the cushion between them and then wrapped her fingers around his. "I'm sorry. I didn't know how to tell you. I don't know what to say to you, even now."

He felt choking emotion. Cold betrayal and loss. Ashleigh was his favorite ballet partner of all time. They danced everything together, in perfect, comfortable harmony. "Why?" he asked. "What did I do?"

"It's not you."

"I know I'm rude sometimes. I know I always touch your tits and pretend it was an accident. I know, it's bad. I won't do it anymore, I swear."

"It's not that," she said, squeezing his hand tighter. "I've loved working with you. These past few years have been a dream, both personally and professionally." Her pale blue-gray eyes communicated the same pain he felt, the pain that had devastated him when Yves broke the news an hour ago.

"Why then?" he whispered. "Why?"

She let go of his hand and picked at the hem of Liam's shirt. "I'm tired, okay? Ballet has always been easy for you because you're a natural, a phenomenon. It's a struggle for me. I want to... I want to try something different."

Liam joined them with two beers. He sat on the arm of the couch beside his wife, passing one of the bottles to his friend. "You realize you're being a total pussy about this, right? A pathetic crybaby pussy?"

"Stop it," Ashleigh said, reaching over to her husband. "It's hard for dancers to lose a partner. Over time you develop this really transcendent bond, almost like brother and sister."

Or husband and wife. Rubio had pined for Ashleigh years ago, when she was dating Liam. Sometimes he still did, even though his friends were happily married and completely devoted to each other. Ashleigh turned back to him, pleading with him to understand. "You taught me so much about ballet and artistry, so much about performance. I feel horrible leaving you, but...Liam and I are having a baby. I'm three months pregnant. I won't be able to dance next season because of that."

Rubio's eyes went wide. A *baby*? "Is this a joke?" he sputtered. "Your belly is completely flat."

"I'm not showing yet, but believe me, I'm pregnant. Remember how I kept throwing up on the summer tour?"

Ruby put his hands to his head. "*Jesus Cristo*. Why you need a baby? I need a partner! What about that?"

"Watch your tone with my wife," Liam said.

Ruby turned to jab a finger at him. "This is your fault."

"Everything is everyone else's fault, huh?" said Liam. "Maybe it's your fault. You introduced us, if you'll remember."

"Yes, but I didn't imagine all this kissing and getting married and making love and...and babies."

Liam shrugged. "That's what grown-ups do."

Ashleigh turned to Ruby, edging Liam out of the conversation. "Look, there are a lot of talented dancers you can partner with at the company. I'm sure Yves will let you dance with whoever you want."

"Except you," he groused. "I can't dance with you."

"A few months from now I'll be big as a whale. Right? You won't want to dance with me."

Ruby couldn't stop the half-smile. "Don't try to be cute. Don't be funny. I'm angry at you."

"I know. I'm sorry." She wrapped her arms around him and hugged him tight. Rubio waited for her to start laughing, to tell him this was all a joke. She didn't look pregnant. She didn't feel pregnant, but Ashleigh, his favorite partner, his soul-mate partner, was pregnant and he didn't know what he was going to do.

"Maybe I'll quit too," he grumbled against her neck. "Maybe I'll stop dancing. Maybe now it's time."

She pulled away from him in horror. "No, you can't. Don't even say that."

"Pussy," Liam muttered from behind her.

"You have years left to dance," she said, truly alarmed. "You're only thirty years old."

"You're only twenty-eight!"

"It's different with men and women. You're stronger than me and..." She put her hands over her belly. "I really want to have this baby right now. It's time for me to do this. I feel it in my heart."

"Stop begging him to understand, hon," said Liam. "It's Rubio, remember? He's obnoxious and self-centered. He'll never understand the impulse to start a family, but eventually he'll get over it. Won't you?" Liam shot him a dire look.

Ashleigh dropped her head onto Rubio's shoulder. "I just feel like...this is the time. I should have told you," she said, lifting her eyes to meet his gaze. "I should have warned you we were making these plans but I didn't want you to be angry."

"Well, I'm angry."

"But Ruby—"

"I gave you so much. So whatever. Maybe I forgive you someday, but not now. No."

At those words, tears filled her eyes. She jumped to her feet and fled the room.

Liam sighed, sliding down onto the couch. "Very nice. Making a pregnant woman cry. I hope you're proud of yourself."

"What did I say?"

"God, you're an idiot." Liam snatched away his beer. "I would make you go apologize, but that would probably upset her more. Plus the pregnancy hormones are making her erratic and she might kick you in the neck." He bent forward and fixed Ruby with his potent amber stare. "But seriously. If you're going to keep coming over here, if you're going to attend the play parties on Saturdays, you're going to have to cut her some slack. She's pregnant and it can't be undone."

Ruby eyed his friend, noting the subtle tension in his voice. "You and her planned this pregnancy? Or it just happened?"

Liam rubbed his forehead. "It was kind of planned. It kind of just happened. She wants a couple kids, and..." He covered his eyes and kneaded his palms into his eye sockets. "I'm going to be okay with that."

"You're going to be, or you are?" Liam's silence was deafening. Ruby sighed and took back his beer. "Ashleigh is a good girl, you know. She won't be like your mother."

"My mother had postpartum depression. Any woman can get it. Ashleigh too."

"But if she does, you'll be there to help. It won't be the same."

"I know." That was all he said. *I know.* He stood and started toward the stairs. "I better go see if she's okay." He turned back to Ruby and gave a regretful half-shrug. "Look, I'm sorry you're losing your partner. I don't mean to be a bastard to you, but I'm on Team Ashleigh. I have to be. I'm asking you friend to friend, and I really hope you hear me: Let her go."

"I will," he sighed. "I don't have a choice, do I? But who the hell am I supposed to dance with now?"

"It doesn't matter who. You're the best dancer in the *world*, Ruby. Pick someone. Don't be a pussy, for fuck's sake."

With those words, his friend went up the wide marble staircase to comfort his wife.

Chapter Two:
Horrible

Petra squeezed her hands in her lap, a mess of nerves in the back of a black sedan. She was just in from New York, where drivers sat on the other side of the car, and cars drove on the other side of the road. She didn't often regret her single status, only at times like these when she would have liked someone friendly sitting beside her telling her everything would be okay.

And everything would be okay. This dinner wasn't an audition. Petra Hewitt had reached the point in her career where she didn't have to audition. She was the world's premier ballerina and she could pick and choose where she wanted to dance. Companies courted her, theater directors begged her for appearances. Last week, out of the blue, she'd been offered a position at London City Ballet, an offer that included an impressive salary, a furnished luxury "flat," and a driver to take her to and from the theater. But those perks weren't the main draw...

Fernando Rubio danced at London City Ballet.

He was called The Great Rubio, for his partnering skills, his graceful strength and instinctive touch. It was a stupid name, but the ballet press had coined it in his heady younger days, and over the years it had stuck. People also called him "this generation's Petr Grigolyuk" because of his sex appeal, and because women congregated outside the stage door squealing and jostling each other to get a look at him. As it happened, Grigolyuk was Petra's father and she didn't consider any comparison to the man flattering. In fact, she hoped Fernando Rubio was nothing like her asshole of a dad.

Well, she would soon find out. She twitched at her plum-colored silk dress and turned her clutch over in her lap. The sedan eased up to the curb of The Gilded Swan and the smiling driver told her in a charming accent to "hold tight, luv." He got out and shooed some photographers away. London had paparazzi, like New York, although not as many, and surely not for her. These photogs would snap Rubio's photo in a heartbeat, but she didn't share his widespread playboy appeal. She was a serious dancer. Once the driver helped her from the car, she strode into the restaurant without cracking a smile.

"Petra?" A tall, thin, middle-aged man with wire-rimmed glasses emerged from the press of elegant people standing inside the door. He held out a hand to her. "How wonderful to see you."

She recognized Yves Thibault at once. He was well-known in dance circles, admired for his work as the head director of City Ballet. She returned his smile as he kissed her on both cheeks. "I'm so glad to finally meet you in person," she said.

"How was your flight? Is the hotel to your liking?"

He pelted her with polite questions as he led her to a table set for three in the corner. After all her nerves, The Great Rubio wasn't even here. Yves pulled out her chair and a waiter came to fuss over them and offer menu suggestions. "What a lovely place," she said, looking around the opulent restaurant. White tablecloths, gleaming china, sparkling chandeliers. It was old world *richesse*, ornate and glittering. Like ballet, it seemed to be trying very hard to be beautiful.

"Mr. Rubio will join us shortly," said Yves, glancing over the menu. "He's excited to meet you. Everyone at City Ballet is thrilled you're considering our company."

Yves' French accent clipped each of the words; perhaps he felt as nervous as she. Petra sat very straight, surreptitiously watching the door. She might look down on Fernando's bad-boy, sex-appeal image, but she was curious to meet him and see what he was like. He could do great things for her as a partner. In some way, they belonged together since they were both acknowledged as the world's best dancers. Their pairing at City Ballet would be legendary. Historical.

She drew in a deep breath and reached for her water as soon as the waiter poured it. That's when she saw him, mid-sip. The Great Rubio crossed toward them in a tailored suit and tie, looking more "fashion-week" than formal. He was the epitome of tall, dark, and handsome— she'd known that—but in person he was so much more. He had an *aura*, a way of moving that communicated both sensuality and masculine power. Female heads turned, mouths dropped open. They all got that *look*.

Petra tried not to have that look when he locked eyes with her, but it was difficult. He was strikingly, alarmingly sexy. His height, his confidence, the way he moved, the way he presented himself. He was gigolo material, with his tousled black hair and dark eyes, and that carved Brazilian jaw line.

Be cool, Petra. He's just a guy. She took another sip of water, reminding herself that they'd asked her here, that they wanted her, not the other way around. She had nothing to prove, nothing to live up to except a pleasant dinner between contemporaries. She glanced up from beneath her lashes as he navigated the last of the candle-lit tables to arrive in their private corner. Somewhere along the line his casual smile had transformed to a scowl. He stopped a few steps from the table and glowered at her like he wished he could throw a knife through her solar plexus. "No," he said, turning to Yves. "I said no. Why did you bring her here?"

Hm, not a knife. An axe. Fernando Rubio wanted to bury an axe in her rib cage, she could see it in the black depths of his eyes. Cold anger washed over her.

"You said he was excited to meet me," she said, turning to Yves.

"Yes, well—"

"Yes, well," Fernando cut in, "sorry you made the trip for nothing. We don't need another principal here."

Yves gave him a harried look. "Yes, we do. We've lost two principals recently. Ashleigh and Mariel have both retired."

"You said we were meeting to talk about the ballets for next year," Fernando said to Yves.

"We will. We are. Now, if you've made enough of a scene, perhaps you'll consider sitting down and behaving like a civil person."

The director's voice never rose above a level tone, but the reprimand was obvious. Rubio snapped his mouth shut and slid into the remaining seat, fidgeting with his jewel-patterned tie. He angled himself away from her, as if to deny her presence. Petra felt gob-smacked. She'd flown all the way across the ocean, only to sit here and endure his scorn?

"We talked about this," he said to Yves in a stage whisper. "You said I got to pick. I told you, specifically, not this."

At "this," he flicked a finger at her, the ballerina-who-must-not-be-named.

"What's wrong?" She shot him an arch look. "Afraid I'll outshine you if I join the company?"

"Outshine me?" Fernando snorted. "Maybe in makeup you outshine me. You have a tragically big forehead."

Yves made a faint, distressed sound as Petra drew herself up to her full height, which was not very high.

"I do *not* have a big forehead," she said. "And I find it hypocritical that you'd talk about my 'tragically big' forehead considering those massive feet you drag around the stage."

His expression hardened. "My feet are not massive. I have the best feet in ballet."

"No, *I* have the best feet in ballet," she corrected him. "Everyone knows that. Your feet are big and square like...like bricks."

"Petra, Rubio, please, people are staring—" Yves tried to interject.

"Me and my big feet do not want to dance with you," Fernando snapped. "I need a partner with grace and lyrical beauty. Not a big-forehead robot like you."

She gasped. "I'm not a robot."

"You dance like a robot. You're famous because you're Grigolyuk's daughter," he said, waving a hand. "Nothing more."

That flippant wave infuriated her. She hated Fernando Rubio, hated him for dismissing her fame and accomplishments like they were nothing. She'd earned everything she'd achieved through her own hard work, not her father's support. Grigolyuk had never even acknowledged her, although everyone knew he and her mother had had a torrid affair when they were partners at the New York Metropolitan Ballet, and that Petra looked exactly like him, down to his light blond hair and Slavic hazel eyes. And yeah, her mom had named her Petra to drive the point home.

But Hillary Hewitt had never demanded a paternity test or financial support. "Petr knows he's your father," she used to say. "If he doesn't want you, we don't want him."

To this day, Petra lived by those words. She threw her napkin beside her plate and pushed back her chair.

"Forget it," she said to Yves. "If he doesn't want me, I don't want him."

The slim, stolid director shot up from his seat and followed her as she stormed toward the door.

"Petra, please, let me explain." He drew her over by the coat room and spoke in a low, urgent voice. "Rubio wants you—he just doesn't know it yet. He's in a bad place right now. He was..." Yves paused, frowning. "He was very close to his previous partner."

Well, that wasn't the way to make Petra rethink things. After all the pain her father caused her mom, she was dead set against partner relationships. She wondered if The Great Rubio had knocked up Ashleigh Keaton, if that was why she'd left ballet.

"He doesn't even know me," she said. "How can he be so rude?"

Yves looked over his shoulder to where his star dancer sat alone, tapping his fingers on the table. "He's a bit rough around the edges. Temperamental, like many artists. You shouldn't take it personally. He doesn't mean anything by it."

"I don't care how famous he is. I'm an artist too, and I'm not temperamental and condescending. I can dance with anyone in the world, anywhere I want to. New York, Paris, Berlin, Moscow." She knew she sounded bitchy but, for God's sake, she did *not* have a big forehead. She felt embarrassed and disappointed. Rejected. "You misled me," she said. "I came here because you said Fernando Rubio wanted to dance with me."

"He does! I promise you he does, it's only a matter of adjustment and change."

"You asked me here knowing he would refuse me. That doesn't inspire a lot of trust."

Yves sighed and removed his glasses. "I asked you here because he chased off the previous four prospects, and you're the only one left."

"What?" That kicked her ego right in the gut. "So I was your last-ditch choice? Really?"

"No, you were the most expensive choice. With Mr. Rubio on the payroll, we couldn't afford another renowned dancer until a certain donor—who wishes to remain anonymous—agreed to foot the bill for your salary. I invited you to come the same day." He put a hand over his lips and looked massively stressed out for a moment. He'd composed his expression by the time he looked up again. "Petra, you of all people must understand. Mr. Rubio needs a certain caliber of partner to inspire and motivate him, and that type of partner doesn't grow on trees. You are his best match in the ballet world at the moment. The two of you could become a legend, one of those pairings that inspires a whole new generation of students to dance."

We could, thought Petra, *if he wasn't such a braying ass.*

"He said that he'd already told you no," she said. "So why—"

"Mr. Rubio is saying no to everyone and everything right now," Yves said, cutting her off. "Again, you shouldn't take it personally."

"It's hard not to take it personally when someone says you dance like a robot."

"We all know you don't dance like a robot. Please, give him a little time and space to redeem himself. You know, he and his previous partner began their acquaintance under terrible circumstances."

"Ashleigh Keaton? But they were—"

"Amazing together? Certainly, but they first met under the pressure of a last minute substitution. She wasn't prepared, he was incensed. He called her a whale, if I remember correctly."

"He called her a *whale*?"

"And she accidentally kicked him during the *pas de deux*, barely missing his testicles," he said, setting off the *accidentally* with air quotes. "He stormed away after the curtain call and she ran to the dressing rooms and vomited. Repeatedly. It was a disaster, but from such beginnings they developed into one of the most notable partnerships City Ballet has ever known."

"So what happened? Why did she leave the company?"

"Ashleigh is expecting a baby in the spring."

She knew it! She shot a vicious glance at Fernando. "By him?"

Yves' eyes widened. "No, by her husband. Ashleigh and Rubio were friends, nothing more. When he gets to know you better, he will be your friend too. Please, don't leave yet. Dance with him tomorrow so he can see all you have to give, what a perfectly matched partner you'd be. We're rehearsing *Romeo and Juliet* for the fall. Perhaps you already know the choreography."

Petra sniffed and pulled at the clasp of her clutch. Of course she knew the choreography. *Romeo and Juliet* was a much-loved ballet, even if the maudlin, misery-of-cursed-love theme was a bit overblown. At twenty-eight, she'd danced the lead role in five different productions.

"If he wants to dance, I'll dance. But if all I get from him is attitude, I'm heading back to New York." She looked past Yves to where Rubio sat scowling at the table. "And I'd rather not stay for dinner. I seem to have lost my appetite."

Yves squeezed her hands. "Of course. I'm sorry. I'll make this up to you, and I promise you'll receive an apology from Mr. Rubio."

Petra wouldn't hold her breath on that one. She climbed into the back of a cab, still fuming. She'd really wanted things to work out here. London City Ballet had great facilities, savvy management, and some of the most lavish productions in the world. There was a history here, a history that extended far beyond that of the companies she'd danced for in the US. Her father had chosen to dance with City Ballet after he left Russia...and he still lived in London.

That wasn't why she wanted to be here, of course, although she'd had fleeting fantasies of him coming to meet her after a performance. Of the two of them hanging out and bonding backstage. Since her earliest years, she'd imagined a scene where her father would come to find her, perhaps in her dressing room, or in the dark hush of the wings. He would hold out his arms and smile and say, "I'm so proud to call you my daughter. I'm sorry now I was never part of your life."

She wanted to jab an ice pick in her brain whenever she had those fantasies. Grigolyuk had turned on Hillary Hewitt as soon as he found out she was pregnant with Petra, destroying her ballet career. He hadn't even come to her funeral a few years ago. Petra had been walking around wearing his face for twenty-eight years without the least acknowledgement of her existence, so why expect him to come meet her now? It was a stupid fantasy and it wasn't even really a fantasy because she didn't want it to happen.

As for The "Great" Rubio, she'd dance with him tomorrow for Yves' sake, but that was it. One chance to redeem himself, or she'd be out of here like Ashleigh Keaton.

No wonder the woman had gotten herself knocked up—anything to get away from him. Four years of Fernando's brand of professionalism, and Petra would be stark raving mad.

* * * * *

Rubio banged open the elevator and stepped into the stillness of his soaring, cement-walled loft. He threw his keys on a table and collapsed on the couch, running his fingers through his hair. Petra Hewitt. Damn it.

He'd only seen her perform two times, but that was enough to know he didn't want her as a partner. She was too perfect, horribly perfect, and he didn't like it. She danced like a robot, like an alien from some ballet planet where no one made mistakes. Her body was perfect, her balance, her technique, her face, her hands and feet, all perfect. She was so flawless that she shook his normally unshakable confidence, and he didn't need that in his life right now. Petra Hewitt danced like she was tiptoeing over the skulls of her enemies—and he was pretty sure he'd made an enemy of her tonight.

He bit off a few Portuguese expletives and reached for his phone to message Liam. *Call me, a-hole. U suck.*

He went to the kitchen for an apple and then walked over to the wall of windows to look out at the London cityscape below. He was on the eighth floor of a modernized industrial building. He'd bought this concrete-bound loft because one of the walls was a giant window, but he hadn't realized there would be nothing to see but more concrete and buildings. In the slums of Rio where he grew up, people built houses right on top of each other, rickety, cobbled-together houses that boiled in the summer months, but at least in the *favela*, there had been a view.

His phone rang and he crossed to answer it, his mouth stuffed with a bite of apple. "Li-am?" He swallowed. "You fucking dick."

"I'm working." His friend's calm tone only increased his agitation. "What's up? What do you need?"

"I need you and Yves to stop conspiring against me."

"I have no idea what you're talking about."

Rubio tore off another bite of apple. "I know it was you," he said, gnashing the fruit between his teeth. "*Que droga.* They couldn't afford her without you."

"City Ballet has plenty of donors. Hundreds. How can you be so sure it was me?" Rubio could tell he was grinning, even over the phone.

"I will punch you right in your ugly face."

"Aw, come on," Liam said in his drawling American accent. "She's the best, Ruby. Me and Yves thought you should have the best. She was restless in New York, having some kind of personal issue—"

"Because she is a snotty, perfectionist diva! Everyone in ballet knows this."

"Look, I don't want to hurt your feelings, but you're not exactly known for rainbows and sunshine."

"She is worse than me. Much worse. She told me my feet were bricks."

"Let me guess, it was right after you said something horribly inappropriate to her."

"Is not inappropriate to inform someone their forehead is too big."

Liam sighed. "Your English is getting better but your charm factor sucks. If you're going to dance with this woman—"

"I'm not going to dance with her. No."

"You're going to dance with her, you obnoxious fuck, and you're going to like it. The paperwork is all but signed."

Stupid Liam. He didn't get it. He wasn't there, looking at her regal fucking majesty from across the table. Sure, Petra Hewitt was an amazing dancer. Sure, they belonged together but...damn it. She was just so good. He was used to being top dog at City Ballet. He enjoyed starring in all the photo ops, fielding all the big interviews and television appearances. He was the one with the fanciest dressing room. He was the exalted star the lower-tier dancers were afraid to look on.

"You did this to stick it to me," he said. "You and Yves. You want to stick it to me."

"What the fuck are you talking about?"

"You think I'm too much a diva. Too ego-tastical. Too full of myself." He stalked over to the kitchen and tossed the apple core in the trash.

"Well, yeah, sure, but—"

"You want to take me down a nudge."

"Notch. Take you down a notch, you ego-tastical bastard. And no, that's not what motivated Yves to bring her here. He did it for you, because you need a dancer at her level to continue to develop your art. Look, I love Ashleigh, and she's a great dancer, but she struggled to do the things that came easily for you. Maybe it's time for you to struggle a little. I'm sure you can do it," he said in a bright voice that made Rubio want to kick him in the nuts.

"It's not just that," Ruby said. "I don't like her. She's unpleasant. She's stuck-up and she doesn't smile. Her hair is this terrible yellow color and she has eyes like...like...lizard color. Snake eyes."

21

"Translation," Liam cut in. "She's the most beautiful woman you've ever seen and she wasn't sexually receptive to you, so now you're pissed off."

"No, that is not it at all. I would rather die than have sex with her."

"What are you talking about? You can make super ballet babies. She's already a super ballet baby, isn't she? Grigolyuk's kid? Add some Rubio to the mix and this kid can take over the world."

"We're never having a kid," he groused. "She's horrible. I hate her."

"You adore her," said Liam. "That's good. It will create compelling sexual tension between you while you're performing, sort of how you were with Ashleigh."

Rubio crossed back to the window and looked out at the cloudy, gray sky. No, no view at all. "I don't know why we're friends," he muttered into the phone. "I hate you."

"Sort of how you 'hate' Petra Hewitt? Cool. Well, listen, I'm glad we had this talk but I have a security business to run. Your ghastly little dance partner isn't coming cheap. So try to make it work, okay?"

Ruby hung up on Liam and pressed his head to the window, breathing condensation onto the glass. He'd have to do some thinking about this Petra Hewitt situation. He didn't like her, not really, but he admired her far too much. He wished she was horrible and ugly like a lizard but she wasn't. She was very pretty. Her forehead was completely normal size.

For the first time in a long time, The Great Fernando Rubio felt insecure and a bit threatened, and he didn't like that at all.

Chapter Three:
Mistake

Petra could feel everyone's eyes following her as she crossed the main rehearsal room. She stole a quick glance around to see if Fernando had arrived yet, but no, he wasn't there. Maybe he wouldn't show up. Petra had considered it, after she saw the morning papers. Someone at The Gilded Swan had snapped photos of them snarking back and forth across the table and sold them to the press. There was even one of her storming away with Yves in pursuit while Fernando sneered in the background.

Ballet Battle Royale, one headline trumpeted. *The Prima and the Prince*, read another. *Trouble in Paradise?*

Oh, there was trouble all right. Petra could honestly say she'd never been featured in a tabloid, not until now. Due to the media hubbub, tickets for City Ballet's fall performances were selling out, and the theater was considering adding extra matinees to keep up with demand. She hadn't even signed the contract yet!

Yves had told her about the sold-out shows this morning, with carefully restrained excitement. He didn't mention anything about the photos, but Petra noticed copies of the papers everywhere. In the cafeteria, in the costume room, in the dancers' lounge. Everyone hid them when she was around, which made her feel even more unnerved about the whole thing. Petra Hewitt, tabloid fodder. Ugh.

Maybe your dad will see it, said some unwelcome voice inside her. *Then he'll know you're here.*

No. She didn't care about that. She didn't give a shit about her dad or the fact that everyone was reading about her and Fernando's blow up. She doubted she'd even agree to dance here, although she desperately needed to get away from New York. Gary Paulsen was in New York. Creepy guy, who sent her flowers and chocolate and teddy bears, and letters five or six days a week. Eighty percent of her "fan mail" at the theater had been his bizarrely cordial notes. *You're so delicate, so lovely. Your dancing is like nothing I've ever seen. You are the most beautiful woman on earth.* They disturbed her so much that she never replied to any of them, although the Met Ballet staff sent him the occasional autographed headshot. Near the end, he'd started sending his weird notes to her apartment, to her actual private address. *Why don't you reply to me? I'm your biggest fan. Your artistry gives me a reason to live. I wish I could hold your hand. I wish I could give you a hug. Are you lonely?*

My biggest dream would be to make you my wife.

Uh, no.

For the record, she had never been married, and if she did get married it wouldn't be to the bald, ruddy, creepy man who lingered around the theater exit and sometimes right outside her building door. He'd never said anything threatening to her, or tried to approach her, but he was always there and it really freaked her out.

Petra sprawled on the floor to stretch, and laid her cheek against the resin-scented surface. All studios pretty much smelled the same, but the people here were strangers. She'd known everyone back at Met Ballet, from principal dancers to corps, but she didn't know anyone here yet. Well, she knew one person...

As if on cue, Fernando Rubio entered and swaggered to the far side of the rehearsal room to warm up. He didn't greet anyone or look in her direction, not that she wanted him to. He wore a black tee and gray sweatpants, typical practice clothes, but the way they hugged his finely-honed body...his broad shoulders...his taut ass...

Stop, Petra. Stop it now. It was normal for dancers to check out one another's bodies, but she didn't want to think of him that way. She got to her feet and hid the shake of her knees in deep *pliés*, feeling each muscle lengthen and respond. She noticed Yves standing to the side with the artistic director, their eyes alert. It would be a coup for them to cement this partnership. It would place City Ballet squarely at the top of the world's dance pyramid and guarantee ticket sales for seasons to come. It might even place Hewitt and Rubio alongside the great ballet couples of history…

"Hey, you," Fernando called across the rehearsal room. "Are you going to be ready some time today?"

The entire room went still. Great ballet couples of history? Only if they didn't kill one another first. Petra tapped her toe box on the floor once, twice, before she turned to him with a scowl. "You know my name every bit as well as I know yours, Fernando. I would appreciate it if you'd call me by it, as opposed to 'hey' or 'you.'"

She heard a few stifled titters. His black eyes burned darker, if such a thing was possible. "My name is Rubio," he snapped, "not Fernando." Then he held out his hand, stubbornly refusing to call her anything at all.

She stared at that elegant hand, not moving an inch. If he thought she would come scurrying to him after that display, he was mistaken. She stood where she was, her arms crossed over her chest. He shrugged and, to her shock, tilted forward into a perfect handstand. His shirt fell down, exposing a back of bronzed, defined muscle. Her mouth went dry.

"Nice trick," she said, turning away. She heard his shoes hit the floor as he righted himself.

"Come," he said impatiently. "If we are going to dance, let's dance."

"I don't know if we're going to dance," she said, lifting her chin. "I was told I would receive an apology for last night."

"For telling you about your big forehead?" he drawled, across the entire rehearsal space. "I'm sorry, I shouldn't have said it. Not out loud."

She blew out a breath. "Alrighty then." She turned on her heel and went to get her bag. "I can fly home today if I hurry."

"Ms. Hewitt." Yves' voice sounded hushed in the dead-silent room as he crossed to her. "Please, wait. Mr. Rubio?" He beckoned to the frowning dancer, who glared at her like a dark-haired demon fallen from grace. The director said a few short words in Fernando's—no, *Rubio's*— ear that Petra couldn't hear. With an expression of forbearance, Rubio turned to her.

"I apologize for last night," he said tightly. "Now…please…we dance."

She looked at his outstretched hand but didn't take it. "You don't want to dance with me."

There was some flicker of sadness in his eyes, a tightening of his jaw. "I can't dance with who I want. Forgive me, please. Is not your fault."

That apology sounded a bit less hostile, and Petra felt herself relent. Fernando Rubio was gorgeous and talented, and hell, he was a legend. She'd come all this way. She might as well take a spin around the floor and see what he was like as a partner.

"Okay," she said. "Past is past." She turned to Yves. "What part of *Romeo* are you rehearsing today?"

"Well," said Yves, a bit tentatively. "We've been waiting to rehearse the balcony *pas de deux*."

Jesus, the balcony scene was one of the most romantic pieces in all of ballet, and it ended with a huge, passionate kiss. Was this the director's way of trying to smooth the tension between them? They would have done better to start with the death scene.

She would look unprofessional if she refused, so she deferred to Rubio, who shrugged and mumbled something unintelligible. Yves beckoned to the accompanist, a disheveled-looking guy hunched over a coffee mug in the corner. He scurried over to the piano and banged a handful of keys as he sat. The tuneless, dissonant sound seemed an appropriate opening coda as Rubio reached for her hand. Their eyes met and held, and for a moment no one in the room seemed to move or breathe, including the two of them.

Was this the start of history, or disaster? Rubio turned her hand over and their fingers laced, and in his gaze, some connection flowed to her, some recognition of their rightness for each other. No matter her misgivings, no matter his gruff rudeness, as artists they belonged together, as did their hands, their feet, every part of their painstakingly trained bodies. Rubio was the dark to her light, the strength to her grace, the premier to her prima.

Damn it. Why did it have to be him?

If Rubio felt a similar pang of connectedness, he gave no sign. He looked away and pursed his lips, and she became aware again of the world around them, the soft chatter of other dancers and Yves' consultation with the pianist. Petra did a few *passés* while Rubio supported her, to give him an idea of her weight and balance. He was taller than her, perhaps six-one or six-two to her five-four. Though his touch was light, his manner was as forceful and imperious as ever.

"Turn," he ordered, touching her waist.

Petra hesitated. She was used to respect and deference, not commands. His dark eyes bored into hers, waiting with the sense of someone used to being obeyed. What had Yves called him? Rough around the edges? It was a little more than that. Rubio stepped closer, right into her space, molding his hands to curves of her waist, and she felt her nipples tighten against the sheer nylon of her leotard. *Please don't betray me, body. Don't get hot for him. No, just no.* How could she be sexually attracted to this man?

She pushed those disturbing thoughts from her mind and launched into a neat series of pirouettes. She could assert her own dominance in this arena. She twirled eight, nine, ten times in a row. He attended her cues, his touch every bit as deft as it was reputed to be. He didn't stand too close or too far away, but perfectly right. She forced one last pirouette, just to see if she could trip him up. He made a sound of irritation but they pulled it off, the way partners pull things off when they have to. She liked that he helped her when he could have left her to wobble to a stop in front of everyone.

Then his hands tightened on her waist and he lifted her, a cold lift with the strength of his arms. She hadn't expected it, and the landing jolted her. She looked over her shoulder at him with a frown. "Sorry," he murmured. "Lift, again," and this time she was ready. It felt like flying when they were in tune. He set her down and stepped away from her. No comments, no words, just a grunt and a hooded look.

So that was that, a quick assessment for both of them. She wondered what he thought of her lines, her technique. How did she compare to his other partners? And how did she feel about him? She wasn't sure she could judge. She felt curiously shaken-up at the moment.

"Are you warmed up enough?" she asked, bending down to fiddle with her laces. "This *pas de deux* has a lot of lifts."

She straightened to find his lips curled in an unpleasant sneer. "Don't worry. I won't drop you."

"I never said you would. I was just asking if you were warmed up."

"I've been dancing as long as you. Longer. I can manage my own preparation."

"Fine." She waved a hand at him and they backed away from one other. This was a rehearsal studio, not a boxing ring. They weren't going to accomplish anything by sniping at each other, aside from feeding the gossip mill. She watched as he bounded to the other side of the room, executing some astounding cabriolets.

"Okay," he said, returning to her. "You ready?"

She was more "ready" than she wanted to admit. He emitted some chemical or pheromone that was making her crazy, or perhaps it was the close physical contact with his body. She could feel his hard abs through his shirt, and smell the fresh, clean scent of his cologne. Or was it only soap?

God, why did she care? With determined concentration, she pushed everything out of her mind but Juliet's adolescent excitement and emotion, and the precise execution of the steps. This balcony scene was lyrical and romantic, a stolen interlude between two lovers who desired each other desperately but were never meant to be. Her partner fell easily into the role of Romeo, and seemed to become a whole other person.

She'd hoped this rehearsal might be a disaster from beginning to end so she could hop on a plane and put this whole thing behind her, but she found herself impressed with his partnering. He made everything so easy. He gave her the emotion she needed to lose herself in the role, so it felt natural, almost magical, and he gave her only as much support as she needed, so all her energy might go to the dance. As for him, he performed his steps with such finesse, even now in a casual rehearsal. *He could make you a better dancer*, she thought to herself. *He's that good.*

At least he was good until the second series of lifts. He absolutely did not have to put his hand *there*. A mistake, she hoped. They moved on to more sweeping movements, to balanced poses that felt easy and graceful.

"Beautiful," he murmured when she stretched into a taut arabesque. "So pretty, your extension."

"Thank you." She felt a weird tightening in her chest, some giddy pleasure that he'd noticed and complimented something about her. His partnering made her feel so safe, allowed her to become naive, impulsive Juliet without reservation. She thought if Romeo and Juliet were real, they might have felt this connection as they came together in the dark of Verona's night. In the middle of an intricate series of lifts she met his gaze and some recognition passed between them.

But then, damn it. He groped her again, and this time she knew it was intentional. Was he testing her? Her limpid gaze turned into a glare.

"Stop," she muttered under her breath. "I know what you're doing. Stop it."

"Not doing nothing," he said. "You're taller than my last partner. Hands in the wrong place. Sorry."

That was a bald lie, because Ashleigh Keaton was the same height as her. Irritation propelled Petra through an abbreviated solo and made it easy for her to shy away in character when Romeo tried to kiss her. But then, oh God, how he made her fly. It was impossible to stay angry, to not be drawn back into the emotional flow of the piece. His hands were a miracle, such a miracle.

I wonder what else he can do with those hands...

This part of the ballet was meant to be innocently provocative, but with Rubio it took on whole new shades of sensuality. His dark eyes caressed her, his arms clasped her close and then propelled her into beautiful movements. On either side of the room, dancers stared at them, still as statues. Yves appeared to be holding his breath. Petra met Rubio's gaze and found such intensity, such tenderness that it shook her.

It was a *moment*, as they said in the theater. It was the beginning of them, of their legendary partnership. Yves was right—they only had to dance together to understand each other. Petra thought she would remember this first dance forever, the emotion, the perfection, the soft, flowing legato of the piano, and the preternatural stillness of the room. They began the final turns leading up to the big kiss but then—again—his hands weren't in the right place.

His palm brushed over her breast in such a way that Yves wouldn't notice, or the accompanist, or any of the two dozen or so dancers arrayed along the walls. But she noticed, because she felt the betrayal of trust down to her toes.

She stopped mid-step and spun on him. He grinned at her, a filthy, knowing grin that felt like a kick between the legs, especially after the magic that had come before. Without thinking, she reached out and cracked him across the face. The slap echoed in the silence of the room.

"You're an asshole," she said.

He didn't reply, only stared at her, his hand held over the red mark of her blow. Why did she feel like crying?

Because he'd showed her the prince and then turned into the toad, like she wasn't good enough for the prince. Like she wasn't good enough for him. But God help her, she'd gouge out her eyes before she cried in front of him. She shoved the tears down, beneath her anger and her outrage. "If you want to dance with me," she snapped, "you need to act professional out of respect for my art. Out of respect for all the hours I've put in to get to this fucking place."

In her peripheral vision, she saw Yves start toward them, then stop again. The rehearsal room grew even quieter than before. "You know what I mean," she finished in little more than a whisper. "You know what I'm talking about."

"I'm sorry," he finally said, rubbing his fingers across his cheek. "I made a mistake."

He looked at her with his head bowed a bit to the side, like a chastened boy. A gorgeous, chastened boy. How could he be so beautiful and so awful at once?

"Yes, this is a mistake, all of it," she said, looking away from him. Emotions assaulted her—anger, disappointment, confusion, and worst of all, horribly inappropriate lust. She could still feel the pull to him, the agitation of all her erogenous zones, but she thought she'd die if she had to dance with him again. She'd die if he ever groped her crotch or her breast again with that leer on his face. If she had to kiss him, even on stage...

No, she couldn't sign a contract here. She ducked her head and started for the door, but he followed, catching her wrist.

"My mistake," he said. "Let me fix it. We go again. Please."

"No, you were right about us. This isn't going to work—"

"I think this will work," he said, speaking over her. "A good partnership doesn't start until the first slap."

She stared into his dark eyes. The lurid mockery was gone, replaced by an apologetic gaze.

"That's the stupidest thing I ever heard," she said, pulling her hand from his. "A stupid way to start a partnership."

"I didn't start nothing. This just happened. This... This..." He gestured helplessly. This *magic*, she supplied in her mind. He lowered his voice and took her hand again. "You know what I mean," he said, borrowing her earlier words.

Yes, she did know what he meant, but her courage had left her. She felt too vulnerable now, too afraid. "You don't really want to dance with me," she said, staring at the middle of his chest.

"I need a partner and you're here." His fingers tightened on hers. "And there's a lot to do before the season gets underway. So...we go again, Petra. Please."

She might have had the power to leave if not for that *please*, because she understood how much it cost him to add it. "I don't know," she said, deeply conflicted. "I'm not sure about you and me. I'm not sure it will work out."

He gave her a look that said *liar*. And she was lying. She was grasping for any way out of this, because his artistry cowed her and his enigmatic sexuality seduced her. This must have been how her mother felt when she danced with Petr Grigolyuk, and that had ended so badly. Dancing with Fernando Rubio would be hell for her, a constant struggle against feelings she didn't want to have.

He glanced to the side at a stifled outburst of giggles, and Petra remembered everyone was watching this private moment. Would this story be in the tabloids next? *Slappily Ever After.* She wouldn't put it past any of these dancers to sell a play-by-play of this interlude to the press.

"Is because you don't want to kiss me?" he said in a loud voice, bringing the audience in again. "I'll take a breath mint first, if you want."

She understood she had to play along, if they were going to put this episode behind them. If she was going to forgive him, it had to be public, so they could all move on. "No breath mint on earth could compel me to kiss you," she sniffed with playful derision. "Maybe at the final rehearsal, I'll take a stab at it. Not before."

The room erupted in appreciative laughter, and Yves visibly exhaled. Petra squared her shoulders. *Take a deep breath and smile at him. Everything will be okay.* She would find some way to survive working with Rubio, because they really did belong together. Her suffering seemed like a small thing when measured against the beauty they could bring to the world.

"Okay. We do it again?" he prompted, all business now. He turned to Yves, who nodded in agreement.

Petra angled her face to Rubio's so no one could see. "Don't disrespect me," she said. "From now on, keep your grabby fucking hands where they belong."

He regarded her from beneath his lashes with a disconcerting shadow of a smile. "If you say so. If that's really what you want."

Oh Jesus, he *knew*. He sensed the attraction she felt to him, she could see it in the teasing glint of his eyes. What a fucking situation. She'd shed blood, sweat, and tears to get to the top, only to end up partnered with this profane virtuoso. Somehow, he made it through the rest of the rehearsal without groping her again.

Afterward, Yves led her to the dressing room set aside for her, with a cozy couch, chair, and vanity, a smallish but private bathroom, and plenty of closet space. She told him there, privately, that yes, they could proceed with the contracts. Yes, she would come.

Yves left in a haze of happiness but Petra paced and fretted, second-guessing, until she collapsed on the beige velvet couch. On one hand, she was thrilled by Rubio's talent, by his consummate skill as a dancer, but on the other hand, she was too aware of him as a *man*. He'd made sure of it by touching her inappropriately and giving her those knowing smiles. Maybe it was a power-positioning thing. Maybe it was a Brazilian thing. Maybe...

Maybe he found her as attractive as she found him.

No. She didn't want that. She didn't want him to find her attractive. She didn't want him to do anything but partner her through pirouettes and arabesques, and haul her into the air when the choreography called for it.

In the midst of her fretting, a knock sounded. She entertained a flash of fantasy, a tableau of him kicking down the door, pushing her to the couch and ripping off her leotard, and—

"Petra?"

Female voices. She opened the door to find a couple of the other principal ballerinas outside.

"Can we come in?"

"Sure," Petra said, standing back to admit them.

"I'm Hannah," said the taller one, holding out her hand. "And this is Suzanne."

"Hi," said Suzanne, grinning and waving. "So...?"

"So...?" asked Petra, smiling at Suzanne's friendly exuberance.

"Are you going to dance here?" she asked. "We really hope you are, cause we heard that you slapped Rubio in rehearsal. Is that true?"

Petra tried hard to look ashamed. "It's true."

"My God," Hannah cried. "My new best friend." She swept Petra into an impromptu hug. "Do you have any idea how long he's had it coming to him?"

Petra grimaced. "I have some idea."

"Tell us everything," said Suzanne. "How did he react? Did he go mad? Did he start raging at you?"

Petra turned out the back of her pointe shoes to dry. "He didn't do anything. I think he knew he deserved it."

They looked deflated to learn there hadn't been a big scene.

"He was groping me, being sly about it," Petra explained. "He said he was sorry and that he'd made a mistake."

Suzanne snorted. "He's made that mistake an arseload of times."

"Yeah," said Hannah, shaking her head. "And you'll be his main partner, so you'll probably be dealing with his 'mistakes' a lot."

"You guys will still dance with him sometimes, won't you?"

Hannah shrugged. "He'll dance with Suzanne and some of the others, but not me. He has the option in his contract to dance with whoever he wants. He thinks I'm too tall. Whatever. I'm okay not dancing with Rubio. He can be a massive prick."

"Aw, Rubio's okay," said Suzanne. "And you two will work out fine," she added, looking at Petra, "because you stood up to him."

Hannah gazed at Petra in rapt admiration. "I can't believe you popped him. I heard you also called him Fernando." She grabbed her head. "God, why wasn't I there? I should have been there."

Petra looked between the two dancers. "Why doesn't he like to be called Fernando? It's his name, isn't it?"

"It's his name, but we've all learned not to use it," said Suzanne. "And here's another helpful hint. Don't accept any party invitations from him. Ever."

Hannah burst out laughing and made a fake whip-cracking sound. "What?" Petra asked. "What do you mean?"

"I mean that he doesn't go to your average parties." Suzanne lowered her voice to a whisper. "Now you're joining the company, you'll eventually hear this around the water cooler, but your new partner's as kinky as they come. He goes to this orgy-sex-party thing in Regents Park every weekend, at his pal's big white house. I've never been brave enough to try to get in and see what goes on, but I hear Rubio's an eyeful." She waggled her eyebrows. "If you know what I mean."

For a moment, Petra was struck dumb. Literally, she held her breath in a kind of shock. Rubio, kinky? Attending orgy-sex-parties? She put her hands on her cheeks and then ran them down her face.

"Hey, it's okay," said Hannah. "He's not that scary. Just don't follow him to any parties at big white houses."

"And don't get on his bad side," added Suzanne. "He's a Lord-Master-Dominant, from what I understand. I mean, you know, it makes sense."

Hannah made another whip sound and they both collapsed into laughter. Petra managed a chuckle but inside all she could think was *Oh my God.*

She might have guessed he was a Lord-Master-Dominant, from the way he moved, the way he commanded the attention of those around him, even the way he beckoned her by thrusting out his hand. She knew a little about BDSM, but she'd never done anything aside from fantasize about being tied up. She wondered what Rubio was like when he did BDSM with his partners. Rough? Sensitive? Scary?

It didn't matter, because she herself was not into BDSM and she'd never hook up with him anyway, because they were partners, not lovers, and when her mother had taken her partner as her lover, it pretty much ruined her life. Petra didn't want to lose her career, her self esteem, her heart, pretty much everything to someone who turned out to be undeserving.

She owed it to herself—and the memory of her mom—not to repeat Hillary Hewitt's mistakes.

Chapter Four:
Suck

By the end of the first week, Rubio was mentally exhausted. A new partner was bad enough. A new season, shakeups in the repertoire and line ups, all those things stressed everybody out, but he struggled with more than that. Something felt off inside his body. He wasn't sleeping well. He dreamed at night about white-blonde hair that burned him when he touched it, and lightning-fast toe shoes skittering away, always out of reach.

Rubio felt challenged for the first time in years.

He ought to have been grateful for the challenge. Artistically, he was in a great place. Yves was happy, and the City Ballet patrons were happy, buying up tickets like crazy. Maybe he was happy. He couldn't tell because Petra Hewitt made him so tired. When Ashleigh and Liam invited him for dinner, he almost said no, even though he enjoyed spending time with them. He knew they would ask him about his new partner and the *Romeo and Juliet* premiere, and he didn't know what he'd tell them. *Yes, everything is well. Yes, she is a dream to dance with.*

Yes, maybe, a little bit, I am enamored of her.

"I can't stand her," he said to Ashleigh as soon as they brought her up. "Really, she is the biggest bitch ever."

"Ruby," Ash chided. "I heard she's really nice."

"She's about as nice as someone who kicks dogs and drinks baby's blood."

Liam threw a piece of dinner roll at him. "Tell the truth. Everyone loves her. Yves told me rehearsals are going great."

"Oh, speaking of Yves," said Rubio, "he told me to ask if you and Ashleigh would be at the *Romeo* premiere."

"Yeah, we'll be there," said Liam. "Mem too. The Saturday-night revels can wait until you arrive in your triumphant glory. Or...are you planning to take Petra out afterward for a romantic candlelit dinner?"

Rubio scowled at him. Take Petra out? He might as well sit across the table from a big block of ice. She was so cold to him, so standoffish.

"If you don't want to come to the show, you don't have to," he said. "Is just *Romeo and Juliet*."

"And the first time ever that Fernando Rubio and Petra Hewitt dance onstage together," Ashleigh added. "Just in case you've been on Mars, it's a big deal here in town. I saw one of your posters on the Tube. You looked gorgeous together."

"Hm." Rubio shrugged. "Probably, it will be okay. She's a good Juliet for someone who kicks dogs."

Ash made a face at him. "I'm sure Petra doesn't kick dogs, although I heard some gossip that she bitch-slapped you during your first rehearsal."

Liam burst into laughter. Rubio gave him an affronted look. "It wasn't funny. It left a mark."

"And you've never left a mark on anyone?"

"Not in rehearsal I haven't." Rubio rubbed his cheek, feeling the ghostly outline of her hand.

"Well, why did she hit you?" asked Ashleigh.

"Because I felt her up. Three times. Not even bad."

"Is there a way to do it that's not bad?"

"You miss my touching, huh?"

She shook her head at him. "You should be in jail by now."

"I don't mean to do it. It's only that women's bodies feel so good. So smooth and strong, and pretty." Especially Petra's, but he shouldn't think about that right now. He eyed the gentle curve of his former partner's waist. "How is the baby inside you? All okay?"

She put her hand over the barely visible bump. "Everything's good, thanks for asking. I'm starting to feel little *jetés* inside me."

"Oh yeah? Baby is dancing in there?" Ruby chuckled until he noticed Liam's sober face. Liam had grown up in the bad part of L.A., kind of how Rubio had grown up in the bad part of Rio, only Ruby had a great mom, while Liam's mother had killed all his brothers and sisters in a bout of postpartum depression. He knew his friend was worried about Ash having a baby, because he worried about her getting depressed too. "You miss dancing?" he asked Ash, to change the subject.

She shook her head. "I mean, I miss it, and I miss you sometimes, but I'm keeping busy doing other things. I help Liam with work and hang out with my old friends from the theater. That's where I heard that Petra is not a dog kicker or baby blood drinker. Everyone thinks she's great. Everyone's also wondering whether Petr Grigolyuk will drop by at some point. He lives in London, you know."

No, Rubio didn't know. He didn't care, except that Grigolyuk was Petra's dad, so maybe he should care. "She never talks about him," he said. "She never talks about anything. Just does classes and rehearsals and goes home."

"She probably feels lonely, being new to London and everything," said Ashleigh. "You should invite her over here sometime."

"For the party?" Ruby allowed himself to imagine, just for a moment, his uptight partner tied to a BDSM rack, at the mercy of his sadistic whims. Naked, aroused, pleading for release...

"No, silly," said Ashleigh, interrupting his fantasies. "Not for the party. For dinner."

"Oh, yeah," said Liam. "That's a great idea. We'd love to have her. Just don't tell her I'm paying her salary, because that might make things awkward. You haven't told her, have you?"

Ruby didn't think he had. Sometimes he wasn't sure what he said to Petra. He got distracted looking in her eyes, because the color was so unusual, and they were so pretty, the way they slanted upward. "No," he said after he'd considered a moment. "I'm sure I haven't. Is none of her business. Or your business, if you want to finance the salary of a dog kicker."

Liam rolled his eyes, reaching to pour more wine. "You're having a blast dancing with the dog kicker. And I bet in her mind, you're the one who kicks dogs and drinks baby's blood."

Ash put a hand over her belly. "Mind if we stop talking about drinking baby's blood?"

Ruby picked up his wineglass as if to make a toast. "Whatever you say, Ash. But Liam's right. Petra won't come to dinner, she hates me. I think she wants to be...you know...at a distance from me. Detached."

"Give it some time," she said. "You're a hard partner to stay detached from. When it comes down to it, you're a love-him-or-hate-him kind of guy."

"And you love me, yes?" he asked, batting his eyes at her.

"On occasion," she answered, almost keeping a straight face. "But don't push your luck."

He laughed with her when she finally broke into a smile. Liam laughed along with them, but Rubio could sense his mind was elsewhere. Liam was stressed out, as stressed as Ruby himself. Maybe more. He wished he could comfort his friend, tell him everything would be okay with Ashleigh and her baby, but nothing was ever sure.

Even Petra and their partnership. It wasn't settled yet. They still circled around each other offstage, outside the studio, unsure of their relationship. What if Ashleigh was right, what if he was a love-him-or-hate-him kind of guy and Petra decided to hate him? With any other dancer, he wouldn't have cared, but with her...

He didn't want Petra to hate him, cause he had a lot of feelings toward her that he hadn't straightened out yet.

* * * * *

Rubio's hands felt hot on Petra. She felt hot all over.

They rehearsed alone in a cavernous studio with black walls, black as his eyes and his scruffy, glossy hair. They arched as one entity, then he kissed her on the neck. She shivered at the fleeting contact of his lips. She could feel his hard cock against her ass, pressing and poking through her leotard. The bare skin of his chest burned where they brushed against each other.

Like dripping wax, the black studio melted away into a sex dungeon with candles and cages and a pair of shackles hanging from the ceiling. "Down," he said, pointing to the floor beneath the shackles. His face was drawn in stern lines. "Kneel down and raise your arms."

Without thought, she fell to her knees and extended her hands upward. He fixed each of her wrists into the shackles and then he roughly gripped her neck. She gasped, aroused by his force. A rush of warmth flared between her legs. His fingers dug into her hair and then his leggings were gone, disappeared along with her leotard. His cock thrust hot and thick against her face. "Suck it," he said in his languid Portuguese accent. "Suck me, you uptight little bitch."

Oh, but... Why did he think she was uptight? In her fantasies she was sexy and adventurous—and oh, so horny for him. She opened her mouth and tried to fellate him but his cock grew with each passing second, until it was threateningly large, until it choked her. *Uptight little bitch...* She acted like a bitch to him, she supposed. She couldn't help it. He scared her, he endangered her. He could destroy her if he wanted to.

He doesn't want to destroy you, you uptight little bitch.

He wrenched her hair so she swayed on her knees, rattling the shackles. He forced her to take him deeper in her throat, but then the dark walls began to waver like a desert mirage.

"That's a good little slut," he crooned. "Suck me, yes. Just like that."

Her mouth ached. He was too big and it was hot in the dungeon, so hot. She felt frustrated that she couldn't make him come. Then a shrill bell sounded. It was some kind of alarm to signify that she wasn't really kinky, that she'd never done BDSM before. Rubio scowled down at her, shaking his head in disappointment. He was disappearing, fading into thin air. "No," she cried. "I'm sorry. Don't leave me. I need you."

Again, the shrill alarm bell. No, not an alarm bell, the phone. She came awake and dived to answer her cell on the bedside table.

"Hello?"

"Good morning, Miss Hewitt. Just letting you know there's a delivery for you at the front desk."

"Okay, thanks."

She blinked down at the display and then at the clock. It was almost nine in the morning and she was lying in bed having revolting sex dreams about Rubio. *Ugh.* She threw off the covers and headed to the bathroom to shower. She was sweaty and aroused, like she was infected with some kind of fever. Rubio fever. The cool water ran through her hair and over her shoulders, relaxing her by slow degrees until she came to full wakefulness.

What in holy fuck was up with that dream? She'd been dreaming about Fernando Rubio for a week now, ever since they'd begun working together, ever since she'd learned he was a kinky pervert, but that was the most depraved one yet. The wavy melting walls and his ever-growing cock, and the way Rubio had talked to her... He wasn't exactly a gentleman at the theater but he never called her a bitch or slut, at least not to her face, and certainly not with that edge of sexual menace.

She'd been browsing too many BDSM sites, that was the problem. She'd been curious. Maybe too curious. She touched her throat, remembering the firm feel of his hands on her neck. He used the same firm touch when he danced with her. Strong, capable, with the threat of great force or great tenderness.

What did she want? Force or tenderness?

Ugh, these stupid thoughts. Damn the front desk for waking her up. She dressed for work, throwing street clothes over her leotard and tights. Her alarm blared to life and she silenced it. *Yep, already up. Thanks.* She liked her new building, because it had a doorman and good security, and a lobby with marble floors. She looked around her neat and spacious "flat." It was a great, old, oddly shaped space with high ceilings and textured walls. The only reason it was so neat was because she'd barely unpacked anything yet.

Tonight. Tonight she would unpack, before the season started in earnest and things got crazy busy. The premiere was next week and the London arts scene was buzzing with excitement. She and Rubio had posed for professional photos in their *Romeo and Juliet* costumes, for the publicity department to use on posters and advertisements all over town. They'd done interviews and profiles for TV news programs, during which Rubio was faultlessly polite. They'd even managed to stay out of the tabloids, aside from a few candids outside the theater. In one of them, Ruby had been holding the door for her, his head thrown back in a laugh. She remembered that day because they'd happened to be leaving at the same time, and joked about who got to take the company-hired car. He'd suggested they share the ride, and she'd said she was afraid to be alone in the back of a car with him.

She kept a copy of the picture in the drawer beside her bed, because she liked the way they looked in the photo. It was something about their body language—it painted a picture of two close friends, even though in reality they mostly avoided each other. He'd put her into the company car and ducked into a taxi, because he got followed by female fans. All the lurkers outside the theater doors queued up to see him, not her, and she definitely preferred it that way.

Petra headed down to the lobby and asked at the front desk for her package. It was from New York, somewhat large but very light. She received a lot of promotional materials, free shoes and bags and leotards, although they usually came to the theater. She went upstairs and opened the box, pushing aside the packing peanuts. Underneath, she uncovered two fuzzy ears of a gold-colored stuffed bear. Her confusion gave way to goose bumps as she pulled it out.

It was a mess. The eyes were gouged out, threads hanging shorn and bare. The middle was also torn open, with bits of stuffing visible, along with a note. Her first reaction was to drop the thing on the table. It couldn't be meant for her. She poked inside the stuffing and pulled out the crumpled pieces of paper. The first was a printed-out photo of her and Rubio, the very one of them sharing a laugh at the stage door. The second was a note, written neatly in black pen on lined paper.

Why are you doing this? You're tearing me apart.

Ugh. Why did freaky, stalky people have to exist in the world? Who in their right mind would send a ripped-up bear like this to another person? Scary Gary, that's who. The man had developed some weird obsession with her, and with this "gift" he'd shown her that moving an ocean away wasn't quite far enough.

* * * * *

One week later, Petra sat in an office at the local precinct. Not an office, actually, but a cubicle, which was the first sign that she was going to get absolutely no help. The second sign was the age of her assigned officer, who appeared to be just out of high school.

"I don't know what to say, Ms. Hewitt. Gary Paulsen has no criminal record, no known mental illness. Is he behaving badly? Yes, of course he is. Can I do anything to help you stop him?"

His expression said everything. *No.*

"So what do I do?" she asked, trying not to sound like a whiner. "He's writing me, bothering me, sending me packages. He's been doing it for months now. I feel...endangered."

He gave her a patronizing smile. "I don't think you're endangered. He's not even in this country."

"How can you be sure?"

"The IP address of his emails, for one."

"Can't those be manipulated?"

She could tell his patience was wearing thin. "Aren't there laws against harassment here?" she asked.

"There are laws against harassment, but they require a degree of menace. Your guy isn't making overt threats. He's not in a position to confront you or attack you. You can change your phone number and email and refuse anything he sends through the post. It's an annoyance, of course, but his actions aren't significant enough to merit international legal action. Not at this point."

"So if I was in the US, you could do something. But since he's an ocean away he can harass me all he wants?"

"Until he presents a credible threat, yes."

Petra sighed, looking around the shabby police station. Coffee rings stained a pile of reports on the young officer's desk. His girlfriend, or perhaps his wife, grinned at her from behind a crooked frame.

"So I wait, then," she said. "Until he says something threatening or scary."

"There's always the possibility he'll move on to some other obsession. Have you considered..." He shuffled his feet under the desk. "Would it be possible to take a break from the stage? Temporarily retire, so to speak?"

"Temporarily retire? Now? At the height of my career?"

"I know it's not ideal, but if it's the dancer he's attracted to—"

She stared at him. "I *am* the dancer. Ballet is my whole life. I can't stop, I can't retire just because some wacko is obsessed with me."

"It was just a suggestion."

She shouldn't be yelling at the kid. None of this was his fault. He was obviously the poor schlub who got all the cases no one else wanted to handle, and she was one more headache in his day. "Could you send him a cease-and-desist letter, on some kind of official police letterhead?" she asked. "Do you think that would accomplish anything?"

"It would only reassure Mr. Paulsen that he's getting through to you. Ignoring is your best option. Return his packages unopened. If you don't want to change your email, change your filters so you don't have to see the things he sends. Whatever you do, don't engage with him. If you don't respond to him, eventually he'll give up."

"You promise?" she asked, chewing a fingernail.

He gave her a weary smile. "I can't promise, although I understand your frustration. I know this will sound strange, but try not to get too worked up about the whole thing. Put him out of your mind and perhaps he'll come to realize there's no point in continuing to badger you." He stood and fished a card out of a plastic holder. "And if he shows up here in town, or if his overtures to you become violent in nature, by all means, let us know."

"Okay," she said out loud, pocketing his card. *Thanks for nothing,* she thought to herself. *You suck.*

Chapter Five:
Inappropriate

It was opening night of a new season. Not just a new season, but a new era at City Ballet. When he and Petra performed the kiss at the end of the balcony *pas de deux*, Rubio fell in love with her a little, as Romeo should. The audience broke into gleeful, impromptu applause. He felt her smile against his lips and then compose herself.

As for him, he felt transformed.

Rehearsals were one thing, but this opening performance had raised them both to new heights of inspiration. Petra brought bright, light innocence to the role, the needed balance for his dark Romeo. She was vivacious as young Juliet, and later dramatically mournful. During the death scene he was pretty sure she cried real tears. That scene was one of his favorite places to cop a secret feel, but he didn't, not this time. Petra was far too invested in the character, so he laid still and stiff while she sobbed over him, keeping his perverted fingers to himself. Instead he focused on her closeness and her sweet scent.

Petra always smelled so pretty. Her hair smelled like *sonhos*, like vanilla and sugar and good things, even at the end of a long, exhausting day. He liked that about her. He wished she wasn't such a hard ass bitch. He wished she was a horny, cowering, deeply masochistic submissive, so he could run amok all over her delectable body until she broke down and cried. But no, she wasn't. Too bad.

At the final curtain call, the audience went wild. Flowers, whistles, yelling and screaming, a tidal wave of appreciation. When he held her hand and led her forward to take their bows, a stagehand trotted out with a massive bouquet of roses. The bright pink roses symbolized welcome and affection for a new partner, and Rubio presented them to Petra with a fleeting kiss. The already-crazed audience exploded into hysteria.

She smiled up at him in the midst of the furor. It was impossible not to grin back. As he gazed into her pretty, almond-shaped eyes, he felt an attachment to her beyond duty and performance. He felt in solidarity with her. *We can make perfection together.* Afterward, instead of heading off to his own dressing room, he followed her to hers.

Yves joined them, grinning ear to ear. "I have no words. I don't know what to say, how to express my emotions. I felt like I was watching history being made."

"Yes, well," said Rubio, rolling his eyes. "You can watch history made again tomorrow. And the next night. And next week."

Yves ignored him and turned to Petra. "How did it feel? How was the stage, the production? The sound of the orchestra?"

"It was all wonderful. But the partnering..." She winked at Ruby, her eyes dark with an ebony outline of stage makeup. "Horrible. Can I still get out of my contract?"

Yves feigned distress, which wasn't too hard since he was almost always stressed out. A stagehand wove past him with two vases of roses and Petra gestured him to the table beside her vanity where the pink ones already lay. One of the vases overflowed with white roses and the other, significantly larger, with red. He knew the white ones were from Liam and Ashleigh.

Rubio had ordered the red.

He had second guesses now. Was that the expression? Second thoughts? The flowers seemed too garish in her cramped dressing room. Five dozen roses was probably too much. He would have left the room with the stagehand and Yves, but she'd already grabbed the card. *Muitos abraços*, he'd written. *Many hugs*, in Portuguese. He had signed it "R." He had not written *I think you're marvelous*, or *You smell like vanilla and sugar*, or even *I wish you were a horny, cowering, deeply masochistic submissive*, and he was glad for that now.

She read the two handwritten words aloud with an awful accent. He repeated it to her the right way.

"What does it mean?" she asked. "It's from you, right? These are from you?"

Before he could answer she buried her face in the bouquet, taking a deep breath. It was the same thing he wanted to do to her hair. "My goodness," she said. "They're so beautiful." She turned and threw her arms around him. They touched all the time but this felt heightened. Different.

"It means many hugs," he said against her hair. He smelled it furtively. Someday he would ask what shampoo she used. "It's a usual Portuguese greeting or whatever, to be nice."

"But you're only being nice because this was our first time dancing together, huh?"

"Yes," he said. He thought he might be blushing. It wasn't good. To his relief, she turned away to read the card on Liam and Ashleigh's bouquet, which was more reasonably sized. Ruby thought he should leave her goddamn dressing room and go hide, but then the Wilders appeared.

"We came to see the stars of the hour," said Liam.

Ashleigh didn't say anything, just enveloped Petra, tutu and all, in a smothering hug. "Oh my God," Ash cried. "I know we haven't met before, but oh my God, Petra, you were *so* good."

"Petra, this is Ashleigh Keaton," Ruby said over Ash's babbling. "And her husband Liam. They are my good friends."

Petra grinned when Ash let her go. "Thank you for the beautiful flowers."

"You were amazing," Ashleigh sighed. "Both of you were amazing." She hugged him next, an affectionate squeeze.

"Everyone loved it," said Liam. "There was this..." He waved his hands around, almost knocking Rubio's bouquet off the table. "This energy, this buzz. There was this sense of seeing a really momentous thing."

"A really special thing," Ash chimed in, nodding. "The balcony scene, my God. The kiss. Even Liam cried."

"I did not cry."

"You had something in your eye then. I see."

"No, I was laughing because *you* were crying."

Petra watched the couple banter back and forth with a charmed look on her face. Rubio didn't want to like her. He didn't want to want her but he did, with a growing intensity. He wished he could shoo Ash and Liam out of the room and peel Petra's costume off and fuck her fast and rough against the wall. "Hush," he'd say if she tried to stop him. "I need to be inside you."

The chatter in the room fell silent, and for a moment he was afraid he'd said it out loud rather than in his fantasies.

"Well, we'll get out of your hair then," said Ashleigh with sideways look at Liam. "Congrats again for an awesome first show."

She nudged her husband until he said, "Yeah, I think Mem's probably got the car." He shook Ruby's hand and then the two of them left the room. Again, Ruby thought he should flee, get the hell out of there. He had Liam's party to get ready for, his usual Saturday night craziness, but he lingered, not wanting this premiere night to end.

"What are you up to now?" she asked in the lengthening silence.

I wish I was up your pussy, he thought. "I am up to nothing," he said aloud. He wasn't telling her about Liam's party and he definitely wasn't inviting her. But perhaps he could take her for a drink first? What would she say if he asked? The words stuck inside his mouth, reluctant to come out. If he asked, she'd probably say no, which would be really embarrassing.

No, he had to get to Liam's party and get rid of some of his sexual energy. His new partner was not kinky. One encounter between them and she'd be scarred for life.

"Well, I'm out of here," he said, heading for the door. "I'll see you tomorrow, yes? We'll do it all over again."

She smiled at him. Such a pretty smile. Maybe one drink? No. He needed sex, not cocktail hour with a vanilla girl. He was about to leave when the stagehand returned with one more bouquet. This bouquet wasn't white roses or red roses, or even pink ones. It was dead roses. A bouquet of dead, blackened roses drooping amid dry sprays of baby's breath. Petra looked at it and gasped.

"What the fuck is that?" Rubio asked the stagehand. "Why are you bringing her that?"

He shrugged and looked at the card. "It was delivered to the theater. For Ms. Petra Hewitt."

"Take those away," he ordered. "No, wait." He grabbed them out of the grunt's hand and nodded to the door. "Leave. Get out."

Petra made a soft sound as he set the roses down beside the other two vases. "Why do you talk to people like that?"

"Like what?" he asked, rooting though the dead blooms to find the card.

She plucked it from his fingers before he could open it. "Could you please not read my stuff?"

"Who sent you these?"

They fought over the card. He won and opened the folded paper inside. *These roses are as dead as your soul.* It wasn't signed. Ruby turned to her as she read over his shoulder. "You know who this is from?"

"Yes," she said with a grimace. "I recognize the writing."

"Because I would like to punch him out. Ex-boyfriend?"

"No, just some guy. He used to write me a lot of fan mail when I danced in New York." She took the note and stared down at the print. "He's angry that I moved to London, but really, why should it matter? I don't even know him." She bit hard on her lip. "I don't know what he wants."

"I know what he wants," Ruby said. "He wants attention. People see you dance and they think they deserve a part of you. That they own something of you."

"Yes, maybe that's it." She crumpled the offending note into a ball, but before she could throw it away, he pried it from her hand.

"You better keep this. Evidence, for protection order."

She shook her head. "The police won't do anything. They say he's harmless. Just a bit too much of a fan."

A bit too much of a psycho, Ruby thought darkly. Petra's eyes darted around the room as she smoothed back her hair. Her hand shook a little. He noticed these things in his partners. Shakes and trembles, signs that balance was off or concentration wavering.

"You should talk to Liam about this." Ruby crossed to her vanity and picked up a pen, scribbling numbers on the back of a theater memo. "Here's his number and address. He works in security."

She ignored the paper when he held it out. "I don't need security."

"This person is bothering you, yes?" He pressed it on her until she took it. "He sent you dead roses. This is creepy and inappropriate."

Ruby could be creepy and inappropriate, but he'd never sent anyone dead roses. And the note... *These roses are as dead as your soul.* He had his problems with Petra. He'd even called her a robot once, but he'd never said she was dead in her soul. That was just damn mean. That wasn't something a fan wrote to an artist. It was something an angry lover wrote to his ex. He wondered if Petra was lying, if these roses were from someone she used to go out with. Had she broken someone's heart?

"Your friend lives in Regents Park?" she asked, studying Liam's information.

"Yes, big white house. You can't miss it. Go and talk to him about this..." He gestured toward the dead roses. "About this weirdness. He can help you, give suggestions."

"Won't that cost money? To hire a security guy?"

"He's not a security guy. He owns the entire Ironclad agency. They have offices all over the world." He snorted. "He's the one who gave Yves the money to bring you here, so I think he'll help you with this." Shit, he wasn't supposed to say that. "That was a secret. Don't tell him I told you."

"Remind me to never tell you any secrets."

"I'm not reminding you of nothing," he said truculently.

She folded the wrinkled note card between her fingers, then looked at the paper with Liam's info. "I don't know. The police in New York never did anything, but... Maybe I should ask your friend. Do you think he's home?"

"Tonight, no. I mean, he's home, but you can't ask tonight. They are, uh, very busy on Saturday nights. You call tomorrow. Sunday. I think you should call and ask his opinion what to do. He won't mind."

Ruby had to go. Party time. "Well, it was a good night," he said, edging toward the door. "Be careful on the way out, okay? Maybe people still hanging out. Photographers too, taking pictures."

"I'll watch out. Hey." She stopped him just as he turned to go.

"Hey what?"

"Why don't you let anyone call you Fernando? What's wrong with that name?"

He wondered why she wanted to know. The truth was, the name Fernando made him feel like a child, not that she could ever understand about his childhood. "I prefer Rubio," he said with a shrug. "Like jewel rubies. Deep red, dark and dangerous."

"In Spanish, Rubio means blond."

"I am not Spanish," he snapped. "I'm Brazilian." He was sensitive about his roots, his poverty and yes, even his family name. What would Petra Hewitt know about it, with her impeccable ballet pedigree? "Why you don't go by Grigolyuk?" he asked to poke back at her. "If Grigolyuk is your dad?"

The minute he said it, he regretted it. He could tell by her expression it was a very wrong thing to say.

"Grigolyuk is the world's ugliest sounding name, and he's an asshole." She was suddenly very busy, tucking back her hair, collecting her things to remove her makeup. "I'll see you tomorrow, okay? Have a good night."

"I'm sorry," he blurted out. "Sorry I said that."

She didn't answer. She was staring at the roses, drooping hauntingly on their stems, the roses that cancelled out the Wilder's white bouquet and his oversized scarlet arrangement. She touched one of the flowers and a cascade of petals fell to the floor. "What kind of florist would create such a thing?"

"I'll throw them away for you," he said, picking up the vase and tucking it under his arm. He'd throw it away—right after he showed it to Liam. Shit was so fucked up sometimes. He hated all the anger and sadness in the world. He hated asshole fathers and psycho fans, and mean ballet partners like him.

Yes, he was mean to her a lot. She brought out that beast in him and he didn't know how to handle it, except to push her away. He needed distraction and distance from her pretty smelling locks, her witchy green-eyed stare. He needed release, alcohol and partying and beautiful people. That's what Saturday nights at Liam's house were for.

* * * * *

Petra watched him go with the usual feeling of conflicted longing. Why did he have to be so virile and attractive? Why so careless with her feelings? And then so sweet, worrying for her safety?

Why did he have to bring up her father, tonight of all nights?

She'd secretly wished Petr Grigolyuk would be here, secretly fantasized about him showing up backstage. She'd built the whole thing up in her head, the way he'd be awkward, as if he wasn't sure his estranged daughter would accept him. She would have played it cool at first, but then she would have said, "I'm glad you came to see me dance." From there, they could have started a relationship, even if it was just a friendship...

Ugh, she hated herself. When the flowers were delivered she'd pounced on them, thinking surely one of the arrangements had been from him. But why on earth would her father send her flowers after ignoring her from birth?

Rubio had gotten her flowers. Beautiful roses, tons of them. She traced the petals of one scarlet bud. *Muitos abraços.* She'd keep that card forever, just like she'd remember this night forever. If she'd ever given such an inspired performance, she couldn't remember it, and it was all because of him, The Great Rubio, who was truly great as a ballet partner. Was he trying to make her crazy, being utterly charming and talented, and then devastating her with his careless mention of her father? Was he playing some game with her? She wondered if it had to do with his kinky, dominant thing.

Speaking of which... She looked down at Liam's card. *Big white house. You can't miss it.* How many friends could Rubio have who lived in big white houses in Regents Park? Who happened to be "busy" tonight? Busy hosting a BDSM party, she was sure. She never would have guessed Liam was the friend Suzanne and Hannah had been talking about. He seemed too polished and sedate for such depravities, and if he was married to Ashleigh Keaton, then she was a closet freak too.

Right now, probably this moment, Rubio was headed to this party to get his kink on. Inappropriate fantasies crowded her brain, making her feel dirty. She threw down the card and got ready to leave, wiping off her makeup, showering and drying her hair. She had to get over this sexual obsession with him. She knew it was only because of the mystery, because she didn't know what he was into, or what he did at those parties in the big white house.

But there was a way to find out.

A wig from the wardrobe room, some heavy makeup and dark eyeliner, and Liam and Rubio wouldn't know her, especially if she hid herself in the crowds. There'd be crowds there, wouldn't there, if it was such a big house? If she wore dark, nondescript clothing and kept her head down...

No. It was a ridiculous idea. A dangerous idea, because if Rubio discovered her she'd never live down the embarrassment. Or if Liam and Ashleigh discovered her...

But he was heading to that party *right now.*

Petra groaned and put her face in her hands. What else was she going to do tonight? Go home and worry about the dead flowers? After the high of the performance?

She stared at Liam's card, turning it over and over. It didn't take long to convince herself this was something she *had* to do. This was the only way to get over him, to get past the curiosity and craving that dogged her. It was just...necessary. With that suspect rationalization, Petra headed for the wardrobe room before she lost her nerve.

Chapter Six:
You

An hour later, Petra stood outside the Wilders' house, her knees knocking together beneath her black knit dress. She had prettier dresses, and fancier ones, but she wasn't out to get noticed—she needed to blend in. She flicked her synthetic black hair over her shoulder, then reached one last time to be sure all her real hair was hidden beneath the tight cap of the wig. Theater wigs were great because they were designed to stay on and not slide around a lot. She'd added a few pins just in case. In case of what? In case she had wild sex with someone? So it wouldn't come off? She wasn't going to the party to have sex, or even to spy on Rubio. She was going to prove to herself that her fantasies were just that— fantasies. She hoped to God that Rubio was gross and unattractive while he was having sex. She hoped he had a terrible "o" face and no rhythm and a miniscule dick. She hoped the BDSM stuff was cheesy and laughable.

That's what she hoped, but she had no idea what she'd actually see, or if she'd even get in. There were men inside the door checking people against a guest list. Crap. She'd pictured this entire thing being open and anonymous. In desperation, she huddled behind a couple and climbed the stairs with them. The doormen waved the couple through with a greeting. Petra tried to slide in after them but one of the men held out a hand.

"Good evening. Have you been here before?"

She froze. "No... I'm, uh... I'm new in town. But I know some of the people here."

That was true. She knew Rubio and she knew Liam and Ashleigh. A little.

"Would you mind naming names?" the shorter, stockier guy asked. "Did someone invite you? Are you on the list?"

"I work with Fernando Rubio," she said, because it was probably the only way to gain admittance. "I dance with the London City Ballet."

The doormen glanced at each other. "She does have that look about her," one of them said.

"Mr. Rubio invited you?" the other one asked.

She nodded, a flush burning across her cheeks. "He invited me to come check things out. He didn't tell you?"

Please, please, don't find him to validate my story. I'm totally lying to you. The taller one looked at his cohort. "Should we ask Liam?"

She pushed down rising panic. It wouldn't be the end of the world if they called Liam. She could pretend she was here for advice about the dead flowers. Although, with the fake hair, and the way she was dressed... The guys studied her, and it suddenly seemed that everything about her must be completely transparent. That she was wearing a wig, that she was lying, and that she hadn't been invited here at all.

Just as she was about to turn and flee, the shorter one gestured her in.

"How much trouble can she be?" he said to the other guy. "If Liam has a problem with her, he can throw her out."

The tall one grinned. "Have fun, sweetheart. Bar's by the kitchen, play room is down the staircase. Drinks stay in the living room and no scening while intoxicated. Absolutely no drugs."

"I don't use drugs," said Petra, feeling like a suck up. *Just shut up and go in before they change their mind.*

She hurried into the marble-tiled foyer. The house was packed with mingling, well-dressed people, all engrossed in conversations. Her heartbeat calmed as she realized it would be pretty easy to hide in the midst of this noisy crowd. She went to the bar and asked for a vodka shot. The bartender had a thin face and white blond hair like hers, and was wearing a toga made of gold lamé. The other bartender was in full leather. Gold Lamé Toga poured her a generous shot of luxury-label vodka. "How much is it?" she asked over the din of the electronic music.

"No one pays for drinks here." His youthful features twisted into a grin. "Your first time at the ball, honey?"

She nodded and dug for a tip. "No," he said. "Go have fun. Mr. Wilder foots the bill. But we're required to cut you off when you get sloppy."

"So don't get sloppy," boomed the other bartender, tipping his leather hat to her.

"I'll try not to." She smiled and tossed the shot back, then winced as it burned down her throat. The Russian half of her enjoyed vodka, whether that Russian half was legitimate or not. While she waited for the liquor to calm her nerves, she looked around the Wilders' place. The main room had a soaring ceiling and swanky leather furniture, ornate molding, and gold-framed art on the wall. Real estate here must be crazy. Just how big was this Ironclad security company Liam owned?

Petra shrank back as Liam walked by in a button down shirt and jeans, but his attention was on his wife and her group of friends. That crisis averted, she scanned the room, but she didn't recognize anyone else. Either Rubio wasn't in attendance, or he was downstairs. She asked for one more shot, for courage, downed it in one gulp, and skirted the outside of the crowds until she reached the wide marble staircase that led below.

What would she find down there? How hard did this sexy crowd party? She lifted her chin, prepared to see just about anything as she moved into view of the lower floor. She heard the sounds of impact first, thuds and smacks and screams, but they were happy screams. As she neared the landing, the play room opened before her in a series of erotic tableaux.

Wow. Just wow.

The Wilders' entire basement was set up in her image of the classic sex dungeon. There were intricate racks and solid wooden benches, crosses and cages, chains and pulleys and other equipment she'd read about in her investigation into the BDSM "lifestyle." Almost all of it was in use. From the stairs she could see the whole room, but she didn't dare stand there and gawk. She continued down and moved off to the side.

The music was softer down here, so she could hear the pervasive sounds of lust and arousal. The lighting was minimal, which suited her purposes—lots of shadows to hide in. The walls, floors, and ceiling were all black, lit by candelabras that flickered even though the candles were fake. From her vantage point, she could see that the back and side walls were loaded with whips, handcuffs, sex toys, and some stuff she didn't recognize. Aside from the decor and the extensive selection of BDSM toys, the whole room was alive with people, real people doing really intimate and perverted stuff, freely, in public.

Petra watched all of this with a sense of wonder. She wasn't a prude by any means, but...wow. These people were going at it full throttle, with no self-consciousness, at least none that she could see. There were crawling women on leashes, slave men decked out in complex body harnesses, Dom-types with leather floggers and cuffs clipped to their belts. In one corner, a burly man decorated a curvy girl with knotted rope, while his female assistant stroked and teased her between the legs.

Nearby, a man walloped a bent-over, voluptuous woman with a thick strap. The woman cried out at each blow, but she was clearly enjoying it. The woman's ass was scarlet red beneath her sheer pink panties, and her entire body seemed to tremble in fear at the same time she accepted each stroke. As for her partner, his face lit up in a smile at each of her cries and groans. It was so freaky and weird and...hot. The sound of the strap and the impact turned Petra on, even though she didn't want anything like that to happen to her. It was impossible not to react to the intensity of interplay between the couple.

Petra closed her eyes. *No.* No, she didn't want to be that girl. Did she?

No. She was only getting turned on because it had been so long since she'd had sex. It had been too long since anything raunchy or intense happened in her bedroom, unless she counted her sex dreams about Rubio, and they weren't real.

Rubio. Where was he? She searched the room as well as she could, but other scenes caught her attention. A twenty-something girl with long stripey socks clutched a teddy bear while an older couple played with her breasts. A super hot, barely-legal guy knelt in front of a latex clad woman, alternately licking and polishing her boots, while a girl in skin-tight leather writhed and screamed as her Dom paddled her.

If she was that girl, would she scream like that? She wondered what it felt like, to be spanked while screaming her lungs out, powerless to get away. She'd fantasized about it, but these men and women were really living it.

"Hey, Ashleigh!" Arms encircled her, pulling her into a full body embrace. "I thought you went upstairs with Liam."

From his touch alone, she knew it was Rubio. His hands roved over her flat stomach. "*Meu Deus do céu.* What happened to your baby?"

Petra turned and stepped away from him. He took in her face and her hair at the same time she took in his astounding nakedness. He was hard all over, beautifully muscled, his pronounced iliac furrows framing a truly magnificent cock. She dropped her gaze and stared at the ground. *Don't recognize me. Please don't recognize me.*

He put a finger under her chin and tipped her head up. A muscle twitched in his jaw as he scrutinized her face. His voice came low and roughened with surprise. "You!"

She shook her head, like she might still play this off. He backed away and looked at all of her—her dress, her wig, the black pumps she wore instead of her toe shoes.

"You," he exclaimed again, like he couldn't get his brain wrapped around it. Her brain wasn't working that well either. She was stone-cold busted and Rubio was so, so naked. When she turned to flee, he caught her arm.

"Wait. What are you doing here?" He pushed back her hair when she tried to hide her face. "Why are you wearing a wig?"

So you won't recognize me, damn it. "I'm here for the same reason you are," she lied. "To have a good time, to relax, to enjoy myself."

"What in holy fuck?" He seemed outraged, which made no sense since he was here and, from the looks of things, having quite a pleasurable time. "I thought you were Ashleigh," he spluttered. "You looked just like her from behind."

"You run around groping Ashleigh whenever you feel like it?" Petra snapped. "I thought she was married to your friend."

"What are you doing here?" he repeated, ignoring her question. Again, helplessly, her gaze dipped to his half-engorged and wholly-impressive cock. He reached down and covered himself with an affronted expression. "Stop leering at me like I'm a piece of meat."

"I'm not leering. You're the one running around naked." He wasn't the only one, sure, but he was the only one standing two feet from her. And the only one with a body that made her want to cry in its virile perfection. She'd seen him bare-chested, in clinging sweats, and in body-hugging tights that left nothing to the imagination. Even then, she'd never imagined this.

"Come here." He took her elbow and steered her deeper into the dark corner. He backed her against the wall and leaned down, and for a moment she thought he was going to kiss her. Instead he waggled a finger in her face.

"If you came to spy on me, to tell my secrets to everyone, too bad. Everyone knows I come here. I'm not ashamed that I'm kinky."

What? He thought she was here to out him or something? She didn't want him to believe that so she spit out another blatant lie. "I'm here because I'm kinky too." She stuck out her chin, willing her voice not to shake as she lied her head off. "I've been kinky my whole life, as long as I can remember."

"Who are you here with? Who invited you?"

She bit her lip. How long was she going to brazen this out? "No one invited me. I heard about this party and I came to check it out." She shot a longing look over his shoulder, to the stairs and the exit.

"Who you looking for here?" he persisted. "A man? A woman? A top or a bottom?"

His intent questions alarmed her almost as much as her lies. "It's none of your fucking business who or what I'm looking for."

He stared at her a moment, then he snorted. "You have sub all over you like fucking body oil. Is leaking out of your pores."

"It is not."

"I knew you were a sub from the second I met you. I just wasn't sure *you* knew it."

She inched away from him, back toward the activity and noise of the play room floor. "It doesn't matter. Just because you're a Dom—"

"I'm a top," he said sharply. "I don't do all that role play stuff. I top women and make them feel good. I hurt them, give them sex. They like it. End of story for me." His gaze flashed with a way-too-alluring intensity as his lips quirked up in invitation.

"That's great," she managed to say. "Good for you."

She walked away from him, because she needed distance and because she was thinking really stupid and ill-advised thoughts.

"Hey." He grabbed her and pulled her back again. She couldn't help it—her gaze returned to his cock. It was the barest glance, but he noticed.

"How long since you had sex, Petra? Too long, huh? You like what you see?" He slipped a hand around her waist, brought her right against his chest. She hated that it felt so good, so natural to be in his arms. *We're partners, that's why. Don't allow this, stupid girl.*

"I'll top you if you like," he said in a soft, compelling voice. "Tie you up and hurt you and make you feel so good." His cock rose with insistent presence against her front. "Then we could do whatever you like. Fucking, oral, even anal if you're into it. I'm into it," he added in a truly filthy whisper.

She could barely draw breath. "No, I don't want you t-to top me. I was just—just going home. I'm tired."

"But you keep staring at my cock," he wheedled. "Three, four times now you're staring at it like you want it."

Was he teasing? She couldn't read his expression in the dim light. She shrank back against the wall. "I'm staring because—because—"

Because you're completely, ridiculously beautiful and because I'm insane.

And because I want to take you up on every one of those offers right now.

Chapter Seven:
I Don't Know

Rubio could feel her shaking. He felt like shaking himself. Petra Hewitt, kinky? But some part of him must have known from the beginning. That was why he felt the instant attraction to her, the connection.

"I like your dress," he whispered against her neck.

She pulled away from him. "We can't do this. Definitely not. It would be totally...completely... inappropriate."

"Why?"

"Because we're ballet partners."

"Yes, we're ballet partners. This makes it even better. You've thought of it. I know you've thought of it." He pressed his rigid cock against her, so she could feel what she did to him. "I've thought of it too. And now I learn you're kinky... What do you enjoy?" he asked, to plan his scene with her. "What are your fetishes?"

"Fetishes?"

"Spanking, nipple clamps, latex, bondage, what?"

Her eyes darted around the room. "I like... I like a lot of stuff. Yes, spanking. Being tied up...and submission. Submitting to...somebody."

"You can submit to me, Petra." She trembled as he traced along the curve of her shoulder. "Will be fun, I promise. I'm the best one here to play with."

She shook her head, fake black hair brushing over her cheeks. How strange she looked, now that she was dark all over. Dark dress, dark lips, dark hair. She was the dark twin of light, sweet Petra. He cupped her cheek and held her close.

"Don't kiss me," she said.

"Okay. Don't have to kiss to do a scene," he whispered, staring at her lips.

She studied him with so many messages in her eyes. Embarrassment, guilt, panic, denial, but beneath it all, curiosity. Bent over a spanking bench, he thought, with her arms and legs restrained. He wouldn't make it too scary, their first time together. After all, he wanted her to come back for more.

"I would like to spank you," he said, taking the bold and direct approach. "I want to put you in bondage and punish you for being a bad girl. That would be fun, huh?"

Her eyes widened. "I haven't been a bad girl."

"Oh, please," he said. "You're a naughty, cock-staring girl. Everyone here knows it."

She sucked in a deep breath, stealing another glance at his hardening tool. "I don't want there to be any sex."

"Why not? I'm clean. We'll be safe."

She squared her shoulders and tugged at the hem of her dress. "I'll let you sp-spank me if you want. Do a scene with me out there." She gestured to the equipment. "But no sex. I want you to put some pants on. Your hard-on is scaring me." She shaded her eyes, like she hadn't just been leering at his erection.

"No sex at all?" he asked. "You're sure? You don't think I'm sexy?"

"It's the whole...the whole partner thing."

"Okay," he said. "I'll put my pants on, but only if you take your clothes off."

"What?"

He shrugged. "That's my offer. I'll dress if you undress."

"Oh, we're bargaining?"

He made a show of looking around. "No one cares if you're naked. I don't care. I already know your body anyway, all of it. I feel it with my hands every day."

"The thing is, I've never done...I've never done anything public like this before."

"Only your dress off," he said. "My final offer. But it's better if we're both naked."

"No it's not, because we're not going to have sex." She pointed a finger at him. "I'm serious."

"You don't trust me?"

She almost said no, he could see it, but he'd never given her any reason not to trust him. Not in class, not in rehearsals, not onstage. He'd never once been careless or endangered her, or come close to dropping her, or done anything that might injure her. "I trust you," she finally admitted in a grudging tone. "You're just really, really... God, Rubio. You might poke out my eyes with that thing waving loose."

"Come on," he said, taking her hand and leading her across the room. He found his jeans by the back wall and pulled them on, stuffing his erection into the rough denim. It would go down in a minute. Or not.

A horse. He'd make her straddle a sawhorse, secure her arms over her head so she couldn't flail around too much. And then...

He rubbed the front of his fly. This was going to leave him with a horrible case of blue balls, but if she didn't want sex, he couldn't force her. If he played this scene right, they could start a whole journey of pain and submission and, eventually, she'd want something more. Like in ballet, he'd partner her, hold her steady and guide her through the hard parts.

We can make perfection together.

She looked around self-consciously as he led her to the right side of the room, to a padded horse that was currently unoccupied. Strange, to see Petra without her usual confidence, but he liked her better this way. She was letting down walls, allowing him to see a sliver of her vulnerability. A sliver, that's all she would give. When they stopped beside the sawhorse, he started gathering up the skirt of her dress. He could feel her legs shaking.

"Is okay," he said. "We can stop anytime if you don't like playing in public. But I think I can help you forget everyone else."

She looked at him and then she nodded, letting him pull her dress up and off. Nice stretchy thing, like a dance costume. He flung it in the corner and took in the vision of his partner. Her black hair matched a sexy black bra that pushed her tits up in perfect little mounds. She also wore a black garter belt and stockings that had his cock surging against the constriction of his jeans. Who would have guessed Petra dressed like that under her clothes?

He pushed back her false hair when she tried to hide her face. How dark it looked against her pale skin. He would have taken the wig off but he had a sense she needed it, that she needed anonymity right now. Her lips were a dark-plum pout on her face.

Damn you, he thought. *You're killing me.*

He traced the curve of her breasts over her bra, marveling at the silky texture of her skin. "Is okay to touch you?" he asked, beneath the throb of the music. "Even with no sex?"

"I—I guess so."

He ran his fingers down to her waist, tracing the edge of the lacy garter belt, and then down the elastic fasteners to the tops of her legs. He knew her legs like he knew his own, knew their size and strength, but he never knew them like this before, with the sheer tops of the stockings sliding under his fingers. Her panties were black silk, and they covered far too much for his taste. He brushed the pad of a thumb, only one thumb, across the smooth gusset.

Her whole body reacted, drawing up with aroused tension. He just meant to tease her a little, but suddenly their bodies were vibrating on a whole other plane.

"Really, no sex?" he murmured when he had control of himself again. "You're sure?"

She pressed her forehead against his chest. "Please, don't keep asking."

"You have a beautiful body, though. Is too beautiful for words."

He didn't know why he said that. Maybe because he really was having trouble putting words together at the moment. He collected the shreds of his sanity and nudged her toward the horse. She started to bend over it but he stopped her and lifted her, and settled her on it astride. Her feet could reach the ground, but barely, so she had to balance with her pussy pressed against the padded top. She gave a faint moan crossed with a sigh, and he wished he had a recording of it, so he could listen to it a thousand more times. She was kinky. How...*perfect*. He wished he'd known before now.

"Stay," he said. "I'm going to get some things."

He watched her surreptitiously as he prowled along the wall, picking up a pair of narrow cuffs and a riding crop. He wondered why she could bare her soul in front of a massive City Ballet audience, but was afraid to play here without hiding behind makeup and a wig. It made him feel protective, which was something he almost never felt in a typical scene. He liked to challenge his partners, drive them crazy, get them off. Protect them? No.

He returned to her, ignoring the curious glances of his friends. "Give me your hands," he ordered.

She obeyed, staring as he buckled the cuffs onto her wrists. "Are you going to give me a safeword?" she asked.

"I'll give you a safeword if you want. How about *Romeo*? You can remember that word, yes?"

Maybe it was a bad choice. It would remind her they worked together, that they'd premiered their partnership a few hours ago in front of four thousand eyes. Or maybe it was good to remind her they worked together, that she could trust him. He looked into her eyes as he lifted her wrists with one hand and fished for the dangling carabiner with the other. She looked halfway to heaven and halfway to falling apart. Once her arms were fixed above her head, he grasped the curve of her neck and kissed her. He did it meaning to calm her down, but then he felt her straining to press against him, to get closer to him, and he caught fire.

He threw a leg over the horse so he faced her, and pulled her forward into his arms. He could touch her everywhere, anywhere now, and she couldn't stop him. He took advantage, running his hands over all the parts of her he adored. He kissed her while he explored her waist, her hips, her breasts, even the hot silk of her panties. She tasted so sweet, as sweet as the *sonho*-sugar of her hair. He grasped her tight ass in one of his palms and squeezed it, and then gave it a sharp, resounding slap.

She broke away from the kiss with a gasp.

Ruby's hand stayed where it was, curled into a fist. He could see in Petra's eyes that it was the first time in her life she'd been spanked by anyone. He'd bet his life on it. *Kinky, my ass. You're a reckless little vanilla, Petra Hewitt.* He shouldn't play with her. He should send her home immediately and tell her not to come back. But he couldn't.

He blinked, holding her gaze, and then he swatted her again for good measure.

"That's what happens to bad girls," he whispered against her lips.

* * * * *

Petra stared into his dark eyes from inches away. Every time she breathed in, her chest brushed against his solid heat and she was aware of him not as her partner, but as a man. She stretched her arms and pulled at the leather cuffs, but she couldn't get away. Between his arms and his body, and the sawhorse and the cuffs holding her, she felt trapped and powerless in a way she'd never been before. It was a hot, scary feeling exacerbated by the sting in her ass cheeks. He'd done that to her. Rubio had spanked her—hard—with those same hands he used to lift and manipulate her onstage.

That's what happens to bad girls.

Oh God. When he spanked her, she'd been shocked but turned on too. Her whole body responded instantly, her pussy flaring hot and then settling into a nagging, simmering ache. His monster cock was put away, concealed within his jeans, but she felt more threatened than ever. His sexuality enveloped her, intoxicating her—and there was going to be more, much more. She could tell by his expression and the tension in his muscles.

"Ouch," she said, trying to sound light and nonplussed.

She'd lied like a maniac, told him she was into this stuff. At first, it was only so he wouldn't be angry with her, but then she realized it was also because, deep down, she wanted to try it. She wanted Rubio to top her because once he offered it, she didn't think she could survive without knowing what it would be like.

She was in deep shit now. He was so much more intense than in her fantasies. Everything was so much more real: his hand squeezing and slapping her ass, his breath in her ear, his hot skin brushing against hers, and the growing pressure between her legs.

He let her go and stood up, and without meaning to, she pitched forward. The cuffs stopped her and her pussy slid against the padded top of the horse. She felt the teasing pulse of pleasure all the way down the insides of her thighs, and up into her breasts. Her nipples tightened, ticklish, against the cups of her bra. She struggled in the cuffs because she didn't know how else to process all this stimulation. Around them, people turned to look with appreciative stares. They were involved in similar scenes, but Petra couldn't imagine any of them feeling quite as unhinged as her.

She glanced over her shoulder to find Rubio studying her, a thin, whippy implement in his hand. It looked like a riding crop, but not a real one. It was one you used for sexy games, for having fun. She felt self-conscious under his gaze, about how she looked, about how turned on she was. He came closer and ran a hand up the length of her thigh. "Are you ready, little Petra?"

She tossed her head back, trying to be a sexy, wanton BDSM chick like the ones she'd watched earlier. At least she'd worn the damn garter belt. Was she convincing him she knew what she was doing? She jerked as a hot spark of pain landed on her left ass cheek. *Holy shit!* Her eyes flew to his.

"You like?" He wore a speculative expression. "More?"

"Of course, more," she said with false confidence. "Do your worst. I can take it."

His lips turned up in the shadow of a smile. "Dancers are such masochists." He flicked her again with the crop, and this time a yelp escaped. He barely seemed to swing it for the resulting amount of sting. It had to be in the movement of the wrist. Again, and then again, he flicked her on her ass cheeks, concentrated points of pain. Was this supposed to feel good? It felt kind of good, but it frightened her too. She arched her back, pulling at the cuffs and chain holding her. She was acutely aware that her movements were sexual, that anyone watching would find her struggles erotic. She stood on her toes to relieve the pressure on her pussy and then he flicked her on the outside of her thigh.

"Ow." She turned to frown at him. He made a face like, "What?" He strolled around her, slowly, casually, threatening more pain at any moment. He would choose when, he would choose how. She supposed that was the whole "top" thing. She jerked as he flicked the other thigh. It stung but barely left a mark, only a faint pink blush. What if he really whacked her with it? Was that what this was leading up to? She glanced out at the other areas of the basement where some people were playing very hard. The wailing woman on the spanking bench was getting paddled in a terrifying tattoo of cracks.

He came closer, took her chin in his fingers and lifted it. "You watching everyone else?" he said. "I can't keep your attention?"

"There's a lot going on. It's hard not to look."

"Mmm," he said, slipping an arm around her waist. "You ready for more?"

"You've hardly given me anything."

It was probably the wrong thing to say. It was like he'd been waiting for an excuse to go harder. The flicks began again, sharper this time, left cheek, right cheek. She didn't want to struggle and make a scene but it was so hard to be still. Each time she jerked and tried to inch away from him, all she did was turn herself on more. Her panties were whisper-thin, her clit pressed hard against the top of the sawhorse. She hadn't meant to get so turned on, not that it was her fault. He was the one who'd put her in this position. A groan escaped her. Yes, of course he'd put her in this position. He knew exactly what he was doing and she...she was a naïve, inexperienced fool.

He started cropping her light and fast then, with no rest in between. *Tap, tap, tap, tap, tap, tap.* It started out uncomfortable and quickly grew unbearable. She flailed and pressed against him, swinging her arms, but he only held her tighter. *Tap, tap, tap, tap.* Ow, ow, ow, ow...

"Oh God," she huffed. "Really? Ow. Please, stop."

"Use your safeword if you need it."

"I don't need to use a safeword. It's just..." *It's just that my ass is on fire and you smell wonderful and my pussy is about to explode.* "My arms are starting to hurt." What was one more lie? She pulled at the cuffs and made a face like her shoulders hurt, even though she was a dancer and could have held this pose for ages.

He didn't question her, just set to work undoing the buckles. When he freed her wrists, she made a big show of stretching and kneading her arms. It bought some time for the hot ache in her ass cheeks to subside. When she finished she grasped the horse and sat rigidly still, even though what she really wanted to do was grind against it furiously.

"Arms better now?" Ruby asked her.

She nodded, eyeing the crop. "Is that it? Are we finished?"

His brows rose. "Not close to finished. But you can have your arms loose if you can keep them out of the way."

Of course she could keep them out of the way. At least until he started that infernal torture again. *Tap, tap, tap, tap, flick, flick, flick.* "Ah, God," she moaned, reaching back to shield herself. As soon as she did it, he moved to her thighs. *Tap, tap, flick, tap, tap, tap,* right over the garter elastics, right on her tender, bare skin. She put her hand there and like quicksilver, he was back at her ass, harder now. *Flick!* No matter where she tried to shield herself, he found another open spot.

"You're going to get your fingers hurt," he said. "Is not safe." He grabbed her hands and pushed them down against the top of the horse. "Leave them there. Grab and don't let go."

Her fingers clenched on the black vinyl. She wasn't sure why he was so worried for her fingers when he was killing her ass and thighs. She squirmed on the horse, wanting more. Wanting sex. Oh, God, no, no, *no.*

"No what?" he asked.

67

Had she said that out loud? She was losing her mind. "I don't know. I mean, I don't know if I can keep my hands still."

He studied her face. "It hurts too much? You want me to stop?"

No, she didn't. She'd never been so turned on in her life, but if he continued, she was afraid she'd lose control of everything. Her cries, her movements, and especially her sanity. She'd beg him to fuck her, to ride her to orgasm right here in front of everyone.

She stared at him, trying to compose an answer to his question, but she'd forgotten what he'd asked. He gazed back, like a predator not quite certain of his prey. Did he know? She should confess everything to him. That, yes, she'd come here to see him, and that no, she didn't know anything about BDSM. She should confess about her dreams and her fantasies, tell him how much she wanted him even if she couldn't allow herself to have him.

He swung his leg over the horse again, this time so he was behind her, his chest pressed to her back. "Give me your hands," he said. In that fleeting moment, with his sultry, demanding voice at her ear, she could have sobbed with frustration. She let him take her hands, beyond obedience now. There was only him and the crazed feelings he created in her. She was not like this.

Then why are you letting him hold your hands behind your back? Why do you love the way it feels?

He could circle both her wrists with a thumb and finger. With the other hand, he stroked the crop along her thighs, a light, teasing glide. He ran it over both legs, over shimmery stockings and the bare skin above. She heard him take a breath, his chest rising and falling against her back.

Then, again, *tap, tap tap*, but this time it was very sharp and very controlled, on the tender inner skin of her left thigh. The longer he did it, the harder it was to be still. She arched back against him and he tightened his grip on her wrists. He started on the other thigh. Oh God, it hurt. *Tap, tap, tap, flick, flick, flick.*

She made an agonized sound, or perhaps a pleading sound. She wanted to plead on her knees for him to flick it on her center. To rub the crop over her aching sex until she exploded into orgasm.

"What's the matter?" he whispered.

She shook her head violently. *No, no, no, no.*

"It feels good or bad?" he asked in the same soft tone. "You want me to stop?"

She couldn't answer. She bit her lip and turned to him, seeking solace in the arms of her tormentor. He brought his hand up and guided her face until their lips met in a brief kiss. She could feel the crop in his fingers, right against her leg. A moment later, *flick*. A bite of fire landed at the juncture of her pelvis. The other side then, back and forth, on her bare skin. The stockings, her panties, nothing covered that delicate, pale area, nothing except the flicks of his crop.

She squirmed against him, desperate for him to touch her clit. If he touched her now, she would orgasm like a maniac and then she'd die. If he touched her, he'd know everything, and she'd lose everything, because she'd do anything to live like this, with Rubio's hot breath against her ear and his hands cinching her wrists behind her back. She would want this three, four, five times a week. Every night.

He slid a hand down her hip, pinched and squeezed the same sensitive flesh he'd tortured with his crop. One touch on her aching clit, and she'd go off like a rocket...

"No," she cried, cowering away from him. "No, that's enough. That's—"

She jerked her hands hard, and he released them. She vaulted off the horse and backed away. He stood, his face tight with concern.

"What? What's the matter? You okay?"

No, I'm not okay. What are you doing to me? She didn't feel like herself. She felt scared and conflicted, and she was wearing a damn black wig that kept falling in her eyes. He reached out to her but she eluded his touch.

"I just—" She put her fingers to her lips, where he'd kissed her. "I just—I have to—to leave."

He laughed uncertainly. "You didn't like it?"

She grabbed her dress and motioned him back when he tried to approach. "No, it was good. I liked it, but I have to go. Um..." She cast around for appropriate parting words as she yanked down the skirt of her dress. "You probably want to have sex and...and take your pants off again. So, I'm going to go and then you can play with someone else. I mean, someone more willing to have sex."

"I liked playing with you," he said. "I told you, we don't have to have sex."

You idiot. Is that what you think? When he reached out for her, she let him hug her but she was too alarmed to hug him back. She broke away and said goodbye, then headed for the stairs, hoping he wouldn't follow. Halfway up the stairs she started to run, dodging naked, happy guests. She was halfway across the living room when someone stepped in front of her.

"Hey, are you okay? What's the matter?"

She looked up into the concerned amber eyes of the party host, Liam Wilder. Before she could come up with words in her state of distress, his eyes narrowed.

"Petra? Is that you? What are you doing here? Why are you wearing that wig?"

They were the same questions Rubio had asked her earlier, but this time, she didn't bother to lie to him. "Oh God. I don't know what I'm doing here. I don't know."

* * * * *

Rubio regretted letting her go. He prowled around Liam's house three times, upstairs, downstairs, in case she'd decided to linger, but she was nowhere to be found.

He shouldn't have let her go, but he'd been so freaked out himself. He'd tried to be responsible and maintain a safe detachment. He'd tried to stay in control, because she was so delicate. She would have been so easy to hurt.

Once he realized she'd never played before, it made her sensual reactions so much more powerful. He'd almost lost control at the end. He'd been one second from sliding his hand down the front of her panties, one second from shoving his fingers inside her hot pussy and making her ride them until she came. He wanted to conquer her and own her, and torment her until she screamed for mercy—the good kind of screaming. He wanted these things so badly, but somehow, she didn't want him.

No, she'd jumped down from the horse and taken off for the stairs like the room was on fire, and he'd watched her go, helpless, his heart in his throat.

Damn her. He should have left her in the cuffs. He knew her arms weren't really hurting. He was pretty good at reading women and he'd thought she was enjoying everything he did to her. He'd thought she was turned on, right up until the point where she'd fled. He pictured her running down the street, dodging cars and swearing at strangers, her itchy black wig blowing out behind her. Crazy, erratic Petra. Why had she come to Liam's in the first place, in that awful disguise?

"Ruby."

He turned at the strident tone of Liam's voice. "Hey. You seen Petra?"

"I just took her home. She seemed pretty upset."

Rubio stepped back, holding out his hands. "I didn't do nothing to her."

"I know. Relax. I think she was just...confused."

Rubio was confused too. He looked around at the chattering crowds of kinky friends. This was his crowd. She'd been the interloper, the one who didn't belong here. "I don't know why she showed up. I didn't invite her. I didn't tell her anything about your parties."

"They're not exactly a secret in ballet circles, thanks to you."

"I never told anybody," Ruby protested.

"I told you to relax," said Liam, drawing him to a more private corner. "I don't care who knows, as long as they're a friend. And I have a pretty good idea why she showed up here. I expect it's the same reason she ran out the way she did."

Rubio stared at him. "What? What reason?"

"Obviously she's as tangled up over you as you are over her."

Liam's words didn't make any sense. "Tangled up?"

"You, her. Tangled up." Liam intertwined his fingers in a knot. "And before you deny that you feel anything for her, I saw you playing with her earlier. So save it."

Rubio glared at him. He hated when Liam got this way, prying into his business and giving him judgey looks. Liam was always the cool, collected one, the smart one, while Ruby was the fuck-up who swanned around in tights. He waved a hand at his friend. "I'm tired. I'm going home."

"You could go to her place instead, you know. Tell her how you really feel about her, instead of standing here pretending nothing happened downstairs."

"Why would I do that?"

"Why wouldn't you?" his friend answered. "I think both of you could use a good aftercare session. At the very least, you should check on her and be sure she's okay."

He hated Liam. He hated him because he was rich and suave, and judgey, and almost always right.

Chapter Eight:
Please

Rubio knew where she lived. He'd walked her to her door a couple times, when rehearsals finished early and they didn't want to wait for the car. He'd even picked her up here once, for lunch, in some fruitless attempt to thaw the frost between them. She'd certainly thawed tonight, and then frozen up again like a glacier. Why? Liam said Petra was tangled up with him. What did that mean? Why could he never understand anything where women were concerned? All he knew was how to turn them on, and how to hurt them so he didn't really hurt them. Neither of those talents was proving very useful where Petra was concerned.

He knocked on her door with a feeling of dread. "Petra," he said softly. "It's me."

"What do you want?"

He stepped back. She was right on the other side. "Let me in."

"I'm in my pajamas."

He made an agitated sound. "I don't care. Can I come in? Before your neighbors call the police?"

He heard the lock turn and there she was, his sugar-vanilla girl, dressed in a cat shirt and pajama bottoms. She looked defensive, her arms clutched at her waist.

"I wanted to make sure you were okay," he said. "Are you okay? I didn't hurt you?"

"You didn't hurt me."

"But you left so quick. Why did you run away?" Her pretty blonde hair was still wet from a shower. He liked her better this way, in her natural look. She still had the faintest shadow of dark lips. He wanted to kiss them. He almost did before he remembered himself.

"I'm sorry," he said instead. "I don't know how to be like Liam. I don't know how to be a good guy, for you to like, but I like you, Petra. I'm sorry Liam had to take you home. I would have taken you home."

She closed her eyes and hugged herself tighter. "Oh, Rubio. I just had to get out of there."

"If you stayed, I would have taken care of you. Aftercare, is called. I know you don't know anything about BDSM, by the way."

She opened her mouth to protest but he stopped her. "Please, don't lie to me anymore. Is okay. It was your first time to do it, yes?"

"If you knew I was lying, why didn't you say something?"

"Why? Because..." *Because I wanted you. Because the temptation was too hard to resist.* "Because I didn't know at first. Only after, I realized, but then it was too late. I wanted to show you. I wanted..."

She pulled him inside and shut the door. "You wanted to embarrass me," she said. "Admit it. You wanted to show me that you can control me and make me want you."

"Maybe. A little," he admitted. He raised his eyebrows. "Did you want me?"

"No, I didn't, and I don't. I don't want you," she snapped, turning away. "And I don't want you to make me want you when I don't want to want you. I don't want you tempting me to want you just because you can, when I've already said I don't want you."

He held up a hand. "Please, slow down. My English is not so good."

"I don't want this," she cried, backing away as he advanced on her. "And I don't know why you're here now, tempting me, making things worse. We don't belong together. We're nothing alike. I don't want you, okay? Believe me, I don't. Not sexually or otherwise."

He blinked at her, once, twice. She was pretty even when she was angry, but she'd made her position very clear. "Okay, then. I'll go," he said, heading for the door.

"But...wait..."

When he turned to face her, she shook her head. "No. I mean, yes. Go. Ignore me."

"But you said to wait." He shoved a hand into his pocket. "I brought condoms just in case. In case you want me. Because I want you. I've wanted you forever now."

To his chagrin, she covered her face and started crying.

He hurriedly shoved the condoms back in his pocket. "Or, okay. I'll put them away. I was just thinking, safe sex."

"Please shut up," she yelled through tears. "Look, I lied. I don't w-want you to g-go. I'm just afraid I'll fall for you, and I really don't want to fall for you. Why are you making this so hard?"

"Hard? I'm making things hard?" He narrowed his eyes, reaching to caress the curve of her jaw. "You lied to me, Petra, twice now, and you're saying all kinds of crazy stuff. You're such a bad girl." He brushed away one of her tears. "You know, lying is bad. You need someone to make you a better girl. Someone to punish you when you're not being good."

She made a small sound, like she was choking or laughing. "Let me guess, that someone is you?"

"I would be happy to help." He took her in his arms and kissed away her tears, making gentle shushing noises. He patted her back and then ran his hands down over her delicate curves. He didn't even try to hide his erection. He pressed it right against the front of her. Let her feel what she did to him. Oh, and the things he wanted to do to her...

He drew back and pressed his forehead to hers. "What now? You said you don't want sex. You said, because we're partners..."

She took a shuddery breath. "Don't you understand what happened with my mom and dad? If you knew what he put her through, you'd see why—why we can't—"

"Who? Put who through what? Petra—"

"Maybe it won't happen with us, but what if it does?"

"What if what does?" he asked, bewildered.

"My mother...she lost herself in my father, in her feelings for him. Then she got pregnant and found out he'd never really loved her. No one would hire her after that. It was a big fucking mess."

"But...what does that have to do with either of us?"

She shuddered again, even harder this time. "Because I understand how my mother felt now. I'm about to die from wanting you. It's horrible. This is the worst thing I've ever felt."

He gave a quick, bitter laugh. Did she think he didn't understand the wanting? He slid his fingers over the elegant line of her neck. He wanted to fuck her until she couldn't walk, until she screamed and cried, until she came in a rush of breath and begged for more. "I die every time I touch you," he said. He pushed up the back of her shirt and opened his hands against her warm, bare skin. "You torture me, every day, every hour. You're a very bad girl."

She buried her face against his chest. "I don't mean to torture you, but I'm scared. You scare me in so many ways."

"Do you think I'll hurt you?" he asked, sliding his hands down to squeeze her ass.

"Yes. I think you'll steal part of my soul."

He tilted her head back to look in her eyes. "Really? You believe that?"

"Yes. I want you so bad, but I'm scared. I'm so scared of what you'll do to me."

"Ah, *querida*," he sighed, his cock jumping at her softly spoken words. "You know what, though? Is okay to be scared."

* * * * *

Is okay to be scared. Is okay to be scared.

She gasped as he backed her toward the wall, pinning her with his body. While she was still processing his heat and his closeness, his mouth closed over hers in a ravishing kiss. His tongue warred with hers, his hands roving over her stomach, her waist. His palm slid lower to press against her pussy through her sleep pants. Oh *God*, his fingers. He could make her do anything with those fingers. She didn't want him to stop but some self-preserving impulse made her push him away.

"No," she said. "Haven't you been listening?"

"I've been listening. You're just not making any sense."

"Rubio—"

He made a quelling sound and threaded a hand through the back of her hair, massaging her nape. His touch hypnotized her, quieting the alarm bells in her brain. She wanted to stop him, but more than that, she wanted to feel the full force of his sexuality. Just one night. What could it hurt? This was too thrilling not to experience, just this once...

She closed her eyes and gave herself up to the pull between them, the attraction she'd stuffed down since the second they'd first touched.

He kissed her, rough and hard, as she clung to him. His hands strayed to her breasts, squeezing them through her faded tee shirt. The grasping pressure felt so good that she moaned against his lips. There was some wildness in him that made her forget caution and discipline, and the control she'd honed all her life.

"Yes, please," she whispered. "More."

He gazed at her, his lips parted. In one fluid movement he had her tee up and off, so she stood before him bared to the waist. When she moved to cover herself, he took her hands and trapped them behind her back, and bent to kiss her. His teeth closed on her lower lip in a teasing bite and she sucked in a breath. That moment, when he trapped her and bit her, that was the moment she knew she was lost. She struggled against the cage of him, but only to make him hold her harder. She wanted these intense games he played. She wanted him just as he was, commanding and carnal. She wanted him to hurt her and make her *feel*.

He gave a growling sound, the perfect accompaniment to her thoughts. His roving hand found her nipple and pinched until she shied away in agony and desire. She buried her head against the side of his neck, pleading for God knew what. *Please, please, please...* He left her nipple and grabbed her ass, pulling her forward against him. She could feel his cock through his jeans, a thick, threatening outline to go with his brutal grip on her wrists.

"I want to fuck you, Petra," he said, pulling away from her. His dark eyes glittered with mayhem. "That's what you need, yes? To get fucked like a naughty little slut?" He emphasized both *fucked* and *slut* with violent urgency.

Before she could answer that yes, she definitely needed to be fucked like a naughty little slut, he lifted her in his arms. "Your bedroom?"

"Second door down the hall," she answered, clinging to his neck.

Is okay to be scared. Is okay to be scared.

She repeated it to herself as he carried her down the hall and kicked the door shut behind them. She repeated it as he stripped off her sleep pants and panties and pushed her back on the bed, draped her legs over his shoulders, and started licking her pussy like a starving man. *Oh my God.*

She had plenty of sexual experience, but this felt like the first time. The sensation, the surge of erotic excitement felt totally new. She shuddered as his tongue flicked over her clit, his warm breath teasing her senses. No man had ever gone down on her like this, forcing her thighs wide open and exploring every orifice, doing as he pleased to her, so that she felt like the submissive one. His fingers tightened on her thighs and she felt so controlled that, for a moment, she felt a frisson of fear.

Is okay to be scared.

"Oh, please," she cried, reaching to grasp at his hair. *Please don't stop. Please don't ever stop.* He licked her everywhere, from her slick labia to her clit to the sensitive bud of her ass. His mouth was magic. His tongue found her most responsive spots and relished them until she thought the pleasure would break her mind. Flick, lick, nibble. Oh, what the hell was he doing? She was torn between pushing him away and pulling him closer.

He took the choice from her, grabbing her hands and holding them out of the way, so all she could do was cry out and buck under his ministrations. Her pelvis ached with the pressure of quick, fierce arousal.

"Is okay," he said, tightening his grip on her fingers. "Come for me. I want it."

She couldn't move her hands or her legs, or anything without him allowing it. She squeezed her fingers into fists as his tongue flicked and laved the most sensitive spot of her core. "Oh, please, please, don't...don't stop..."

He said something she couldn't decipher, something low and lyrical in Portuguese, and he didn't stop. As for her, she could no longer talk, only make helpless animal sounds. When her orgasm finally broke wide, her walls crashed together in an almost painful release. She cried out, a loud, long sob, which was not at all like her. She was always quiet in bed, self-conscious and controlled, but he had stripped that control from her. He brushed kisses across her clit as the aftershocks rolled through her body, and then he kissed her lightly on the inside of each of her thighs.

"I wanted you," he said against her skin. "I wanted that for a long time now."

She whimpered in agreement. She wanted it too, again and again. He released her hands and she reached for his face, to touch him, to come to terms with the idea of rude, infuriating Rubio bringing her such feverish elation. He pressed a kiss against her palm and backed away from her.

"Don't move," he said. "Rest a minute. More is coming."

More? Of course there was more. There was still his masterpiece of a body to enjoy. She watched as he stripped beside her bed, quickly, without inhibition. Shoes, shirt, jeans, boxer briefs, socks. He was garishly hard. He dug in his jeans pocket and straightened with a couple of condoms in his hand.

"See," he said, holding them up. "Safe sex. No problems."

He keeps condoms in his pocket, she thought. He was a manwhore. She needed to remember that. A few hours ago, he'd been running around naked in a sex dungeon. This would have to be just for play, for enjoyment. It would be all too easy to fall head over heels and sacrifice everything, her entire career, for this hedonistic playboy. *No.*

He came to the bed and crawled over her, his arms trapping her on either side. His heavy cock fell against her belly, a jutting threat that made her feel scared again, but it was a delicious fear. He cradled her and rubbed his cheek against hers. "Is okay," he said. "Will feel good, to have me inside you. Maybe I hurt you a little, but you'll like it." He delivered a sharp slap to her outer thigh, to the same place he'd cropped her earlier.

She struggled in reaction, because it turned her on when he fought back and pinned her down. He slid a hand into her hair and closed his fist. He pulled until he bared her throat and then he licked her from below her jaw to the base of her throat. There was a teasing slide of teeth—he could have bitten her. She kind of wanted him to, but instead he flipped her over and arranged her on her hands and knees. He knelt behind her, his arms on either side of her, his muscled torso along her back like a wall. She'd been body to body with him many times at the theater, in rehearsals and ballets, but never like this.

He leaned back and smacked her on the bottom, right below the curve of her ass cheek. She whimpered and tried to wiggle away but he stilled her with his two giant hands. He spread her cheeks and she shuddered. He could see all of her, every secret part of her as he held her open. It was awful but she felt turned on too, used and manipulated. When he moved his palm down and groped her, she lost her nerve and collapsed on her stomach, trying to turn away from him.

"No, up." Another sharp slap to her ass, then another. "On your hands and knees."

She scraped together her courage and obeyed him because she didn't want this to end. Her knees were shaking and her arms felt like twigs but she held the pose as he spanked her again, and again. Her ass throbbed, the shape of his hand prints like a blazing brand. She didn't know what bizarre mental-physiological impulses were at work, but the more he spanked her, the more she wanted him to fuck her. Despite the fact that she'd come just a few moments earlier, she wanted him deep inside, riding her hard, overpowering her. She heard the sound of the condom wrapper.

Thank you, God. She looked back over her shoulder as he rolled the condom over his thick length.

"I'd make you suck me first," he said, eyeing her mouth with a lurid twist to his lips, "if I didn't want your pussy so bad."

She thought wildly of her dreams, of Rubio's cock growing bigger and bigger in her mouth. As much as she'd fantasized about it, she was glad it wasn't on the menu tonight because she wanted him inside her, not choking off her breath. Once he'd double checked the condom, he grabbed her hips and eased her back onto his rigid cock. He was so big, it felt kind of dangerous. Not dangerous like she wasn't wet enough, or that she didn't want him—it was that he didn't give her any sense of control. She cowered downward, resting her shoulders on the bed.

"No," he said with another slap to the thigh. "Hands and knees."

With some reluctance she resumed the position—hands and knees, naked and pale, scared and vulnerable. *Is okay to be scared.* She was thinking too much now, about how she looked, about whether she satisfied him, about whether she measured up to all his sexy BDSM girls.

His hands squeezed on her shoulders, massaging them as he pulled out and slid in again. "Good girl," he said. "This is the very best part. Don't leave me now."

She tried to obey, tried to make herself relax. His hands moved from her shoulders to her hips and then he gripped her waist. With a long, low grunt he snapped his hips against hers. He held her like she was his toy, his plaything, and she liked that feeling, shuddering on all fours with a smarting ass as he plunged deep inside. She bit her lip and squirmed, squeezing on the length of his cock.

"Oh God," he moaned. "You little—"

He pulled away and flipped her over, entering her missionary style. She closed her eyes, confused by all the conflicting messages in her brain. She wanted to satisfy him, but God, she shouldn't even be sleeping with him. She wanted him to hurt her, but she wanted him to caress her too. Most of all, she wanted to please him more than anyone had ever pleased him before.

"Open," he said.

She parted her legs wider, to accommodate his thrusting hips.

"No, your eyes," he said. "Open your eyes and look at me."

She did, and he fixed her with his dark gaze. "Stop thinking," he said. "Just feel. Do I feel good inside you?"

She squeezed her inner muscles on him again. "Yes, you feel...amazing."

He closed his eyes and shuddered. "Stop doing that with your pussy. I'll tear you up if you don't stop." He slid inside her, all the way, and stopped with a shiver of his own.

"Tear me up? Literally?" she whispered. She stared into his eyes and squeezed on his cock again. She had pretty good pelvic floor muscles, being a dancer. He grunted, a wild, surrendered sound. His pelvis ground against hers, right against her aching clit. She sighed and closed her eyes.

"Open them," he insisted.

She stared up at him, angling her hips to feel the pleasure again. His gaze was burning. Intent. "I don't want you to tear me up," she said meekly, feeding on some dialogue between them, some unspoken dynamic they both understood.

"Stop."

"Because you're so much bigger and stronger than me. You could really hurt me." The hand on her ass pinched until she yelped. "If you hurt me I—I don't know what I'll do."

He buried his face in her neck, licking beneath her ear. "You're teasing me, huh?" He held her ass hard, forcing her to take the full length of his increasingly vigorous thrusts. She struggled with him, wound up tight like a spring. Every time he pressed into her, her thoughts receded a little more. His eyes caught hers and held them and that, more than anything, nudged her toward climax. He was pure male force, pure power, and he wasn't hurting her in any way she didn't like.

"Please," she said. "Please, please, please..."

He groped her breasts, pinched her nipples and then grabbed her waist the same way he did when they were about to do a lift, but he wasn't lifting her, he was pressing her down, impaling her on his cock, touching some unexplored territory deep inside her. She cried out, falling over the edge into orgasm, collapsing and expanding from within. She made fists while tears spilled from her eyes, not tears of emotion or sadness, but tears from a depth of pleasure she'd never felt before. Oh, she'd had orgasms, plenty of them. This wasn't an orgasm. This was a whole-body death and resurrection. He pounded into her and then he came too with a jerk and a harsh groan.

For long moments they lay still together, gasping for breath. He slid his knees under her thighs and held her trapped beneath his chest, and she didn't feel the slightest impulse to escape his weight. She felt so close to him, connected to him in a way that went beyond partnering and professional matters, even beyond a typical sexual experience. This was a universe away from what she and her previous sex partners had done. It simply wasn't the same thing. Rubio's chest felt perfect against her chest, and his legs felt perfect against her legs. His cock felt perfect inside her as she flexed her sore, hot cheeks. Everything was perfect, balanced and aligned. It wasn't exaggeration, it was the truth.

Slowly, as she came to her senses, another truth devastated her.

They could never, ever do this again.

* * * * *

Rubio thought he was crushing Petra. He was almost sure of it, but he didn't care. He wanted to crush her. He wanted to put her in a cage in his loft and keep her there whenever he wasn't using her. He wanted to put his cock in her mouth and shove it in balls deep. He wanted to fuck her again, tonight, tomorrow night, every night until she begged him to leave her alone. He wanted to do every perverted and sordid thing in the world to beautiful Petra.

"*Meu bem*," he whispered against her ear. "What were you saying? You don't want me?"

She smiled, but then she shook her head and buried her face in her hands. This reaction befuddled him. He was still drifting in the afterglow of their luscious, mind-altering sex, but she looked unhappy. Why?

Jesus Cristo, he'd hurt her. He must have hurt her too badly. He must have misread her signals.

"I'm sorry," he whispered in frantic repetition, checking over her slender frame. "I'm sorry, I'm sorry, I'm sorry. I didn't know what you liked. I was too rough. I'm sorry."

She shook her head. "No, it wasn't that."

"What then?" He pulled out since he was going soft, but he still held her in his arms. "What's the matter? You are angry? Hurt? Please, tell me."

"It's just..." She turned away from him. "We can't do this. It's even worse than I thought."

With patient, gentle pressure, he managed to uncurl her from her fetal ball. He nudged her hands away from her face. "What do you mean, worse than you thought? What are you saying? I don't understand."

She stared up at him, her eyes hard now, and bleak. "I thought, just one time. Just once would be okay, to satisfy my curiosity. I didn't realize it would feel so...perfect."

"Is bad? To feel perfect?"

"No. I mean, yes! Don't you understand how dangerous this is to me, to my career? I don't want to fall in love with you, and end up heartbroken and used, and get knocked up with some baby you don't want, and spend the rest of my life crippled with regrets. Crippled and angry and bitter and resentful."

He tried to follow the miserable tangle of her words. "But..." He shook his head. "I didn't make a baby in you. I used a condom. Petra, look." He held up the used, filled receptacle before it occurred to him it was pretty disgusting. "Here, let me up a minute."

He went to the bathroom and threw it away, and washed his hands. When he returned, Petra was propped up against her pillows, huddled in her blanket. He went to sit beside her. He wanted to comfort her, but he was afraid to even touch her in her current mood. "Petra, I know your concerns. But I liked what we just did. I liked it a lot. Didn't you?"

"Yes, but it doesn't matter. I only want to dance with you. We should be dance partners, that's all."

"Sure, we are dance partners," he said to soothe her. He pulled her against his side, and when she didn't shove him away, he pressed a kiss to her temple. "Listen, we can make this work. We don't have to make a baby, like your mother and father. We can dance and then we can have sex sometimes if you like. We can even play at Liam's party, or here, or at my place—"

"No, we can't do that," she cried. "That's what I'm trying to explain to you."

"But it was so fun. You liked it when we played. You liked it just now, when I spanked you and fucked you," he said in sultry flirtation. "You were so wet."

"I know. It felt really good, all of it."

He scratched his forehead. "Is this because I called you a naughty little slut? Because that was just doing dirty talk. It's a sadist thing, to say nasty names and threats and all that. I didn't mean it for real."

That made her bury her face in her hands again, and he decided he better shut his mouth before he made things worse. He ran fingers up and down her arm, resisting the urge to grope her tit. He breathed in the scent of her sugar-vanilla hair and sighed.

"Ah, Petra. This makes me very sad, your rejection. I'm sorry," he said, because he didn't know what else to say. "I thought you wanted it. I'm sorry I made you angry."

"I'm not angry." She flung her arms around his neck. "The sex was good. Too good. It was spectacular. That's why we can't do it again. I don't want to lose my head and act stupid, and go chasing after you—"

"You don't have to chase me. I'm right here. If you like, we can do it again. And again."

She made an irate sound and got up from the bed, taking the blanket with her and revealing the fact that his cock was stiff, ready for an encore.

He pulled the corner of a sheet over the evidence. "I would like to do it again," he said. "But I understand you don't want to. Okay. Because you don't want to get hurt or...because I will do to you like Petr Grigolyuk do to your mother? But I don't like when people say I'm like him. I'm me. Different person."

She walked over to get his clothes with the blanket wrenched tightly around her. "It's not your fault, okay? It's me. It's my issues, my fears."

"My cock was so happy inside you." He stepped into his jeans, thinking about all the possibilities. "We could do it whenever you liked. Before class, after shows. During rehearsal breaks in my dressing room."

"No."

"I don't care if you want to live your own life. I won't make any demands. Only tease you and hurt you and fuck you, and maybe sometimes I'll pee on you in the shower—"

"No!"

He frowned. "But...then...where will you get sex? From someone else?" He scowled at her as he shrugged into his sweater. "When you could be with me? This isn't fair. There is so much more we could do together. Restraints and toys, and nasty sex, and whips, and all kinds of fun stuff. God, Petra. You would love it, to play with me. It makes no sense."

"It makes sense to me."

He glared at her with his arms crossed over his chest. "Right now, you are being a very, very bad girl."

She looked apologetic but determined. "If you care about me, please don't push this. Please, just pretend this never happened."

Somehow that hurt him most of all. Pretend it never happened? Impossible, for him anyway. He could count on one hand the number of women who'd affected him this way since he'd come to London. One finger, really. There was so much promise between him and Petra, so many possibilities to explore. So much perversion to wallow in. But she was his partner. If she pouted and fussed at him all the time like this, they'd both go mad.

"Okay," he said. "I don't have a choice, do I? But I'm not happy about this, and I won't pretend it never happened, because it did happen. I'm not good at pretending."

"You pretend all the time. When you dance, and act on stage. That's all pretend, isn't it?"

He glared at her. Why was she doing this? He wasn't Petr Grigolyuk, and she wasn't her mother, and partners slept with each other all the time. It wasn't exactly professional, but it was common.

It had happened with him and Ashleigh. Almost.

But that was ancient history, and he'd stopped thinking about Ashleigh that way as soon as he realized she loved his friend. Rubio had his quirks but he did have a sense of honor, of goodness. He didn't want to be like his father, for instance, who abused women, and dealt drugs, and died in a hail of gunfire when he pissed off the wrong man. He was not his father and he was not Petra's father, and all of this was a huge disappointment.

When he tried to kiss her goodbye, she turned her head so he only brushed her ear. He grabbed her face and made her turn her head back, then held her chin until he caught her gaze. "One kiss, damn you. That's the price if you want me to forget."

She stiffened and he thought she would refuse, but then she let him take her in his arms. Her lips opened and they got caught up in the same magic of their earlier kiss. She sighed into his mouth and he pressed her to his front, groping her strong, lithe silhouette beneath the blanket. His fingers stroked over her tight, heart-shaped ass. He'd barely gotten a chance to know that ass. It wasn't fair to offer up an ass like that and then deny him further access. The kiss lasted a long time, but not nearly long enough to suit him.

It was the most mournful kiss he'd ever shared with anyone. All of this was completely unfair.

Chapter Nine:
Disturbing

Petra's sleep had gone to shit ever since the Rubio incident. Not only that, but her stalker was writing to her five, six, seven times a day. She stared at the number of emails that had accumulated in the "Paulsen" folder. If anything, he was writing her more, not less, no matter how much she ignored him.

Whenever news about her and Rubio hit the papers, the influx of emails doubled or quadrupled. Even if it was just some generic blurb about an upcoming ballet, or a review, or some interview about their partnership on a ballet website, Paulsen saw it and emailed her about it. *This Rubio guy is an ass. I don't know how you don't see it. Be careful— he's bad news.*

Another reason not to strike up some big relationship with Rubio. Any evidence of interaction between them seemed to incense Gary Paulsen, which was really scary when she thought about it. Her blood rushed faster whenever she saw someone with his coloring and build on the street. She checked the IP addresses of his emails the way Officer McGillivray had showed her, and scanned them for violent overtones, but the notes remained cordial. Cordial and creepy. She was creeped out all the time now, and lonely and sad. The only time she really felt okay was at the theater with Rubio, and then it was in a wistful way, because she still wanted him and he made it all too clear he was still available to her.

He gave her looks, glances, touches she knew were meant to remind her. They plowed through rehearsals for *Giselle*, a ballet that required a lot of angst and soul-gazing. Rubio danced Albrecht, the handsome, playboy duke who toyed with Giselle's affections and broke her heart. As Giselle, Petra got to stomp around the stage in a soul-broken fit before dying at Albrecht's feet. A lot of dancers found the ballet cheesy and melodramatic.

For Petra, it was the perfect time to play a role about losing her shit.

"Giselle is easy for you, no?" Rubio asked one day as they took a break from practice. "Easy for you to play the crazy lady." He teased, but his voice held a brittle edge.

"And you'll be good at Albrecht," she said to get in her own dig. "You're more or less playing yourself."

Ruby ignored her comeback, tipping into a neat handstand before he vaulted down and sprawled beside her on the floor. His showy handstands and flips used to impress her, but they'd grown familiar over the past weeks. He gulped some water and then helped her stretch, offering resistance as she pushed with each leg. "Albrecht is not so bad," he murmured. "He redeems himself in the end."

"Because she forgives him? He's still an asshole. It would be a better ballet if she didn't forgive him."

He narrowed his eyes as she lowered her legs to the floor. "She has to forgive him. It only has a happy ending if she forgives him. Otherwise, is just depressing and sad."

"Like real life." She picked at the edge of her pointe shoe.

He touched her knee, a soft, fleeting touch. "You sad, Petra?"

She shouldn't have looked at him. If she hadn't looked at him, he wouldn't have seen the longing in her gaze. She looked away and busied herself re-tying her ribbons. "I'm not sad. No."

"You thinking about when we were together?"

She shook her head, taking refuge in stretching even though she was already warmed up.

"I think about it," he said. "Constantly." He bent down until he caught her eyes. "You seeing any other guys? You getting sex? You probably need sex."

She sighed and turned her back on him, but that didn't dissuade him. He popped his head over her shoulder. "We could be together, you know. I think you're out of balance. Too much work, not enough play. You have sad, horny eyes."

She tsked. "I do not have sad, horny eyes. That's not even a thing. Some crazy shit comes out of your mouth, you know that?"

"If you let me come back to your bed—"

She clapped her hands over her ears. "I know. Believe me, I know. Don't say it." She stayed like that until he drew back, a ponderous frown on his face. Let him frown. She didn't need the temptation of hearing how fun and sexy it would be to hook up with him on a regular basis. She didn't need to hear it. She *knew*.

He leaned back on his hands, studying her. She wished Gennady, the director, would call the rehearsal back to order.

"Hey, Petra," he said in a more serious tone. "Is that man still bothering you? The one who sent the dead flowers?"

"No," she said shortly. "Well, I'm managing it." She didn't want to pitch into that conversation, not when she already felt so bleak.

"He send you any other things? Things that are weird and creepy?"

She hesitated a moment. "No."

That miniscule hesitation was enough. He could read her subconscious signals like other people read print in a book.

"What?" he prompted. "What did he send?"

"Nothing. He hasn't sent anything else." She didn't know why she was lying. Maybe because confiding in him would bring them closer, endanger this necessary distance between them. She wanted to confide in him, especially when he looked so concerned for her, but she was afraid she'd end up throwing herself in his arms and acting like an idiot.

Rubio watched her, seeing far too much with his acute gaze. "If you need help—"

"I don't need help, okay? Everything's fine."

He took a swig from his water bottle and flipped back into a handstand, clearly unconvinced.

* * * * *

A month went by, and another. They did their final performance of *Romeo and Juliet* and opened *Giselle* to rave reviews. Three or four nights a week Ruby watched in awe as Petra danced the "mad scene" in front of a sold-out house, her arms flying, her long black wig streaming wild down her back. That damn wig taunted him. Too many memories.

Sharing the stage with her was bittersweet bliss. During performances, she was his to control and to grasp, to hold and manipulate until the final curtain call—then she'd vanish into thin air.

He tried to respect the professional distance she wanted, even though it killed him to hold her so close at work and not be able to have her. He went to Liam's parties hoping to forget, but soon realized no one measured up to Petra. It was a special kind of hell.

But at least she was right there in hell with him.

Sometimes he went out of his way to make her suffer. He'd give her a smoldering look or touch her a certain way he knew would arouse her. He'd spank her ass—playfully—even though Yves had warned him for years that it wasn't appropriate company behavior. With Suzanne or Meredith or Hannah, he'd just give a light tap, but with Petra he flicked his wrist so he cracked her a lot harder than it looked. Whenever he did it, she'd give him a look halfway between fury and ecstasy. It was the same look she gave him in his fantasies.

His life had become an endless, burning dream from which he couldn't awake. If she ever gave him permission to fuck her again, he'd probably kill her from all his pent-up desire. He tried to vent his needs on other women but it wasn't the same. Petra was the one he couldn't have.

"*Bonita*," he would say in his dreams. "Beautiful girl..." And he'd stroke her soft, white-bright hair, and touch her all over her body. He'd hold her down and spread her pussy lips and make her wet, but he wouldn't let her come. Instead he'd cuff her hands over her head so her body was stretched in a long, delicate line, and then he'd make marks on her, sometimes with a whip, or sometimes with a belt. Sometimes with a long, elegant cane or a riding crop. She would beg him to stop, his beautiful ballerina, as she hopped on her toes, but he wouldn't stop until she was sobbing in true distress. And then...

Then he would release her hands and take her face between his fingers and taste her salty tears. He would kiss her and squeeze her thighs, and press his palm into the hot crevice between her legs. He'd make her beg for his cock and then he'd thrust it into her. Sometimes in his dreams he rode her in a wild fervor, and other times he was cool and deliberate, tormenting her with slow, measured thrusts.

Sometimes, rather than dream-fuck her pussy, he'd part her ass cheeks and tease her bottom hole until she begged him to fuck her there. Or begged him not to, which he liked more. He'd push inside her tight asshole anyway as she whined and cried, and then he'd drive in and out while she struggled against him. Every noise, every plea aroused him beyond bearing. He'd pin down her shoulders, snapping his hips against her bucking ass—

"Ruby."

He spun in the half-dark rehearsal room to find his partner standing near the door. He brushed a hand over the bulge in the front of his sweat pants. "Hey. I thought you went home."

"Not yet." She stepped inside, hugging the wall. "What are you doing?"

"What does it look like I'm doing? Some practice. I have energy, you know, when there's no performance."

"I know," she said with a faint smile. A very faint smile. She was so sad, but he didn't know how to fix her. He hated the way her body drooped.

"What's the matter?" he asked.

She forced a bigger smile. "Nothing. I just don't feel like going home."

"You got your shoes on? Come practice with me."

For a minute he thought she'd say no, but then she walked across the room to join him. "What do you feel like practicing?" she asked. "*Giselle?*"

He made a retching sound. "I'm sick of *Giselle*. I want to dance something fun. Maybe...you know *Theme and Variations*? Is one of my favorites."

"I danced it once, but it was a while ago." She scrunched up her face and looked at him sideways. "It's kind of hard, isn't it?"

"Is not too hard. I'll help you remember the steps. Come on," he said when she balked. "We do like Baryshnikov and Kirkland. I have the music." It was a fun piece and he wanted to see her smile. He cued the music and turned it up, and finally she took his hand and let him lead her through a few combinations. She was made for dancing like this, for precise, musical steps. They reached the part where they danced in unison, and they laughed together, trying to beat one another at quickness and elevation.

"If I remembered the steps," she said, "I could do this a lot better."

"You're doing good. Keep going."

They circled one another, bungling the choreography. She stopped and shook her head. "I can't. I don't remember it."

"I'll help you. Here, try again. Leg up." He tapped her thigh and she performed the requisite arabesque. He walked around her, admiring her balance. "Is it hard to do that?" he asked. "Does it ever hurt your toes?"

"Why don't you try it?" she asked with a touch of pique.

"I like better to watch you do it." He slid an arm around her waist. The choreography called for it, but he held her much closer than necessary. They ended up face to face. She fell off pointe, dropping her hands.

I want you, Petra. I miss you. He had to clench his teeth so he wouldn't blurt out the words.

She dug a toe into the floor, glancing at the clock. "That was fun. It's a cool ballet, but I should probably go."

"Why go? What are you going to do?"

"I don't know. Go home," she said, drifting away from him.

"What's wrong?" he asked again. "You always look tired, sad. Something is sad for you?"

"Nothing is sad. It's just..."

He tilted his head. "You look terrible."

"Why do you have to say I look terrible? That's mean."

"Mean but true."

She bent forward, rotating her shoulders. "I haven't been sleeping well. Bad dreams."

He could understand that. He had bad dreams too. Well, good dreams about Petra, but they were bad dreams because they left him frustrated and desperate to have her. He turned her around and started kneading the tension out of her upper back. "I massage you, yes?" he asked, not really giving her a choice.

She blushed, her cheeks reddening as she stared at him in the mirror. "That feels...oh man...really good."

I could give your whole body ten times greater pleasure, he thought. *Silly, stubborn girl.* "What you dream about, Petra?" he asked as she stifled a moan.

"I, uh, I don't remember. I got a call this morning and it wrecked my sleep."

"Who called you? Your mom? Don't she know dancers need rest? Your shoulders feel like a pile of knots."

She shuddered as he dug his thumbs into her spine. "My mom died a few years ago."

"Oh, I'm stupid," he said. "Sorry."

"It's okay. She got cancer. I miss her. She was a great mom."

"I miss my mom in Brazil," he said, massaging down to the base of her back. "She is a great mom too, very loving. Still alive though." He made a sound and scrubbed his hand over his face as she turned to him. "I'm sorry. I don't know what things to say."

"No, it's okay." Petra was blinking really fast, like she was angry now, or trying not to cry.

"You need a hug?" He swept her up, impulsive, playful, but she clung to him in earnest. He held her closer, lifting her against him. "If you tell me, you'll feel better," he said. "I won't tell nobody. For you, I'll keep secrets. What's wrong?"

She was quiet for so long he didn't think she was going to tell him, but then she turned her face and whispered into his ear. "So much is wrong right now. My stalker's started calling me, every hour. Calling and texting and emailing and writing…" She shivered, holding him tighter. "It's too much, Ruby. Way too much. I'm scared."

Chapter Ten:
Scared

Rubio paced Petra's living room, back and forth, back and forth. He could tell by Liam's expression that something very bad was going on. He could read the seriousness of her situation in the deep lines of his frown.

His friend looked up at him from Petra's computer. "Do you mind? The pacing isn't helping."

It was hard for Ruby to be still under normal circumstances. It was impossible when he was stressed, but he forced himself over to the couch. Petra sat beside Liam at the table, squeezing her hands together.

"Paulsen sent you eight hundred and fifty-six emails in the past month," Liam said to Petra. "So, that's about..." He scratched his pony-tailed hair. "Twenty-eight emails a day on average."

Petra stared down at her lap. "I stopped tracking them. They were so repetitive. I got annoyed, so I set them up to go straight to the trash."

"What? Out of sight, out of mind?" snapped Ruby.

Liam held up a hand. "If you don't stop, I'll make you leave. She doesn't need you bitching at her on top of everything else."

Calm, collected Liam. Ruby wanted to punch him in the jaw. No, he didn't. Liam was too good a friend. He wanted to punch something though, a wall or a punching bag, or the asshole responsible for the stressed look on Petra's face.

"The police said not to engage, so I was trying not to engage," she said.

Liam pursed his lips and looked back at the screen. He clicked a few times, his frown deepening.

"I really screwed up, huh?" said Petra in a wavering voice. "I just didn't— I didn't want to deal with him. I'd almost forgotten about him until he c-called this morning. I picked up because I didn't know who it was." Her phone pinged. Another text, the tenth so far this hour. She looked at Liam. "What do I do now? I don't know what to do."

Ruby crossed to take her in his arms. "Is not your fault, okay?"

He could feel her scrunch her eyes shut against his cheek. If she started crying he didn't know what he'd do. He shushed her and petted her hair until she pulled away from him. Liam was still clicking and frowning at her computer.

"I don't think you should read these," said Liam. Her phone pinged again. Liam stopped and squinted at the screen, and sighed. "These emails and texts...this barrage...this is not rational behavior. How did he act when you saw him in New York? Did he seem like a normal person?"

"I guess he seemed normal. Even kind of nice. It only got weird when he started showing up wherever I was, even at my apartment. Almost all my mail came from him, but he never did anything bad enough that the cops could get involved."

Liam took off his glasses and rubbed the bridge of his nose. "This guy's convinced himself he has some personal connection to you. He's being protective and possessive when no relationship exists."

"I don't understand why he latched on to me," said Petra. "I don't get any of this."

"There's nothing to understand. He's delusional. From what he writes, he thinks someone is conspiring to keep you apart." He flicked a glance at Rubio before he looked back at the screen.

Ruby narrowed his eyes. "Me? He talks about me in those emails?"

"Yes. He doesn't like you very much."

Petra paled and walked over to stand behind Liam. "What does he say? Is he threatening him?"

Liam ignored her question, turning to her with a kind but frank expression. "I need to have someone look at all these emails. I need another opinion, but what I sense is, this is a frustrated and jealous guy.

He's angry you're not honoring whatever fantasy relationship you have. Judging from the amount of emails and his tone, he's putting a lot of energy into this, and he's not going to stop until he gets what he wants."

"Which is what?" Her voice trembled on the question. "A phone call? An apology?"

You. He's not going to stop until he gets you. The word pounded in Ruby's brain, along with the knowledge that he was one of the people standing in this psycho's way.

"It's hard to know what he wants, just from glancing over these." Lies. Liam was flat-out lying to her. Rubio locked eyes with his friend.

Later, his expression said. *Not now.*

Liam looked back at the computer screen. "I need to do a deep background check on this guy, take apart these emails and see what's going on. If you don't mind, I'll change your filter to have all his future emails forwarded to an Ironclad server."

"You can do that?"

Liam nodded. Ruby stood with anxious energy and moved to Petra's bookshelf, poking through novels and non-fiction while Liam showed Petra what he was changing, as well as the Ironclad email address he was forwarding them to.

"We'll need to have all this evidence backed up," said Liam, his fingers clicking over her keyboard. "For when we start putting a case together. But I'll take care of that. I'll let you know what I find, but it's time to start documenting every call, every text. Every email. Don't delete anything. Any suspicious packages, call me first. I want you to document every single point of contact to show the judge."

Petra let out a quick breath. "The judge? We have to go to court?"

"We might," said Liam. "If it escalates into—"

Rubio spun and silenced him with a look.

"If it escalates into something that crosses the lines of legality," said Liam carefully. "With the scope of his behavior, and the content of the emails, I think you could at least file for a harassment notice. A restraining order. I'll take care of that too."

Ruby turned back to her bookshelf, because he couldn't bear to see her beleaguered expression. So many Russian language books. What was that all about? Her father was Russian, but he never talked to her. And at the end of the row—a Portuguese language book. For him?

Petra's cell phone rang. "It's not him," she said with relief. She excused herself to her bedroom to take the call, leaving the two of them alone. Rubio slid into her chair.

"So, he's threatening me in those letters?" he asked his friend. "Be honest."

"He holds no love for you. I'll put it that way."

"How soon can you make him stop this?"

Liam closed down Petra's email and rested his elbows on the table.

"I'm going to work on it. Get some good investigators on the case. I need to learn more about him, see if there are angles we can tweak. If he has a spouse or an employer, we can threaten to out his activities if he doesn't leave Petra alone. Sometimes that can discourage stalkers, provided they're not complete psychos."

Ruby watched Liam's fingers tap, tap, tap on the table. "But he's a complete psycho, isn't he?"

Liam nodded. "He's a psycho, yeah. I'm one hundred percent sure he's a psychopath. How close are you two?"

"I don't know him!"

"No, you and Petra. Are you...?"

Rubio stared at him. "Are we what? Together? You're this world class investigator guy and you can't figure out that she can't stand me?"

"Can't stand you? Anyone can see the connection between you, even on stage. But I take it you're not in an intimate relationship?"

Ruby sprawled back in his chair and rubbed his chest. "When you stop asking stupid questions then I will start talking to you again."

Liam pulled at his ponytail. *Men with ponytails*, thought Rubio. *Pfft.* His friend pushed back some escaped strands and glared at him. "You frustrate the hell out of me sometimes. When I was hooking up with Ashleigh you were all in my business. You had to know it all."

"And you didn't tell me nothing. How does it feel? Not that there is anything to tell about Petra. She doesn't want a relationship with me."

Rubio ignored Liam's assessing look. "Well, whatever your relationship," his friend finally said, "you need to watch out for her. At work, at lunch, during breaks, whenever. Don't let her leave the theater alone, especially late at night. Even if she's getting in a car. You never know."

"He's not in London, is he?"

Liam gave him a dire look. "I wouldn't assume anything about this guy."

They both fell silent as Petra returned from the bedroom. "My grandma," she said. "She has the occasional crisis, when she thinks someone's spying on her through her cable box. I should have let her talk to you," she said, pointing at Liam.

"I would have set her straight," he said. "People spy through cable boxes all the time."

Petra laughed at his deadpan joke and Ruby felt a stab of jealousy. Liam had it so easy with women. Good looks, good manners, a solid grip of English, and that ridiculous ponytail hair. If Liam was Petra's partner, she'd be sleeping with him around the clock.

"Well, it's late," Liam said. "I better get home or I won't see Ashleigh before she heads to bed. She's keeping pregnant-lady hours." He took out one of his cards, wrote an additional number on it, and tucked it under her laptop. "You can call my cell any time, twenty-four hours, and I'll pick up. If Paulsen sends anything else, if any more emails get through, dial my number. You won't be bothering me. Any friend of Rubio's is a friend of mine."

"Thank you." She shook his offered hand. "I hope you'll let me pay you for all this work you're doing for m—"

He waved her off before she could finish. "The best way to pay me is to stay safe. Don't walk home from work without a friend, be alert to your surroundings, and report anything suspicious to the police. It's best to err on the side of caution."

"All right, slick," Rubio said. "We got it. Give Ashleigh my love, okay?"

Liam shot him a look that communicated a great deal of "fuck you" and made his way to the door. As soon as he left, Rubio turned to Petra. "It's okay," he said quietly. "*Vai dar tudo certo.* Everything will be okay."

"*Vai dar tudo certo,*" she repeated. "I hope you're right. Hey, can you stay a while?" Her voice sounded strained. "Stay and have some coffee with me, or...do you want something to eat?" She headed to the kitchen and looked in her refrigerator, which was mostly empty. "I can call out for something."

"I'll stay as long as you want. You don't have to feed me, or make up excuses to keep me here."

"But I have to make up excuses. I have to keep my brain busy." Her lower lip trembled as her hands fluttered against the counter. "I keep thinking, what if you're involved too? What if you're in danger? One of the first things he sent was that picture of me and you. What if—" The words choked off in her throat.

He walked over and put his arms around her to make her still. "It's okay. I'm not afraid of him. Liam will take care of all this. Try not to worry."

"But I'm worried," she said against his shoulder. "I don't want anything to happen to you." She gave a wild, nervous laugh. "I don't want anything to happen to me. I should have been keeping track of his emails. I was so stupid."

"No, you weren't stupid." He rubbed her back, feeling an inappropriate erection rising where he pressed against her. Damn her for how she affected him. He shifted back and looked in her eyes. "You didn't do anything wrong. He's the psycho here, not you. He's trying to make you feel scared and threatened, I don't know why. Because he imagines too much, and he's a big loser. I had a woman like this once, writing, constantly, constantly. Is so stupid. One day she jumped in my car and kissed me and—" He shuddered, remembering the feel of her slobbery lips.

"What did you do?" asked Petra.

"I told her to get out. I yelled at her to get out and leave me alone, and she did. But she was not—"

Not like this guy. He didn't say it, but they both heard it. Rubio was twice Petra's weight. He was big and strong, a product of Rio's streets. He knew how to fight. He'd have no problem defending himself, even against another guy. But Petra... He tried not to let his thoughts show in his expression. He probably didn't succeed.

"Will be okay," he said again, as if saying it enough times might make it true.

"What if it's not okay?" Her voice broke on the last word and she started to cry. She was so strong, always, so assured, but now she was cheeping and chirping like an injured bird. He made sympathetic sounds and stroked her hair. He didn't know what to do, how to fix this. He really wanted to kiss her. He wished he could kiss her until she felt better, until that haunted look left her eyes.

He touched the sides of her hair, brushed his fingers over the soft, sweet-smelling strands. "He is very bad," he said. "I know he's so bad, but I can understand why he feels so strong for you. You're so beautiful, Petra. I'm sorry you're sad."

She turned her face up to his, her cheeks streaked with tears. "I'm so tired," she sobbed. "I'm tired of worrying about this."

"I know, *querida.*"

"It's so stupid. It's not fair. I mean, that he wants me, and I don't want him." She buried her face in his chest. "And I want you, but I can't..."

"You can't what?"

She pulled away from him and smeared tears across her cheek. "Forget I said that. I'm really emotional right now. I want everything I can't have."

He stared at the curve of her cheek, the pretty pouting shape of her mouth. "You can have me," he said. "If that's what you want." She shook her head, trying to pull away from him, but he wouldn't let her go. "Petra—"

"We can't, Ruby. Just—please—"

"You can have me," he said again, taking her face in his hands. "I'm right here, damn you. If you want me, why don't you take me? Nothing bad will happen. I don't understand."

"Really?" She looked up at him, her expression racked with torment. "You don't understand? Of all people, you should understand. My entire life has been driven by dance. Every decision, every relationship has been weighed against how it will affect my career. How *you'll* affect my career."

"And?" he asked in frustration. "I'm your partner. I try to help you be your best."

"I know, but I've created this structured life. There's only room for me and dance in it. I'm afraid to upset the balance, you know?"

Yes. In some way he did know. Their dedication to their craft consumed everything, leaving room for little else. No hobbies, no leisure, no relationships, no peace except for Saturday nights at Liam's, and thanks to Petra he couldn't even enjoy that any more. "I know," he said, pressing his lips to her forehead. "Is lonely to live like this."

Petra covered her face and started crying again. He held her against his chest, twining his fingers in her hair. He was lost without her, and she was lost without him. "Don't you think..." He nuzzled against her cheek, tasting tears. "Don't you think we have to find a way? If you want this so much, if your feelings are so strong..." He eased her back and cupped her chin, brushing away her tears with his thumbs. "Listen, we both understand what's at stake. We're both at a time in our lives when our careers must come first. We understand that, yes?"

He waited for her to stop crying and answer. "Yes, but—"

"So we know. We can be careful. I won't make a baby in you, I promise. I won't let you stop dance, no matter what. You won't be your mother and I won't be your father, we'll promise each other this. We can do it. We know better."

She gazed at him through misty green eyes, considering what he'd said. "I—I don't know."

He made a soft sound, tracing the bare skin above her waistband. "Do you want me? Tell the truth."

She shuddered against him. "Of course I want you."

He moved his hand lower, over her form-fitting leggings to the smooth vee at the top of her thighs. "We have so little besides dance. Why can't we enjoy each other? Give one another pleasure?" He moved a couple fingers beneath her waistband and when she didn't stop him, he slid his whole hand in, down to the secret, slick warmth of her pussy. She sighed and pressed her head against his chest as he teased her, stroking over her clit. "It's so lonely to be a dancer," he said, curling his fingers into her tight sheath. "So much discipline. So much sacrifice. No one understands, but we understand each other. There is something between us, Petra." She moved on his fingers, tensing and pressing against him. "Ah, yes, you know it. We understand each other so well."

He caught her moan in a kiss, then pressed his tongue inside her mouth as he pushed his fingers deeper. He'd die if she didn't let him in. She was killing him, slowly but surely.

"But you're into BDSM," she said against his lips. "You're kinky and I'm not."

"Liar." He gave a wild laugh. "You can't stop thinking about how good it felt when I hurt you. How good it felt when I held you down and fucked you." He punctuated each word with a probing thrust of his fingers, his thumb against her clit, pressing and stroking it. "I could teach you everything about dominance and submission. About pain and pleasure and giving yourself up." His fingers closed over her clit in a tightening pinch. "You want to give up control, I know it. You want to be my special toy, my lover. My sweet sex slave. Only for me."

She ground hard against his hand and touched the front of his pants, tracing the thick evidence of his need. It was all the answer he needed.

He flicked open the button of his fly, tore the zipper down and fisted his cock. "Wait," he said. "Don't move."

He went to his gym bag and rooted through shoes and clothing. He came up with the box of condoms and tore one open, rolling it onto his cock at the same time he kicked off his jeans. Petra took care of his shirt, tearing it over his head. He wanted to undress her next, undress all of her and lick every inch of her body, but he found he couldn't wait. He pulled her to the floor and stretched her leggings down somewhere below her knees.

There would be time for seduction later. Tonight, tomorrow, later. For now it was enough to grab her arms and jam his cock between her legs and slide into her inch by torturous inch. She was so tight, so wet. He tried to spread her legs wider but the leggings had her cinched below the knees. They arched together, fucking like animals. Later, he could seduce. For now, he wanted ownership. Possession. He wanted her to understand that she was his. He held her hands to the floor and pounded into her, moving her hips with the force of his thrusts. She pressed against him, bucking her pelvis.

"Oh God," she moaned. "You're hitting...just...the right...spot."

"Don't come yet," he bit out. "Wait."

She made a plaintive sound of protest.

"Not yet," he repeated. "Wait for me."

He could feel her legs straining at the leggings. Spandex made nice bondage. He kissed her hard, snapping his hips against hers. He could go off like a rocket any time, but this reconnection was so exciting, so pure and wonderful, that he didn't want it to end too quickly.

"Soon," he said, as her nails bit into his hands. "Be patient. If you're mine, you do what I like. You come when I say."

"Please," she gasped. "I can't hold off much longer."

He only made her wait another minute, although she groaned like he was subjecting her to torture. "Okay, now," he said, tightening his grip on her wrists. "Now you come. We come together."

They were already so in tune physically. He knew her body, every muscle and tendon. He knew her scent and how she breathed and how she moved. When he heard her gasp and clench around him he was ready, his body resonating on the same frequency as hers. It was like a well-executed arabesque, everything in balance, elegant and beautiful. His orgasm felt better than any applause, better than any performance, because it arrived in perfect concert with hers.

"Oh, you fucking...you fucking..." He clamped his lips shut before he blurted out something rude. He couldn't believe she'd kept this joy from him for so long. He couldn't believe the time they'd wasted. "You fucking *bad girl*," he whispered, gazing down into her sex-dazed eyes. "You made me ache. You made me suffer."

She squeezed on the still-hard length of his cock and gave him a weak smile. "I'm sorry."

"You are not sorry," he chuckled, pulling out of her. "Not yet, anyway."

He went to the bathroom to take off the condom while she stewed on those words. By the time he got back, she'd already pulled up her leggings.

"Oh, no," he said. "No, no, no."

He marched her over to the couch and threw her across his knee before she knew what he intended. He took a moment to yank her leggings back down as she squirmed over his lap. The smack of his hand sounded loud in her apartment. "Ouch," she yelled, throwing her arm back to shield her ass.

"Rule one of BDSM..." He took her wrist and trapped it firmly between her shoulder blades. "Bad girls get spanked. That's my rule, anyway."

Smack!

He wasn't hitting her full strength, but he wasn't pussy-footing around either. He gave her another smart slap, and a couple more just under the curve of her buttocks. She half-laughed and half-screeched, trying to jerk away. This would get her nice and primed for round two of fucking, and he'd make sure that lasted longer. So many things to teach her. So many perverted things to do to her...

Smack!

She wailed, grasping his leg. "Okay, God. That hurts. Ow. I mean, don't stop but...that hurts."

"That's kind of the point, bad girl." He began to spank her in earnest, in a steady, stinging rhythm, thrilling to her rising cries. *The neighbors*, he thought briefly, before deciding not to care.

"Please," she squealed. "Oh, God, no, no!"

With a crash, the door flew open and Liam came bounding in. He stopped short, staring at the two of them. Rubio jumped up, shoving Petra behind him.

"What the fuck are you doing here?" he asked. "And did you ever hear of knocking?"

Liam averted his eyes, staring at the ceiling. "I heard her yelling 'no.' I thought..." Liam looked past him to Petra, now that she was dressed. "I wouldn't have barged in, except that I started reading those emails. Paulsen is en route to London. He wrote that he'd be arriving tonight."

"You couldn't call and tell us that?" Ruby growled.

"No one was answering phones," he replied with a harried look. "And I didn't think you'd still be here. I was coming to help Petra get her stuff."

"What stuff?" she asked.

"All your stuff. Whatever you need to get by for a few days. If Paulsen's coming here, he's coming for you." Liam looked back at Ruby. "And you too. Mem's headed to your place right now."

"Who's Mem?" asked Petra, her voice thin and high.

"Liam's live-in assistant." Ruby crossed to her and rubbed her shoulders. "He's a silent ninja type."

"I don't want to sound alarmist," said Liam, "but I think you should both relocate until we figure out what this guy's up to. I'm inviting you both to stay at my place. It's cheaper than a hotel, and it's the most secure choice."

Ruby looked at Petra. This wasn't how he'd expected their erotic reunion to end. At the same time, if Paulsen was headed to London, she couldn't stay here. Her safety and security was more important than spankings and sex and his wrecked plans for the evening.

"Where are your bags?" Ruby asked her, springing into motion. "I'll help you pack. Me and Liam can carry it. Bring enough to stay for a while." He turned back to smooth away the tension lines between her brows. "*Tudo bem, querida.* Will be okay. I'll be with you. It will be safe."

"What about you? Will you be safe?" She took a deep, halting breath. "This is all because of me, all this disruption."

He tried to reassure her with his smile. "Liam's house is not so bad. The basement is fun, anyway." He kissed her, quick and tender, not caring that Liam was watching. He wanted her to know that nothing bad would happen. He was determined to keep her safe.

Chapter Eleven:
At Liam's

Petra watched the nighttime lights of London slide across the backseat of Liam's car. It was just after midnight and the party people congregated on the street corners in their short skirts and skinny jeans, heading out to go dancing or have a few drinks. She'd never been one of those people. She wondered what it felt like, hanging out in noisy nightclubs and getting wasted with friends. She was too old for that now, anyway.

She felt really old tonight, and tired and numb. Not scared though. She wasn't scared, not with Rubio and Liam sitting in the front seats. Liam assured her everything would be okay, and he lived in a big house and owned a huge international security company, so he was probably right.

"You still awake?" Rubio asked, looking back at her over the seat. In the dark, his black eyes reflected the glittering lights from outside.

She sat up a bit straighter. "Yeah. I'm not tired." She stifled a yawn in spite of herself.

"Little liar," he murmured, turning away. He and Liam started another conversation but she couldn't make out the words over the hum of the engine. This wasn't the same sporty car he'd used to drive her home from the party. It was a different sporty car, something older and vintage. She wondered how many sporty cars he owned. Judging by the size of his house, as many as he wanted.

They'd already swung by Rubio's place, but she hadn't had much time to check it out. He literally grabbed one bag of belongings. One whole bag. But then, she hadn't brought much either. Some clothes, her leotards and shoes, her e-reader. She and Ruby were dancers. There wasn't room for a lot of other things in their lives. His loft was a study in uncluttered simplicity. Unadorned concrete walls, a soaring ceiling, and a massive window.

All she could think of was Paulsen watching Rubio through that window. Loading a gun. Aiming.

She shook those thoughts away. They had no evidence yet that Paulsen was bent on murder, at least she didn't think they did. But it was sinking in that she'd endangered Rubio by coming here, by taking a position as his partner. He might say it wasn't her fault, but that didn't change the fact that it probably was.

She stared at the back of his head, then his profile as he turned. He had beautiful lips and such finely sculpted features. She loved his nose. She dreamed about his nose, about him looking down at her over its haughty perfection. He came from the slums, supposedly, but there was nothing cheap or coarse about him.

Well, maybe the way he had sex.

But she liked the way he had sex, and apparently he liked sleeping with her too. She didn't think of herself as great in bed; sex had always been an afterthought for her. Most of her amorous experiences had taken place while she was half-asleep, or thinking about other things. Rubio didn't do sex like that. When he was fucking her it was impossible to think about anything else, and definitely impossible to float along half-asleep, barely participating.

She was still digesting their conversation back at her place, and the haphazard coupling that followed. And the spanking, which she'd absolutely loved. She hoped against hope he was right, that she could be aware and guard against getting too wrapped up in him. She was so much like her mother in personality, in her tendency to be obsessive. *Please, don't let me be like her in this.*

She shifted on the seat. She could still feel the smallest twinge of lingering ache from when he'd spanked her. She felt lingering embarrassment too. Liam Wilder had gotten an eyeful. *It's nothing he hasn't seen before. He has a dungeon in his basement, for God's sake.*

And him and Rubio were close friends. Liam had probably watched Rubio spank and fuck countless women at his parties. She tried not to feel jealousy, but she did. Not jealousy of Liam, but jealousy of all Ruby's phantom partners. She wanted him to be exclusive with her. Even if they weren't getting serious, even if they weren't going to get lost in each other, she didn't want him flaunting other women in her face. They'd have to discuss that at some point. Maybe. If things worked out.

They reached Regents Park and crawled along hoity-toity streets to Liam's place. They drove around to the back, to a large garage. Five cars then. Not so very many for a gazillionaire like him. An elderly, dark-haired man came out to greet them and help with their bags. Rubio introduced them, his arm around her shoulder.

"Hi, Mem. This is Petra Hewitt."

Mem took her hand in a welcoming grip. "I'm honored to meet you. I have seen your lovely dancing." He gave a slight bow. "You're an artist, Miss Hewitt."

"Please, Petra's fine." She blushed and thanked him while she tried to place his ethnicity. He wasn't Indian or Asian. His soft-spoken accent wasn't British, but not American either.

He was also pretty far from her image of a "silent ninja type." With that said, there was some edge about him suggesting he could be menacing if circumstances called for it. Liam had the same edge behind his mild, reassuring smile.

Liam urged her into the house with that smile, and Ashleigh greeted Petra with a hug that dispersed some of the tension of the evening. Petra respected Ashleigh Keaton like crazy. She wasn't a self-made ballet star—Rubio had made Ashleigh's career—but she was still noted as a skilled emotional and lyrical dancer. She was also pregnant, so whatever career she'd had was done.

Ashleigh didn't seem depressed about it though. She invited them into the dining room for coffee and chatted about City Ballet without any apparent regret. Happy, married, and pregnant by a rich guy. Was that what all ballerinas secretly wished for? Their careers didn't last forever. Petra was twenty-eight, the same age as Ashleigh, and she hadn't thought at all about her future, about marriage or children or anything else. *Tunnel vision,* her teachers used to say. *You will only be great with tunnel vision. You must focus and work.* Her mother had gotten distracted by Petr Grigolyuk and lost everything. If only she'd been like Ashleigh and fallen for some businessman or security tycoon instead. Her life could have turned out so differently...

"What's the matter?" Rubio asked. Petra realized she was scowling into her coffee cup. Had someone asked her a question?

"I think I'm tired," she said.

"Of course you're tired." Ashleigh hopped up. "It's late and you must be exhausted. We prepared some rooms for you both upstairs. And you shouldn't worry," she added, leading Petra over to the staircase. "This place is security-wired like crazy. The alarm is always armed. Not that you're in any danger." Her eyes moved past Petra to Rubio and her husband, climbing up the stairs behind them. "I mean..."

"She means that you're going to be perfectly safe here, whether or not extra precautions are necessary," said Liam. "And they may not be necessary. Until Paulsen arrives, until he surfaces, we don't really know."

"Until he surfaces?" Ruby snorted as they reached the landing. "How many guys did you send to the airport?"

Liam silenced him with a glare. "I sent the necessary amount."

"Here you go," said Ashleigh, ushering Petra into a suite down the hall. "This is the biggest guest room. Do you think it's okay?"

Petra stared around in awe. Okay? It was magnificent. It was pale blue, with designer furniture and a striking canopied bed made of tangled iron branches. "Why wouldn't it be okay?"

"I guess because we're right across the hall. But the other guest rooms aren't as big and—"

"This'll be fine," Rubio cut in. "I'm sleeping here too."

Petra slid a look at him. The room was more than large enough for two, as was the beautiful bed, but...wow. A couple hours ago they'd still been debating whether they should sleep together. Now they were...kinda...moving in together.

Ashleigh looked between the two of them, blushing beneath her long, black hair. "Sorry. I wasn't sure what the arrangements were going to be. But that's fine if you both want to stay in here. Half these bureaus are filled with Ruby's stuff anyway."

He walked over to one of them and opened a drawer. "I haven't left that much here."

"Yes, you have," said Liam. He turned to Petra. "If he starts to threaten your sanity, kick him out. There are other guest rooms down the hall."

She laughed as Ruby made a face. She wished she had friends like these. She envied their easy camaraderie. She needed this feeling of warmth and support tonight. She wondered if Paulsen was heading to her apartment right now, or to Rubio's loft. She wondered if Liam had stationed men at her apartment. At her door.

She wondered what was in those hundreds of emails, for Liam to take all this so seriously. Was it just precautionary, as he claimed?

She studied his face but she couldn't find any answers. A moment later, Rubio left with Liam to get their stuff from downstairs, and Ashleigh sat on the edge of the bed, tracing a finger over an intricately crafted branch.

"This bed is amazing," Petra said. "I've never seen anything like it."

Ashleigh glanced up into the twisting tangle of the canopy. "Liam bought it for me shortly after we met. The first time I saw it, I thought the same thing."

Petra couldn't help staring at the pronounced curve of Ashleigh's belly. She forced her gaze away and toward the door. "Speaking of beautiful things, you have a very attractive husband. Not that I'm a home wrecker or anything."

"I'm glad to hear it." Her grin broadened. "While we're on the subject, you have a very attractive boyfriend. Very talented too."

"Rubio's not my boyfriend."

Ashleigh threw back her head and laughed. "Liam wasn't my boyfriend either when we started hanging out together. They need that distance for some reason, at least in the beginning."

Ashleigh thought it was Rubio insisting they keep things casual, and Petra let her think so, because she didn't want to explain the whole deal. How could Ashleigh understand? She'd already given up dancing, quit the company to settle down and have kids with her fine, rich husband. "It is what it is," said Petra with a shrug. "I don't think we have a future together. We're both so focused on our careers, and besides, we're so different."

"Careers don't last forever in this business. And he obviously cares about you." Ashleigh shook her head and looked sheepish. "Forgive me. I'm trying to match-make for my friend. The truth is, I completely understand the need to keep a distance. Good luck doing it though, with Rubio's super grabby hands."

Now Petra was the one laughing. "He's awful, isn't he? He gropes me during every lift."

"Yep," agreed Ashleigh. "Does he still do that thing where he spreads his fingers out on your waist and then accidentally brushes his thumb over your nipple?"

"He does that all the time. Sometimes he just blatantly feels me up. Like, we'll be in a break from rehearsal and he'll reach out and literally fondle my boob, and then pretend it wasn't intentional."

"He always told me he had to do it so he could get to—"

"—know my body. Yes, he tells me the same thing. He's a deviant."

"Who's a deviant?" asked Rubio, returning with a suitcase and his own bag slung over his shoulder. He dumped them on the floor by the bed. "Is not very nice to talk about Liam while he's away."

Petra and Ashleigh exchanged looks while Liam brought in a couple more bags. Mem brought up the rear with Petra's box of odds and ends. "If you forgot anything, we'll go back and get it," Liam assured her. "I want you to feel comfortable here, even if it's a short stay."

"I hope it's a short stay," said Petra, and then she flinched. "That didn't come out right. I mean that I hope Paulsen leaves right away. It's not that I don't want to stay here. I just feel terrible for causing all this trouble."

"It's not trouble," Ashleigh said. "Our house is yours for as long as you need it, and we hope you'll make yourself at home. To that end..." She stood and took her husband's arm. "We'll get out of your way. If you need anything, you have the run of the house. Kitchen, laundry, gym—"

"Play room," Ruby interjected.

"Just ask one of us for help if you need to leave," Liam said, talking over him. "So we can show you how to disarm the security system first."

After smiles and good nights, the married couple and Mem excused themselves, leaving Petra and Ruby alone. She glanced down at her bags, thinking she should unpack, but she was fading fast. She took a shower instead, only faintly complaining when Ruby climbed in with her and took up all the space. She pushed Paulsen out of her head. If he wanted to come all the way to London to stalk her, that was his problem. His money, his time, his inconvenience.

She had other things to think about right now, like adjusting to having a roommate for the first time in a decade. Not just any roommate. As soon as she dressed in her pajamas, Rubio walked across the room and took them off her. No words, no cheeky flirtation, just his hands pulling them off and throwing them over a chair.

"I want you naked," he said. "I want to hold you and sleep with you with no clothes."

I want. There was something assured and confident about the way he said it, like he'd never expect her to say no. She loved the way he took whatever he desired, or at least went after it. He drew her over to the bed, his hands spreading out over her breasts, her skin. He kissed her neck and pushed her back on the sheets. "You want me, Petra?"

The way he said her name, with that catch on the 'r' and the long, breathy 'a'—it was an aphrodisiac. She wanted him like crazy. "Yes," she said. "I want you."

"Say please."

She stared at his lower lip. She wanted to be good at these games, like him, but he was way out of her league. "Please," she said, but it sounded desperate, not flirty. His face changed, his expression softening. He held her face and nuzzled against her, giving her a kiss. "It was a hard day, yes? Maybe you're too tired."

"I'm not too tired." Now she really sounded desperate, but his closeness made her crave more. She wanted him. As tired as she was, she couldn't just fall asleep. His *I want* and his *Say please* had started a drumbeat of desire in her veins.

He traced a finger down the curve of her jaw. "Little liar. You lie so much. Okay, then. I'll make love to you soft and slow, and put you to sleep before I'm done. Yes?"

"I don't think I could sleep with you inside me."

"Hmm. A challenge." He turned and opened the bedside drawer, rooted around and pulled out a condom. *Manwhore.* He kept condoms in this room, just a couple floors above the dungeon. He stayed here often. He might have slept with two hundred women in this bed. Five hundred.

Five hundred, Petra? Really? It didn't matter. She wanted him anyway. Rubio fished out the box of Magnums and showed her the dates. "See? I check the expiration to be extra careful. No babies for you. Not like your mom. Not like Ashleigh."

Petra felt a sick, nervous feeling every time she thought about Ashleigh Keaton being pregnant. She didn't know why. Pregnancies were supposed to be happy things. "Did she get pregnant on purpose?" she asked.

He paused in the act of rolling on the condom. "Yes. She wanted a baby. Liam...I don't know." He smoothed the latex the rest of the way down. "It's a long story. But they'll be good parents. They're excited to try this new thing."

"Do you think she'll dance again?"

He leaned over her, stroking her hair. "I don't know. I don't think she wants to dance anymore. Someday, you will be tired of dancing too."

Petra shook her head before she even thought about it. A world without dance made no sense to her. Stopping, losing her talent, losing the physical ability to do her work...horrifying.

"You don't think so," he said, "but there's so much more to life than what you know." He held her gaze, smoothing his palm down her belly to the cleft between her legs. "There's a lot besides dancing. But it's okay. For now, no babies. Just sex."

He held her close, stroking her, soothing her with his skillful touches. After a while he turned her so they spooned together, her back to his front. His cock nudged into her from behind, filling her with a long, slow slide. While this coupling wasn't as frantic and forceful as their previous ones, she felt as controlled as ever cradled within the heat and strength of his chest. He parted her pussy lips and toyed with her clit, and then moved his fingers up to whisper across her sensitive nipples, before delving them down between her legs again.

Petra felt impatient in bed sometimes, maybe because she often didn't enjoy what her partners were doing, but oh...she liked this. He was so calm, so firm and steady as he fucked her. She really did start to feel a strange combination of sleepiness and arousal. Pleasure built alongside relaxation. He kneaded her shoulders and she reached back to grip his thigh, squeezing the hard muscle when he located a particularly delicious spot.

I want...

Petra had never known she wanted this. Or maybe she'd wanted it forever. This warmth, this gratification. This closeness. She'd never, ever felt this close to someone before. Finally, with no real effort on her part, she reached that point where her breath grew short, and her body strained to achieve completion. He pressed his cheek against hers and sighed. "Mm, yes. Come for me."

The deep, gruff timbre of his voice vibrated down to her core. His hand spread out on her pussy like he was saying *this is mine*. He slipped his fingertips over her clit and her breath left in a rush. An orgasm started there, right where he touched her, and rolled over her entire body, from her breasts to her shoulders to her head, to her knees and calves, to the tips of her toes. She clamped down on his thick cock as he buried himself deep inside her. One of his hands squeezed in her hair, to the point of pain, past the point of pain, until he unwound behind her.

Then there was nothing. Only satisfaction and his strong arms, and safety...and sleep.

Chapter Twelve:
Okay

Rubio dreamed he was at home in Rio, standing outside a bakery near his neighborhood. Cinnamon and vanilla scents wafted in the air. He was a child again, wishing for sweet buns and pastries he couldn't afford to have. He stretched and came to a slow realization that he wasn't in Brazil at all, but lying in bed beside Petra with his nose buried in her tousled blonde hair.

He blinked, looking toward the window, and stirred gently so he didn't wake her up. It was still early. Growing up in the hustle and noise of the *favela*, with the shouting of his brothers and sisters and mother and father, he'd never mastered the art of deep sleep. He could appreciate quiet though, and peace. He gazed down at the girl in his arms, watching the subtle fluttering of her lashes. He wanted to put his cock inside her but she was tired. Last night had been difficult, and she'd been restless for hours before she settled down.

He slid from the bed and pulled some sweats from the bureau across the room. He padded downstairs and found Mem making coffee in the kitchen. The old man nodded to the dining room and Rubio drifted into the large, formal space. Liam sat at the head of the table with papers spread out in front of him. He didn't even look up when Ruby sat down.

"Petra still sleeping?" he asked, his cheek resting on his palm.

"Yes. Dreamland."

Liam passed a grainy eight-by-ten photograph across the table. "Paulsen went exactly where we thought he'd go, to Petra's building. He buzzed for about ten minutes, and then snuck in behind another resident."

Rubio studied the photo of Petra's stalker. He was a normal-looking guy, with light hair and a slightly rounded, forgettable face. If he passed Paulsen on the street, he'd look right through him.

"What happened at her door?" Ruby asked.

Liam took the photo back. "He knocked. And knocked. And knocked. Eventually he slid a note underneath."

"You put a guy inside?"

"Yeah, I put a guy inside. I didn't know if he'd try to break in and make himself at home. After he left, he checked into a hotel halfway between her place and the theater. She won't be able to walk around town for a bit. Not without crossing his path."

"Thanks for letting her stay here," Rubio said to his friend, feeling uncharacteristically somber. "Me too. But especially her."

"It's safer here." Liam tapped restlessly at the note. "I'm worried though, and I don't worry easily. I have a really off feeling about this guy."

"What does that mean? Odd feeling?"

"No, *off* feeling. Like something's off. I can't figure out where this guy's head is at. He's angry with you, that's a given. My worry is what happens when he starts to feel angry with her."

Mem came in with coffee and joined them. As Liam's assistant, he'd already know the details of the case. He might even have been the man who stayed at Petra's apartment last night.

"What about the theater?" Ruby asked. "There's a security system, but people slip in, invite friends. There are visitors and deliveries, always outsiders wandering around."

"That's gonna have to change, at least while Paulsen's in London. Based on the obsessive nature of his behavior and his actions last evening, Petra's been granted an emergency restraining order. Next move is to get him bounced back to New York."

"How do we do that?"

"Through legal channels. I'm working on it. It might take a few days or a couple weeks. It depends."

"Can I see the note he left her?"

Liam had photocopies in front of him but he handed Rubio the original. He expected blood-soaked drawings and curse-laden fragments but it was handwritten in very even, neat print.

Since you don't seem inclined to come back, or answer my emails, I decided to come here. I think you're very confused about what's going on between us. I've come here to make things a bit more clear.

I know you're busy with your dancing, and I have patience—to a point. I have less patience with continually rude behavior. If you don't meet with me soon, or start replying to my emails, I'm going to assume you have no respect for me and do what it takes to rectify that. Whatever it takes.

Dearest Petra, you belong with me. I'll take good care of you and in return I know you'll take good care of me. You'll always be my pretty little girl, but you're being awfully headstrong right now. I don't want to hurt you because that will hurt me, so let's hope this is only a rebellious phase. Your "friend" Rubio is probably putting ideas in your head that aren't true. I don't want him touching you. I'll do what I have to do to make that stop.

Talk to me, Petra. Let's straighten things out between us.

He concluded with his number and the address of his hotel. Ruby re-folded the note. "*I'll do what I have to do to make that stop.* What does that mean?"

"I don't know. The threats are so vague. It would be easier if he diagrammed out his diabolical plans in detail. *I'm going to ambush you outside the stage door and slit your throat with a serrated knife.* See, then we'd know what we're dealing with."

Mem made a chiding sound. "Don't joke about such things."

Rubio rubbed his neck. "Jesus, Liam."

"I'm kidding," he said to his friend with a sympathetic half-smile. "He hasn't said anything like that. He hasn't said anything useful at all, except that he disapproves of you, and he's disgruntled with Petra's behavior and he wants her to return home to live with him. Happily ever after, etcetera."

Ruby shook his head. "I never understood this stalking thing, how people can be so...out of reality. '*You'll always be my pretty little girl. I don't want to hurt you because it will hurt me.*' Is ridiculous, silly. Melodramatic."

"But look, Ruby, this is a guy who, for whatever reason, has taken an extended vacation from reality. He comes from a wealthy family, probably has always gotten his way from day one. He has no job, few friends, just his fantasies and desires racing around in his head. He believes, literally, that he owns Petra. That she's run away from his loving care and that he has a right to collect her. What if his ultimate plan is to drag her back to New York and chain her up in his place?"

Rubio scoffed, stirring cream into his coffee. "He could never do it. She wouldn't quietly get on a plane, or quietly go to his place and cooperate."

"No, she wouldn't. So what do you think happens then? When she doesn't go quietly? When she stands up to him and tells him to go fuck himself? What have sociopathic, scorned men done to women throughout history?"

Mem shifted in the silence, his face a fathomless mask. Rubio stared down into his coffee. Petra was in danger. Real, honest-to-goodness danger.

"How long will she have to worry?" asked Rubio. "How long will this go on? Forever?"

Liam hunched over the papers, shuffling them into a disorganized pile. "I don't know. I wish I could tell you that this will be over next week. That he'll come to his senses and fuck off back to New York. I wish that would happen, but I doubt it will. Maybe the restraining order will make a difference. Maybe he'll go on some meds and get over her. Maybe he'll get hit by a bus. Problem solved."

"You can make that bus thing happen, can't you?" he asked his friend hopefully.

"I could, except it would be first-degree murder, which is against the law." Liam pushed the papers away from him with a sigh. "It would be easier if she could disappear for a while. If she wasn't so accessible to the public. There's nothing to stop him coming to watch her perform every night if he wanted to. He could sit in the front row, practically reach out and touch her. He could slip backstage while the lights are low—"

"I'm not quitting ballet because of him," said Petra.

The two men turned. She and Ashleigh stood in the doorway, still dressed in their pajamas. "You don't have to stop," said Ash, putting an arm around her. "You shouldn't have to rearrange your life because of him."

"I never said she should stop." Liam made a helpless gesture. "I just wish you were something a lot less flashy, like a dry cleaner or a pest control technician."

"A pest control technician?" Ashleigh echoed, giving him a look.

"Petra cannot stop being who she is," said Mem in his low, clipped voice. "It will be important for Paulsen to discover his arrival does not impact her life at all."

"Yes," agreed Liam. "You have to keep dancing, Petra. You have to keep going to the theater as if nothing's changed."

"What about staying at my apartment?" Petra asked as she and Ashleigh took seats at the table.

Liam shook his head. "Sorry. That, I can't let you do. Not alone anyway. I have guys there, if you want to—"

"You have guys in my apartment?" asked Petra at the same time Ruby made a protesting sound.

"She's not staying there with your 'guys,'" he huffed.

"My guys are trustworthy," Liam said. He turned to Petra. "And they're only there to protect your property. I wouldn't put it past Paulsen to break in. They can also monitor how often he stops by to knock on the door, and whether he leaves additional notes."

"Additional notes?"

Liam touched the folded-up missive on top of the papers. "He went straight to your place from the airport last night, which we expected. He snuck upstairs and slid this under the door when you didn't answer his knock. You don't need to read it. It says the same stuff all the others say."

Ashleigh gave Petra a sympathetic look. "Don't give him the satisfaction of listening to his words. I have no patience with men who do asshole stuff to women. Put me in a room with this guy and I'll shear off his shriveled nuts with a rusty saw."

Ruby's lips twisted into a smile. Ash was so sweet and cute until she lost her temper—then all bets were off. He'd had that temper turned on him more than once in their dancing career.

"Ash, honey." Liam pulled her into his lap. "It's too early in the morning for your graphic imagination. But if I remember correctly, Mem, we have a rusty saw down in the garage."

"Yes," said the old man. "We do."

117

"I have to go in today," Petra said. "We have rehearsals, and *Giselle* tonight. I'm also expecting a shipment of shoes. I can go to work, can't I?"

"Of course you can go to work," Mem said. "You must continue with your life while we endeavor to fix this problem. Mr. Rubio will be with you," he added, nodding in his direction.

Mr. Rubio would definitely be with her. Until this crazy man left the country, Rubio wasn't letting Petra out of his sight.

* * * * *

Petra swept across the stage, her expression blank and grim. In Act One she danced happy, vibrant Giselle, but in Act Two she danced dead Giselle, drifting aimlessly about the Kingdom of the Wilis. The Wilis were an army of bitter, ethereal bitches, all the heartbroken women who'd been jilted by their true loves. Her mother could have been a Wili. With Rubio in her life now, her mother was on her mind all the time. *I'm sorry, mom. I'm sorry Grigolyuk didn't love you, but you have to be happy for me. Rubio's a wonderful man.*

A week had passed since they'd moved in with Liam and Ashleigh, and like *Giselle*, Petra's life had split into two acts. Act One was normal, busy daytime and Act Two was the dark night, dying in Fernando Rubio's arms. Not literally dying, but something like it.

She glanced over to find him watching her from the wings. It didn't escape either of them that Rubio, as Albrecht, spent a good part of the second half kneeling at Giselle's grave. It was creepy for both of them, a constant reminder of the very worst that might happen.

They dealt with the danger in their own ways. Petra funneled her energy into dance, and Rubio hovered constantly, all over her. Since her stalker showed up in London, Rubio literally didn't let her out of his sight. They woke together, ate together, roamed the halls of City Ballet together, performed together, and left through the stage door to go home together.

All this togetherness translated into very unhelpful tabloid headlines. *City Ballet Romance! From Enemies to Lovers! Wedding in the Wings!* As a result, Paulsen's notes became angrier. He started calling her cell phone twenty or thirty times a day, until she turned it over to Liam's people and got another one. It was a hassle but she wasn't willing to stay away from Rubio just to keep Paulsen happy. If anything, she wanted to rub her happiness in the man's face. Her fear had long since turned to fury. She wanted to annoy him in any way she could. She hated Gary Paulsen.

And she was falling in love with Rubio a little more each day.

Later, after the final *reverences*, after her tutu and black wig were put away and they returned to their room at Liam's, she trembled naked against him.

"Beautiful girl," he whispered, stroking between her legs. "My good girl." He punctuated the "my" with a squeeze of her slick pussy lips. "You're so wet for me. You're mine, aren't you?"

He captured her moan of assent in a kiss. She couldn't bear the thought of Paulsen wanting to own her, but Rubio...totally different story. When he turned her around to face the wall, she obeyed with a delicious pang of fear. He gave her two sharp slaps on the ass and she hopped onto her toes. He gave an appreciative chuckle and began to grope her again, pinning her to the wall so she couldn't move. She bucked her hips as he teased her clit, drawing moisture from her pussy up over the aching button.

"Oh, please," she whined.

"Please? You do what *I* please," he taunted her. "It feels good, no?"

She whined again, at an even higher register. He was killing her and they'd just gotten started. "It...yes...it feels good."

He hummed as his fingers found the opening of her sex and drove inside. She tensed and skittered sideways when he probed her asshole with the pad of his thumb.

"Don't pull away," he said. "Let me do it, if it pleases me."

"I'm embarrassed."

"Of your asshole? Jesus, girl, I'm going to fuck it some day. Soon. You won't be embarrassed much longer, not when I'm done with you."

Now she'd gone from embarrassed to terrified.

Is okay to be scared.

She repeated the words to herself like a mantra, whenever he did scary stuff she'd never experienced before. "Relax," he said sharply, spanking her ass again. "Don't be a naughty girl."

That was easy for him to say as he worked his thumb all the way into her ass. She squirmed at the unfamiliar sensation. It felt uncomfortable. Invasive. There wasn't a chance in hell of his cock ever fitting in there but if he wanted to threaten her with the possibility, she'd play along. His other fingers still pumped in her pussy. She rode his hand, wishing she had something to rub her clit against. When she tried to grind the wall, he stilled her hips.

"No, not yet. No coming yet."

"I can't help when I come."

"You'll learn how to help it. I'll teach you. But not now."

He drew his fingers out of her body, leaving her feeling empty and horny. "Stay here against this wall," he said. "Don't move and don't dare come. Don't touch your pussy. You understand?"

"Yes."

"*Yes, Sir.* Say it."

"Yes, Sir," she cried, not even thinking twice about it. *Yes, Sir. Whatever will make you let me come.*

He went into the bathroom to wash his hands, then came out and moved around the room, doing God knew what. She turned to peek and was rewarded with a reproachful glare. "When I told you to stay still, I meant to face the wall. Stay there while I think what to do with you tonight."

She turned back with another anxious shiver. She heard a swatting, slapping sound of something against his palm. He crossed to her and shoved it into her hand.

"Here. Hold this."

It was a thick black leather strappy thing. She breathed fast, in and out. When she tried to turn around he made a sound that stopped her. He started spanking her ass with his palm, not single spanks like before, but a steady, allover distribution. She squirmed at the sustained, stinging pain. After a few minutes, her squirms turned to protests as she danced around to avoid the smacks.

He put a hard hand on her shoulder. "Stop that," he said. "This is just the warm-up. You're going to need it," he added on a dire note.

"Just the warm-up?" Her ass was already throbbing hot. "I don't know how much more I can take."

"I do," he said. "But you have your safeword. Use it if you need it."

Oh God!

"Give me the strap." He held his hand out. "It's a hard spanking for you, little girl. Brace your hands on the wall and stick your ass out."

He slapped her burning cheeks again as soon as she did, then ran his hands over the sting. Her knees shook with fear and longing. She was terrified she'd collapse into a heap before he even got started.

He came around the side of her, grabbed a handful of her hair, and drew his arm back. *Thwack!* The strap connected with her ass, sounding almost as awful as it felt. The leather left a rectangle of pain across both cheeks and she jerked, causing his hand to tug at her hair. Tears sprang to her eyes. Another blow fell, and another. Oh, God, it hurt so bad, like fire across her bottom. She reached back with a cry.

"No. Hands on the wall," he said. "Don't move them again."

The strapping resumed. It was so tempting to end it, to say her safeword and make the pain stop, but then she wouldn't get the reward of sticking it out. She knew her suffering turned him on, just as his power and force excited her, but she could barely keep her hands still on the wall. He paused just as she was about to throw in the towel.

"So hot and red," he murmured, leaning closer to inspect the damage. "You like it?"

She blinked away the sheen of her tears. Did she like it? Yes and no.

"Answer me," he prompted.

"Yes, Sir, I like it."

"Bend more," he said, nudging her downward. "I want to see your pretty pussy." He made a pleased sound and knelt behind her, spreading her cheeks and running his tongue over her exposed cleft. She shivered, three seconds from melting to oblivion. He laved her clit, flicking through the hot wetness there. She was instantly transported from aching, stinging pain to sweet bliss. "Please don't stop," she begged.

He pulled away, pinching her labia. "Not time to come yet. Put your hands back on the wall."

She moaned as he straightened and began strapping her again. "Ah," he said to the accompaniment of her stifled cries. "Your ass is so tempting when it's red like this. When you're tensing away from me. When do I get to fuck that ass?"

"I—ow—I don't know!"

"Wrong answer," he said, with another sharp crack. "Try again."

Petra pressed her forehead against the wall, working to put together a complete sentence. "Whenever—whenever you want. Sir," she added, remembering.

"Oh, very nice." He paused and tilted her head back for a kiss. "Good girl," he breathed against her lips. "For reward, I lick your pussy again."

She almost cried from the relief of his lips on her, and the questing pressure of his tongue. He made sounds like her pussy was the most delicious thing in the world, avid, sucking sounds and hums of approval. When he stopped, she barely suppressed a cry of protest. He responded by pulling her up and covering her mouth with his palm.

"You know Liam and Ashleigh and Mem can hear you." She squirmed against him, feeling shamed and excited. "They hear you being spanked like a bad girl and they hear you groaning like a slut. How does that make you feel?"

She knew it was a rhetorical question, since his hand was still over her mouth. But if he'd prompted her to answer, she would have told him it made her feel the same as when he talked about fucking her ass: part horny and aroused, and part horrified. She squealed against his palm as he trapped her against the wall and resumed the strapping with the most intense strokes yet.

She danced on her feet, danced to the choreography of erotic pleasure and pain. She didn't want it to end, but oh, it hurt so much. When she shied away from the blows, he let go of her mouth and trapped her around the waist. Now, no matter how much she bucked and twisted, she couldn't get away. *Crack! Thwap! Crack!* The pain was awful, but it was tempered by the warmth of his closeness, and his enigmatic power melting her inside.

His pace increased, along with the intensity of the smacks. Her cries of protest became real crying, tears trailing down her face and into her mouth and nose. She clutched at the arm trapping her, not the graceful ballerina now, but the frantic submissive enduring an ass-beating she wanted but could barely tolerate. As much as she wanted to please him, she would have to stop him soon. She shuddered through another stinging stroke and let her legs go limp. Down. She wanted down. She'd taken all she could stand...perhaps a little beyond what she could stand. He stopped at once, releasing her so she could fall to her knees in surrender.

"Romeo," she whispered. "I want more, but—"

"It's okay," he said, tipping up her chin. She stared into approving black eyes. "I'll give you more. Something else, nicer. Kneel up straight and open your mouth."

She obeyed without the slightest hesitation, even though a month ago, a year ago, she would have said she despised giving blowjobs. Somehow that was no longer the case. He left her to go for a condom, then returned to stand with his thick cock jutting in front of her. Without prompting, she opened wider.

"That's right," he said. "Serve me. Let me fuck your pretty face."

Serve me. He'd said that to her in one of her sordid dreams. She remembered the exact words, and fought a sudden feeling of disequilibrium. Was this another dream or was it really happening? She made some small sound of panic and he touched her face as if to soothe her.

"You can do it," he said. "Suck me. You're starving for me, aren't you?" He massaged her throat as she took his length as deep as she could. Dream or reality?

His fingers felt too warm and real for this to be a dream. She cupped her hands around his rigid length, over the part she couldn't fit in her mouth, then reached down to stroke his balls. At his urging, she drew back to lick them with broad strokes. He groaned and put his hands on the sides of her head. "*Jesus Cristo,*" he said. "You're getting too good at this. Turn around. Open your legs."

He knelt behind her and yanked her into position on her hands and knees. She barely caught her breath before he impaled her on his cock. He drove against her hot ass, riding her, manipulating her for his pleasure. He was so greedy and demanding. Heat built in her pussy, her innate response to his mastery. He stroked and pinched her breasts and pressed his chest against her back. When she begged *there, there, there,* he gave it to her there, thrusting deep and sliding his fingers over her swollen clit.

Is okay to be scared. Is okay to be scared.

The deep strokes of his cock were scary exciting, and scary rough. Add his muscles, his grasping hands, and the seductive lilt of his accent, and she found herself in that wondrous world again, the world where she and Rubio fit together like two pieces of a puzzle. His cock and her pussy, his force and her submission. His darkness and the light he opened up inside her, the light that pulsed and made her shudder until she fell apart. He licked the back of her neck and yanked her hair hard.

"You smell like sugar," he said against her ear. "I dream about it..." His voice went out on a gasp and he drove into her harder, faster, lifting her from the floor with the force of his thrusts. Her pussy clenched around him as her orgasm erupted without conscious thought. It was a reflex, a natural outcome of being joined to him. He wrapped her in his arms, and she thought she could feel his heartbeat beneath her own heart's frantic pounding. He ground his hips against hers. His whole body tensed and shuddered, and then he grabbed two handfuls of her hair and pressed his forehead to her back.

"Petra," he sighed. "What do you do to me?"

He drew back and flipped her over, and kissed her as she clung to him, basking in the feeling of his hard body pressed against hers. After a while, he pulled away to take off the condom.

"Careful," he said. "So no baby. Right?"

She nodded, so appreciative of the care he took. She had to look away, or she was afraid he'd see everything she felt about him. *I love you. I'm trying to fight it but I can't.*

He wrapped his arms around her and held her close, right there in the middle of the hard floor. Neither one of them spoke for a moment and then he said, "That was good. Good scene." He ran a fingertip up her arm, raising goose bumps. "I like to be with you, Petra. You make me happy. This is okay, isn't it?"

Petra chose the vaguest answer possible. "I think it has to be okay."

"Hmm." He answered that tentative statement with a kiss. "Everything is okay. Very okay then. Are you happy too?"

She didn't have to think twice about it. "Yes, I'm happy."

"Maybe soon..." He paused. "When we have a day off, maybe it's time to visit the play room together. Try out some of the equipment."

She wasn't sure whether her shiver was born of excitement or anxiety. She just knew "soon" couldn't come soon enough.

Chapter Thirteen:
Ten Minutes

Rubio expected it to be tedious, watching out for Petra, going with her everywhere and constantly monitoring their surroundings. But the truth was, he'd been watching her for weeks, attuned to everything about her. Back then, he'd been watching for any signal she might reconsider their sex-free partnership.

He was so, so glad she'd reconsidered. She wasn't as hardcore as some of the women he'd played with, but she excited him in other ways. She *connected* with him. She made herself vulnerable for him—and he knew it wasn't natural for her to let her guard down. He rewarded her as best he could. He gave her orgasms and eased her into trying new things, new adventures to bring her pleasure. *Nutcracker* rehearsals—which were normally excruciating—took on a new air of sensuality. As they moved together, he'd gaze into her eyes and they'd both remember the previous night's sexual encounter—a cropping that had her begging for mercy or a wrestling match that ended with raunchy sex.

Sometimes as they rehearsed together, he'd whisper what he planned to do to her later, very quietly. He'd move his hand across her ass cheeks, across hidden welts no one else could see. He never kissed her. She wouldn't let him kiss her in front of anyone because she wanted their relationship to be a secret. She didn't want them to become a company "item," didn't want to be the object of speculation and gossip. She didn't want to become her mom.

Rubio understood that. He understood a lot more about her now that they'd grown closer, and he felt a lot about her, but he kept it inside because he didn't want to upset her, or scare her away. Once he started blurting out his feelings all hell would break loose, because he never said things right. He didn't have a lot of smooth manners, and it wasn't easy for him to talk.

He listened to her though. That, at least, he could do. He held her at night as she poured out her fears about Paulsen, and her fears about getting older, her fears about work, or a difficult ballet, or company politics. One frown from Liam, and Petra would fall into a tailspin. Liam kept them loosely informed about Paulsen's activities and correspondence, but Rubio could tell he was selective about what he shared.

Somehow, some way, this stalking crisis would pass. In the meantime, Ruby tried his best to distract her from troubling thoughts. Today, he was taking her on a private tour of Liam's play room—a tour he'd been planning for days.

"Come on," he said when she stalled on the stairs. "Is not so scary. I'll turn on the lights."

He flipped a switch and the "lights" came on: sconces of flickering LED candles. The play room looked the same day or night, thanks to thick black walls and a lack of windows. Petra stood at his side, scanning the equipment. He took her hand and smiled at her. "It looks different, huh? When it's just us?"

She nodded. "It looks empty. You're absolutely sure Liam and Ashleigh won't come down here? Or Mem?"

"I put a sign on the door. *Ocupado.* It's just you and me." He crossed to the sound system and put on some music with a low, sensual beat.

Petra drifted over to a towering iron rack, studying the rails and eye bolts. "How long has Liam been giving his parties?"

"As long as I've known him, which is a pretty long time. Almost ten years now. The parties started out smaller. They've grown over time. Liam likes to make a safe place for people to play and meet new partners. Before Ashleigh, he used to play with..." He made a careless gesture. "Hundreds of women. He was a player."

She looked at him from under her lashes. "You're a player too, aren't you?"

He was about to agree when he realized it had been weeks since he'd been with a party chick, with anyone besides Petra. He shrugged. "I'm not so bad. Not anymore." *Not since I met you.*

The unspoken words danced around them. He shoved out his bottom lip. "Well, pretty soon I'm going to tie you down and do dirty things to your body. So if you want to explore, or ask any questions, you better do that now."

She strolled along the wall, checking out all the various implements. "How long have you been into BDSM?" she asked.

He'd been ready to do tutorials on equipment, not answer questions about himself. "I don't know," he said slowly. "I don't remember a time I wasn't into it. I always had this...this mean stroke. Is that the expression?"

"Mean streak?"

"Yes."

"I wouldn't say you're mean, though. You're a little rough, but underneath, you're a caring person."

"Don't tell that to anyone," he said with a threatening glare. "Is not true, anyway."

"It is true." She grinned at him, so cute and sweet. Pretty Petra. What would she think of his background, his childhood? The impoverished neighborhood where he grew up?

"In Brazil..." He paused, wondering how to explain such things to her. "In Brazil, when I was young, I saw a lot of injustice. A lot of weak and poor, and powerful and rich. There were great divides. From an early age, I thought...I want to have power. I don't want to be weak. When I started ballet, the teachers said I had talent. I wanted to quit. I thought ballet was weak but my teacher showed me it can be strong. It can be powerful. I saw that ballet could bring me power, that I could use my talent to rise out of poverty. I was determined, even when kids teased me and threw rocks at me."

"They threw rocks at you?"

"They threw worse things, but I didn't care. I wanted to be the best, I wanted to have power. With sex too, when I started, I wanted to be the one in control, all the time, for everything. I had this feeling of wanting to protect women, but wanting to hurt them too. But for pleasure, not to be cruel." He shook his head. "I can't explain. My English isn't good enough."

"No. I understand what you mean. I see that all the time in you, the protective-yet-hurty thing."

He locked eyes with her over the space between them. It occurred to him that outside of Liam, Petra knew him best. He glanced away, scanning the room full of BDSM equipment. "I can't say why I like to hurt women in sex. I don't know why I like to hurt you. I can't explain why I want that, when I—" He almost said, *when I love you.* He did love her, he was almost sure. He also knew he couldn't tell her that. Instead he shrugged and said, "I don't know where it comes from."

She turned her head a little, the light of the candles reflecting in her hair. "Pain is a very effective way to exert power. I'm sure that's all it is. But...does it upset you? That you like to hurt women?"

He looked away from her probing gaze. "It only upsets me when it makes me uncompatible with someone I like."

"Incompatible."

"Yes, because I know a lot of women don't like to be hurt."

She looked past him, toward the corner where he'd played with her on the horse. "I didn't think I liked to be hurt, but you make it sexy. Exciting. I liked it from the very first time."

"I remember," he said, forcing a smile. All this serious talk. He tried to refocus her attention to fun things, leading her over to the wall of BDSM implements. "What do you think? See anything interesting?"

"I see a lot of things that are interesting. And scary."

He reached for a clear Lucite paddle and turned it over in his hand. "This hurts bad. Want to feel it?"

He brandished it at her and she ran off. He followed, his laughter rising over the low hum of the music. She was short but she was quick and she fit into spaces he couldn't. She hid behind a cage in the corner and peeked out at him.

"You know you want it," he said, grinning.

"How long did it take Liam to collect all that stuff?" she asked.

"It's not all his. People donate toys they don't want anymore, or leave their gear here for the parties. My private stash is in a trunk over there." He lifted a brow. "Wanna see?"

That got her out from behind the cage. He gave her a crack on the way over just to hear her yelp. She kept her butt covered until he hung the paddle back up. They moved to his custom-made, leather embellished trunk, and he was glad to see curiosity in her expression, rather than dread. He unlocked it with the code and opened the lid. It was designed like a tool chest inside, with lots of shelves and compartments for holding all sizes of evil things.

"So," he said, "you've probably seen a lot of this stuff on those websites."

"What websites?"

He gave her a look. "I know you been checking things out, but that's good." He showed her rope, cuffs and bondage straps, paddles and whips and nipple clamps, fluorescent vibrators and stainless steel butt plugs. "You know what those metal plugs are for," he said, watching the blush spread across her cheeks. "I think today we'll try some. But don't worry. With you I'll start small."

He studied one that was anything but small, just to mess with her. When she cringed, he put it back and got a smaller one, for a beginner. It would do for the moment. He got some nipple clamps too, along with a whip and a vibrator. "You carry these," he said, shoving them into her hands. "I'll get a bigger plug, and the lube."

"A bigger plug?" she asked nervously.

"Yeah, and lube." He nudged her in the direction of a padded bondage table. "For now we'll use lube. Until your ass is better trained." He always used lube for anal—he was just messing with her. "Don't be scared," he said. "Nothing today will hurt too much."

"What are you going to do?" she asked.

He pulled her to a stop beside the table. "Whatever I like. You understand that by now, yes? But if you want to know, I'm going to put a plug in your ass and a vibrator on your clit, and I'm not going to let you come. I'll hurt you with the clamps and the whip too, I think." He had her dump the items on a nearby table. "It'll be fun."

"Fun?" she repeated forlornly. "To not be able to come?"

"It's fun for me, to see you suffering and struggling. Maybe, at the end we can do some bargaining, if you really want an orgasm."

She ruffled up. "Orgasms are physiological. Sometimes they just happen. What if I just...go off?"

He picked up the set of nipple clamps and turned them over in his palm. "If you knew you were going to get twenty whip strokes for coming without permission, could you hold off?"

"I...I don't know. It would depend what you were doing to me."

"I told you. Anal plug. Vibrator. Nipple clamps, of course. Think you could do it?"

"For how long?"

"Ten minutes. Ten short minutes. Easy. Take your clothes off," he said. "Let's try."

She shook her head. "I know I couldn't do it. I'd mess up. And twenty strokes with a whip sounds way too hard for me."

"Ten then. You're a beginner. And I wasn't offering a choice, I was telling you what was going to happen. So take your clothes off and we'll get started."

She shifted, staring at him. She was so beautiful when she was afraid. He picked up the whip. It was a small one but it had a sharp bite. "You need help?" he asked, brandishing it in front of her. "Motivation?" He flicked it against one of her breasts.

She took a step back and pulled off her tee. He unbuttoned her jeans while she took off her bra. "Everything," he said when she paused in her panties. "I need all of you." He undressed too, throwing his clothes on top of hers. "Get up on the table," he said. "Spread your legs for me."

After the slightest hesitation, she obeyed. He made her wait there, legs spread, worried and horny, while he laid out all the items he planned to use. He checked the batteries on the vibrator, turning it on so the low hum curled around them. He set it down and turned back to her, running a hand down to her pussy. "Let's see how my pretty Petra feels. Oh..." He pretended to be shocked. "Wet as an ocean. Wet and horny. It's a waste though. We're not using your pussy today."

One look at her face, and he knew he had her. She was so aroused—and so curious. Her soaked pussy gave all her secrets away.

"Okay," she said. "I'm scared."

"I like when you're scared, baby."

She tensed as he pushed her back and lifted her arms over her head to cuff them to the table. They were Velcro cuffs, lined on the inside and attached to the table with adjustable straps. He tightened them, not allowing her much leeway. That done, he reached below the table to find the leather waist restraint. He pulled it tight across her stomach to fasten her down. "There. Can't have you turning or trying to get away." Her muted moan of nervousness sent blood rushing to his cock. He turned back to the table to pick up the whip. "Open your mouth."

When she did, he placed it between her lips. "Hold this. I have a feeling I'll need it later."

Her chest rose and fell. He gazed at her nipples, tight and hard as little rocks. "You ready for the clamps?"

She gazed at him, unable to communicate with the whip between her teeth. He'd used some mild clamps on her already, up in the bedroom. Today he'd picked out a slightly harder pair. When he attached the first one, her entire pelvis rose off the table, making the leather restraint pull and creak. "Don't you break Liam's stuff," he warned with a tsk. "He'll punish you." He attached the other clamp and fisted his cock as she moaned behind the whip and arched against the restraints. She looked so delicious, so helpless and vulnerable, but this was only the beginning. He picked up the smallest plug and eyed her as he coated it with a sheen of shiny lubricant.

She'd be bargaining by the end, all right. Bargaining for exactly what she wanted. She stared as he approached her with the gleaming sex toy. "Open your legs," he said in his gruff, obey-me voice. "Wide. Pull your knees back. Ah, yes, that's my good girl."

* * * * *

Is okay to be scared. Is okay to be scared.

She spread her legs wide, because she had a bendy little whip in her mouth and she was terrified of being hit with it. He moved closer, masculine feline grace, and probed at her bottom with the plug. It was small, as promised. It didn't hurt, but she automatically tensed her legs as the cool tip touched her skin. He shoved her thighs open and pressed the plug forward until it was fully seated. Her initial nerves subsided. It was no thicker than his fingers, and she'd had those inside her bottom already. Honestly, the clamps hurt a lot worse.

"Good girl," he said. "Okay?"

She nodded, then shook her head. He took the whip for a moment so she could answer him. "I think I might orgasm before you even touch me."

"Don't dare. You better control yourself."

"Please, just let me come," she begged. "Don't punish me. My ass is still sore from last night."

He made a soft sound and placed the whip back between her teeth. "Who said I was going to use it on your ass?"

Oh God. Oh, no.

He stepped back to get his phone, and pushed a few buttons. He held it up and showed her a timer. "Ten minutes," he said, setting it back down. "Don't come."

She closed her eyes, trying not to think about the orgasm already building inside her. She was a dancer. She could control her body if she had to. Ten minutes or ten strokes of the whip. Ten minutes...she could survive that.

Just as she thought it, she felt his fingers slide between her pussy lips, and then his tongue in a long, slow stroke, right up to her clit. Her whole body convulsed in a spasm of pleasure. Her ass clenched on the plug and she tried to arch toward him but she couldn't.

"No, please," she said, dropping the whip from her mouth. "That feels too good. This isn't fair."

"Not fair?" He frowned at her. "I haven't even used the vibrator yet. If it feels too good, maybe you need something bigger in your ass, and tighter clamps. We'll have to stop the clock."

"What?" Her and her big mouth. He took off the clamps and laid them aside, then took out the first plug and methodically began lubing up the second one.

"Think before you speak, huh?" he said, winking at her. "But maybe if you hurt more, you won't come. Still eight minutes and forty-eight seconds to go."

Eight minutes and forty-eight seconds? She was going to die. He picked up the whip and flicked it against her left flank before waving it in front of her face. "Don't drop it again," he warned. "No talking. No begging and saying please. I do what I like, yes? Answer me. *Yes, Sir.*"

"Yes, Sir," she squeaked as he flicked her other thigh. He put the whip back in her mouth and ran his palms over the twin stings on either side. "If you come, I'll whip your pussy. Okay? Ten strokes. You understand that?"

Oh my God. Yes, she understood. She also realized what he probably already knew. He could make her come twenty times in the next eight minutes and forty-eight seconds if he wanted to. She knew it, he knew it. He was going to whip her pussy—it was a foregone conclusion. She rested her head back on the table and moaned in frustration. She could try not to come—she was going to try her very best—but she'd put the odds of success at a thousand-to-one.

At that bleak thought, he approached with the larger plug and pressed her legs up and back in some bastardization of a ballet pose. She felt the blunt head of the plug probe her ass. "This time it will go easier," he said. "But it's bigger. You have to let it in."

It felt okay at first, but the middle part was definitely thicker. She wiggled, curling her toes against the pain. It wasn't sharp pain, like the bite of the whip, but a dull, awful stretching. Her eyes locked with his. Beneath the dominant posturing, beneath the stern glare, Ruby was there, watching to be sure she was okay. Watching, always watching. She forced herself to relax, and with slow, twisting movements, he eased the plug the rest of the way in.

She could feel this one, for sure. Her ass felt stretched. Filled. She held his regard as he studied her, letting him see the pain and discomfort in her eyes. *Yes, I hate this. Yes, I love you.* She bit down on the whip, disturbed by the uncontrolled feelings he aroused in her. He pinched her ass and turned to go, and for a moment she felt panic. *He's leaving. He's leaving me here like this!*

But he'd only gone back to his trunk of toys. He returned with another set of clamps, a more intricate pair that looked a lot more threatening.

"Clover clamps," he said, swinging them in front of her. "Maybe too hard for you. But we have to make you hurt if you don't want to come, yes?"

Yes, yes, make me hurt. But oh God. I'm scared. She had the "Romeo" safeword if she needed it. She squeezed her eyes shut as he pinched her nipples.

"No, open," he said sharply. "Open your eyes. Let me see."

He watched her as he closed the first biting clamp on her sensitive peak. She didn't think she'd ever get used to nipple clamps, with their instant, piercing pain. She keened behind the whip, clenching her teeth so she didn't drop it. "Hurts, yes?" Ruby crooned. "Too much?"

Yes, it was too much, but she still wanted it. She worked to calm her breath, and when she thought she could bear it, she lifted her shoulder toward him, offering her other breast. His expression deepened, turned almost feral. He grabbed her face and kissed her mouth, right over the whip. He bit her bottom lip until it stopped trembling, then he leaned back and drew down the chain of the clamps. He tried to thread it under the waist strap, but there wasn't room. "Suck in your breath."

She knew what he was going to do. He was going to hook the chain through the strap at her waist so the clamps constantly pulled down and hurt her. She almost shook her head but in the end, she lay very, very still and let him do it without a sound of protest.

He laced it under and drew it back up, flicked her other nipple and closed the clamp on it. Through the haze of pain, she saw him check the slack and felt a harder pinch as he gave the chain a tug. "You better not move too much, huh? Or, if you're going to come, move a lot and make it hurt. You see how I try to help you?"

She managed a weak smile behind the leather implement in her mouth. He was pure evil. She tested her predicament, drawing her chest up. The clamps tightened as the waist strap caught the chain. *Fuck me. I'm toast.*

She was overloaded on sensation: the thick plug in her ass, the restraints, the hurting clamps, and the ever-present threat of the whip in her mouth. He watched her, teasing her clit with a deft, light touch.

"Control, baby. When it feels too good, think about that whip in your mouth, and how it's going to hurt on your pussy. You think about that."

Not helping, she wanted to yell at him. *You're not helping at all.*

He picked up the pink vibrator. It was slim with a curved edge, a cute little thing. A cute little horrible torture toy. He started the timer on his phone and flicked on the vibe with a flourish. "Eight minutes and forty-eight seconds."

Ha, thought Petra. *More like thirty seconds. But if you want to keep up this farce...*

As soon as he touched the vibrator to her clit, her body started moving. Trembling, tensing, undulating. She felt sharp tugs at her nipples but it wasn't enough to dull the arousing sensation of the vibrator. She twisted her hips, tiny movements impeded by the leather waist belt. Her attempts at evasion were useless. He circled her clit, observing her torment with a faint smile on his face. *Evil, evil, evil...*

When her legs started kicking, he turned it off. He put it aside and shoved three fingers inside her pussy. She was soaking wet, drowning in her own juices. He drew his fingers out and licked them, then shoved them in again. He finger-fucked her a few times and then withdrew them, pressing them in her mouth this time, beneath the handle of the whip.

She licked them eagerly. Any time spent sucking on his fingers was time without the vibrator. She swirled her tongue around the tips, flicking them, mimicking a blowjob. His eyes widened. His cock was purple-hard as he fisted it.

"Be careful," he said. "Don't tease." He pressed against the flange of the anal plug, then eased it slowly in and out...in and out. She tensed, which made it hurt worse. She couldn't help thinking how it would feel if he fucked her there, if it was his cock moving in and out of her instead of the tapered toy. Her gaze dropped to his thick length. She'd never thought it possible, but now... No. God, no. He was too big for her.

When she looked back at him, she knew he'd read her thoughts. "If you want it, just ask," he said. "If you want me to fuck your little virgin asshole."

She shook her head, the whip shifting in her mouth.

He picked up the vibrator again. With a glance at the clock, he said cheerfully, "Only five minutes to go. See? Control. You can do this."

Was he going to let her do it? Because she knew the control was all his. He would decide if she succeeded or failed. She steeled herself not to come.

"Is okay," he said, placing the buzzing tip against her clit. "Take deep breaths."

Deep breaths weren't going to help. The vibrator set off reactions she couldn't control. Her breasts throbbed and her nipples taunted her with sharp, tugging pains. Her ass clenched around the plug in intermittent pulses as her legs strained against his hands. Her pelvis ached, heavy with arousal. Within seconds, she was going to fall over the cliff into orgasm. Unless he turned the vibrator off, she was lost.

She began to shake her head violently. "No," she begged behind the whip. "No, no, no."

"Yes, yes, yes," he murmured.

She tried to twist her hips away and got a good strong nipple tug for her troubles. He looked over at the clock. "Three minutes, thirty-two seconds," he said. "Think of other things. Don't come."

Just before she reached the point of no return, he switched off the evil toy and cupped her pussy. "You think you might make it?" He grinned at her and then nipped her clit with his teeth. She wailed in protest. "What? You don't like when I taste your pussy? I can't help it."

She shuddered, restrained and burning with arousal, as he teased her exact point of destruction with his warm, agile tongue. She heard the vibrator click on and then she felt both sensations, the tugs and flicks of his mouth combined with the buzzing stimulation of the vibrator. In an instant, it was all over. She gave a cry, a furious, frustrated cry, and surrendered to orgasm. Her whole body shook in violent pleasure to the accompaniment of her blood beating in her veins. Her wail died to breathless moans and then silence as her limbs jerked through the intense climax. She heard the vibrator click off.

"Oh, no," he said in feigned disappointment. "So close. You almost did it."

She spit out the whip. "You were never going to let me do it. You— You cheated. You're a cheater."

He turned the flange of the plug, then reached to take off the nipple clamps. "Five extra strokes for calling me a cheater when you are the naughty one here."

"I'm not naughty," she said, but she felt pretty naughty. She strained against the pain of the blood rushing back to her nipples. "I was trying to be good."

He shook his head and made a disapproving sound. "No control. You're a horny, naughty little slut, aren't you? Say it. *Yes, Sir, I'm a horny, naughty little slut.* Say it or I'll add even more with the whip."

It wasn't fair. It wasn't fair, but they both knew it wasn't supposed to be fair. She pouted and muttered, "Yes, Sir, I'm a horny, naughty slut."

He pressed his fingers inside her, twisting them within her clenching walls. "Say it nicer. Be a good girl for me. This is your last chance."

She took a deep breath and met his eyes. His fingers filled her, a probing, carnal manifestation of his power. "Yes, Sir, I'm a horny, naughty slut," she said in a clear, respectful voice.

"And you deserve a whipping, don't you? Right on your horny, naughty pussy?"

She shivered, wondering what that would feel like. "Yes, Sir," she said after a moment. "I do." He reached to retrieve the whip from where she'd spit it on the floor. "But I'm afraid," she added in a whisper.

He stood and paused, gazing down at her. "This will hurt, but at the end you'll be happy." He brushed a fleeting kiss across her lips. For someone bent on punishing her, the kiss was so sweet. She wished she could kiss him for hours. *Oh God, I'm falling in love...*

"Fifteen strokes," he said against her cheek. He ran his fingers across the strap holding her waist, as if to check that it was still secure, and then opened her legs wide.

"You'll have to keep these still," he said in his gravelly Portuguese accent. "If you close them, I'll add more."

She made a strangled sound. "Can't you tie them open or something?"

"No. This is how we learn control, yes?"

He straightened and she braced for the first blow. She didn't think he'd injure her but she wasn't sure how you got whipped on your pussy without some serious hurt going on.

"Wait," he said. "I have something to help."

He left and returned a moment later with a blindfold. That was supposed to help? Help what? Help break her mind? He smoothed it over her eyes so she was plunged into blackness. In some way it helped, because she didn't have to watch him standing over her with the whip. But now she felt everything so much more intensely. She felt the hold of the restraints and the pressure of the plug in her ass, and the solid table at her back.

"Open your legs wider," he chided. "Open for what you deserve."

Oh my God... The first stroke flicked against the inside of her left thigh, over her labia. "One."

The sting of it shocked her. She pulled at the cuffs, snapping her legs shut.

"Now you added one," he said. "Is like starting all over. Fifteen strokes. Open your legs."

"I can't. It hurts too much."

"I know it hurts. Open your legs."

She could use a safeword, but she didn't want to. With a moan she let her legs fall open, and waited in darkness. The next flick landed on the inside of her other thigh. "Two."

She cried out but she kept her legs open. His breathy "good girl" felt like a caress.

"Three." *Holy motherfucking Christ.* The third stroke landed right on her clit. She jumped but stayed silent, gritting her teeth. He wasn't hitting her too hard, but oh, she was so sensitive there. "Four." Another on her clit. She made a begging sound, then yelped as he hit her two more times in succession, right on the tender folds of her pussy lips. Her skin pulsed and her pelvis felt heavy and achy, like she might come again if he caught it with the whip just the right way.

Then the next stroke fell, and she cried out. "Seven."

That one was hard. Eight was harder and nine had her legs snapping shut again. He slapped her outer thigh. "Now we do nine again. You're making things worse for yourself."

"Please..."

"Open your legs," he said in a dire voice. She wished she could see his face, see the intensity and control she heard in his voice. With a sigh, she opened her thighs against the table.

She struggled at nine, tensing her legs to keep them open as the whip landed on her clit in a spark of fire. "I can't," she said. "I can't take all fifteen of these. Please, I can't."

"Are you ready to bargain?"

His quiet words stilled her. Bargain with what? *Her virgin asshole...* She knew it even before she felt his fingers on the plug. He pressed the flange against her body, wiggling it. "One more stroke, and then you open your asshole for me. You let me fuck your asshole until you come."

Not until he came. Until *she* came. A shudder wracked her body. "I'm scared."

"I know you're scared," he said calmly. "That's why we're bargaining. Pain or pleasure. You decide."

He brought the whip down on the table in a loud snap so she jumped. "Okay." She squeezed her eyes shut behind the blindfold. "Okay. I'll let you."

"You'll let me have your virgin asshole. Say it."

"I'll let you have my virgin asshole," she said, her voice wavering on the last two words.

"Spread your legs then. One last whip on your clit."

His voice was sharp and businesslike, impossible to contradict. He was so good at this. She opened her legs and arched her pelvis so he could get in a good parting shot. She could feel the plug in her ass, soon to be replaced with something altogether larger. In the midst of that thought, the whip flicked against her swollen button. If anything, her legs spread wider for him as she panted through the stinging aftermath. *Until you come.* Oh God, she wanted to come so badly.

He stroked her legs, tapped her pussy a couple times with his fingers, then tugged at the flange of the anal toy until he could ease it out. The pain sharpened as the thickest part slid past the ring of her sphincter.

"You know," he said, "this toy lets your ass close around the narrow part. My cock won't do that. Just something to think about." She flinched as he pressed a finger inside. She felt cool liquid, more lube, and then she heard the sound of a condom wrapper. *Is okay to be scared...*

She felt his warmth above her. His lips lowered over hers for a kiss. Then he was gone and his hands were pressing open her thighs, tugging her closer to the edge of the table. When he touched the head of his cock to her hole she tightened up.

"No," he said. "I won't hurt you. Not too much."

She let out the breath she'd been holding and willed herself to be brave, to accept this intimate act.

"Oh, yes, baby," he sighed. She felt the head of his cock ease in and stretch her in an intensifying burn. "So tight. You're so tight. Is okay, hold on. Soon, it will feel better."

Breathe in, breathe out. He held her legs, massaging the backs of her thighs. "Let me in, baby. I want to be inside you." With every word, he pressed deeper, prying her open, taking up residence where she'd never thought he could fit. She felt an unbearable fullness, but it was thrilling, not bad. The lubricant eased his passage, as he worked himself forward in small movements. "Okay?" he asked.

She squeezed on his girth, impaled by him in her dark world. "Yes, it's okay."

He moved deeper, not violently or roughly. This act didn't need any violence to communicate power—the violence was the very act of being there, demanding entrance into that tight, cramped space. Now that he was there, she understood she was his. His to use, his to hurt, his to please as it pleased him. He palmed her clit, massaging it as he drove in and out.

"How does it feel?" he asked. "It hurts?"

"A little," she whimpered.

"You're scared?"

Yes, she was so scared, but turned on too. Her breath felt heavy, caught up in her chest. Her whole body felt tight and vulnerable, but he was in control now and all she could do was trust. After a while, as he slowly fucked her, she felt her tightness open, felt her limbs relax. His cock wasn't hurting her anymore, only possessing her deep inside. The lube made it slick, so it wasn't friction, just intrusion. He pressed back on her thighs, opening her even wider.

"Yes, baby, that's good," he said, encouraging her as she arched her hips for more. "I want to be all the way inside you."

Her toes curled as he pressed deeper, until his pelvis butted up against her ass. She felt completely stretched, completely full. "Oh God. Oh God!"

He shushed her cries, gripping one hip as he took her ass with measured strokes. The other finger explored her pussy, dipping inside before traveling up to graze her clit again. Her clit and labia were still smarting from the whip, so each touch was more than a caress. It was a memory of his punishment, and her submission to his will.

"You want to come?" he asked. "This time you're allowed to. But I want it to be good."

Oh God, yes. She might have said it out loud or she might have just breathed it out. *Yes, yes, yes...* His voice sounded low and gruff, and wonderfully raunchy. She wished she could see him standing over her, driving into her, but she also loved being swept away on sensation, on the pure hedonism of taking it up the ass. All this time she'd been afraid of anal sex for a myriad of reasons. Now, she was pretty sure it was her new favorite thing.

As she pondered this reversal of opinion, he squeezed her breasts and pinched each nipple. She could feel them harden between his fingertips. She heard the clink of metal and thought, *oh, no, he wouldn't.* But he did. With a searing blast of pain, the clamps resumed their torture, one at each nipple, falling down against her breasts. Her burgeoning orgasm fled.

"Ow," she said. "Oh, God...why?"

"Poor baby," he said, and she knew he was smiling. "Maybe you can't come now?"

He touched her clit, just one fleeting stroke, and she shuddered, nearly incapacitated by the combination of pleasure and pain. He drove deep while he fondled her, taking everything he wanted, doing whatever he wanted. She drew her legs wide, thinking, *I'm yours, I'm yours, I'm yours.* He was enjoying this, hurting her, defiling her, and for her part, she would have submitted to this treatment for hours if he asked it. Her nerve endings were barreling toward orgasm, but she held back, wanting to enjoy the blending of erotic sensations just a moment more...

"Oh God, oh God, *oh God,*" she gasped, clenching her ass. "I'm going to come soon. I can't stop it."

"Come on," he said. "I want it."

The clamps jerked on her nipples. Her arms strained against the cuffs and the leather strap holding her down, and then her body fell into a climax ten times stronger than the previous one. She couldn't speak, couldn't do anything but ride out the waves that engulfed her.

"God, yes." Rubio groaned as she pulsed around his thrusting cock. He said more things, low, in Portuguese, as he surged deep inside her, as deep as he could go. Then he tensed and held, jerking through a series of tremors. At last, he came to rest.

"Oh baby," he whispered, falling down over her. "You're such a good girl. But...I think now...no more virgin asshole."

She laughed weakly. "No. No more virgin asshole, for sure."

He stroked her shoulder, licked her jaw and her neck while her ass squeezed his cock in intermittent aftershocks. "That was crazy," he said after a while. "Just crazy."

She shifted in her bonds. She needed to hold him and touch him, and be close to the man who'd done this intimate, amazing act to her. "Ruby, let me go. Let me see you. I want to see you."

He started to work at her restraints, releasing the clamps and cuffs, and undoing the strap at her waist. When she reached out, he caught her and dragged her against his chest. She flung her arms around his neck, clinging to him. The blindfold came off last, and she blinked in the dim dungeon to find him watching her with a combination of amusement and dread.

"You okay?" he asked. "You survived?"

Had she survived? This time, perhaps, but what about next time? It seemed he could make her do just about anything, which was a dangerous talent to have. What would the next "ten minute" session bring? What if he stretched it to an hour? A day? A week? Her entire life? She couldn't bear to think about it.

She couldn't bear to think about anything beyond this moment, beyond his arms around her, cradling her, and the look in his eyes that said *wow* and *oh, man* and *good girl*, all at the same time.

"I think I mostly survived it," she said. "This time."

His lips spread in a slow smile, and she knew he was already making plans for next time. Which was completely, perfectly fine with her.

Chapter Fourteen:
Is Good

Petra jerked awake to a muttered *merda* and a hand clamped around her wrist. "Crazy girl," Rubio grunted. "Watch your *port de bras.*"

She blinked at him. "What?"

"You're dancing in your sleep." He loosened his grip on her wrist and slid a hand up her arm. His eyes shone in the dim morning light. "Are you finished, or you're going to kick me again?"

"I didn't kick you."

"You kicked me. You whack me on the side of my head all the time."

"I'm sorry," she said, even though he wasn't really angry.

He brushed her hair back with a sleepy smile. "It's okay. Is funny but painful. Maybe I'll start tying you at night, huh? Tie you to the branches of the bed?"

She snuggled into his embrace, feeling all melty at the erotic threat. "But then you could do whatever you wanted to me and I wouldn't be able to stop you."

"Mmm." He kissed the side of her neck, then ran his tongue up to the underside of her chin. His arms were iron bands around her, firm and secure. "I think I like the sound of that," he said.

And I think I love you, she thought. *I'm really afraid I do.*

"I'm sorry I kicked you," she said aloud. "Maybe I can make it better." She slid under the sheets to caress his muscular legs. She kissed his bronze skin, licking over the ticklish texture of his leg hairs. "Is that helping?"

"Ah. Yes. Is better. But somewhere else is hurting." With a mischievous grin he pumped his rigid cock. "Could use some kisses to make it all better."

She grinned. "Just kisses?"

With a grunt, he manipulated her until her face was in his crotch and her ass was stuck in the air. "Ah, that's right," he said, stroking fingertips down her thigh. "Arch your back. Make it pretty for me."

Petra licked her lips, feeling loose and sensual at his softly spoken words. She kissed the tip of his cock, reveling in his halting intake of breath.

"Is good?" she teased, looking up at him.

He gave her ass a lazy slap. "Yes, is good." He reached lower to tangle his fingers through her hair and push her lips down onto his length. "Get busy. Suck me, you hungry little slut."

There was a time when "you hungry little slut" would have infuriated her. When she would have punched someone in the face over it. Now, it excited her. It made her feel sexy and submissive. His fingers tightened, gripping the back of her neck.

"Deeper," he said. "Open that mouth."

She strained to draw him farther into her throat. They'd done some experimenting with deep throating but she wasn't great at it yet. She always gagged like crazy, which Rubio openly enjoyed. At least they didn't have to use condoms anymore, except for vaginal sex, as a backup method.

"Yes, good girl," he said when she coughed and sputtered. "I love when you choke on it."

The "love" was guttural, vicious and forceful. She'd come to live for these Rubio endearments. *I love when you choke on it. I want to hurt you. I love how you cry when I hurt you.*

You're so beautiful when you come.

His fingers trailed over her ass cheeks, then down to probe between her legs. "Open," he said. "Let me look at your pussy."

The old Petra never, ever would have obeyed such an order. The new Petra squirmed sideways to comply. In the last few weeks he'd explored every inch of her, inside and out. Not just explored it. Taken possession of it. His fingers toyed through the moisture between her legs as she licked around his erection. Every so often he'd flick her clit just to make her buck.

"You know," he said in a low voice, "under my bed at home, I keep a pretty Plexiglas cane. It hurts so much. Maybe someday I'll use it to mark you right here."

He pressed his palm against her pussy and she moaned. A pretty Plexiglas cane sounded agonizing, especially between her legs. He slapped her and then drove two fingers inside her wet sheath, forcing her to arch her ass up.

His cock was so solid, so velvety and thick. She sucked the tip like a lollipop and then opened her throat for him to slide deep. She gagged a moment later, hacked out a cough and pulled back for air. With a chuckle, he fisted his balls and nudged her head down to lick them. "Into your mouth," he prompted. "Suck them nice."

She burrowed her face between his legs, breathing in his musky male scent. As she tongued and teased him, his laptop chirped on the table across the room. "Jesus," he groaned. "Bad timing."

A moment later, a ring-notification sounded. He sighed. "Is my mother calling. I told her to call today." He squeezed Petra's shoulder, drawing her away from her task. "Don't go anywhere. We'll finish this very soon."

He slid off the bed and loped over to the table. He slid a finger over his touchpad. "*Mãe, um momento.*" He walked back to Petra with an apologetic look. "I haven't been calling home," he said, pulling on a pair of shorts. "Too busy with other things."

"Like dancing?" Petra asked, deadpan.

He tugged a black tee over his head. "Dancing and fucking you," he said softly, in his throaty lilt.

His voice alone could take her halfway to orgasm. Something of her thoughts must have shown in her face because he said, "Don't look at me like that. Not right before I talk to my mother." He kissed her forehead, then went back over to his laptop. It was angled away from the bed, toward the window, so it was safe for Petra to get up and get dressed. She pulled faces at Rubio across the room, doing an impromptu bump-and-grind. He wagged a finger at her, talking all the while to his mother in rapid-fire syllables she couldn't understand.

She shouldn't hover around and distract him. She didn't know how much his mother knew about his personal life, or whether she knew about her. Did she know they slept together every night? She probably knew they danced together. Petra went into the bathroom to brush her teeth, listening to Rubio chatter in Portuguese. It sounded impossibly sexy, his native tongue. He went from animated to quiet and back to animated, sometimes asking his mom questions. She didn't know the words but she could sense his fondness for his mother, and his concern.

He was a good son. She'd read something once in some women's magazine, about how to tell a good man from a bad one. One of the indicators was how well a man treated his mother. She knew his mother had had a hard life and that he tried to take care of her now. She knew that he sent her money so his mother never had to go without, and he'd bought her a new house and a new life. *She deserves it*, he told her once. *She went through so much.*

Petra understood the subtext, that Rubio had been through so much too. Petra drifted back into the bedroom to eavesdrop and watch his face, his exaggerated expressions and animated smiles. He looked over and beckoned her with a wave of his hand.

"Come here. Say hi to my mom."

Petra didn't want to think too hard about the sentimental thrill she felt at his words. Meeting the parents. Wasn't that a big relationship step? But they weren't in that kind of relationship...

She went over by the laptop and Ruby pulled her into his lap so she'd show up on the video chat screen. His mother gave a delighted whoop when she saw her.

"Wave hi," said Ruby in her ear. "She's been learning English."

Petra waved to his mom. "Hi, Mrs. Rubio." The dark-haired woman looked so much like her son. "How are you?" Petra asked politely.

"Oh, my dear," said his mom with a heavy accent. "You are dance with my son? Very good, yes?"

Petra nodded. "Yes, he's a very good dancer. Excellent."

"He send me pictures," said Mrs. Rubio, fluttering her fingers. "Very pretty."

"Thank you. We have fun."

"Yes, all kinds of fun," he said, smiling at her in agreement. Petra knew exactly what kind of fun he meant, but she didn't want to give that away in front of his mother. He turned back to his mom and said some more stuff in Portuguese, and his mom smiled and laughed. Were they talking about her? His mother chattered for some time in response, then Ruby snorted and made some "Aw, mom" kind of sound.

"*Nando*," his mother chided. "*Juízo, meu filho.*" She looked at Petra. "Is good, for love? Yes? To be in love?"

Petra stared at the screen, at the thumbnail of Ruby's face beside hers. He was blushing all the way through his bronze complexion. "*Chega, mãe*," he said sharply.

Mrs. Rubio and her son launched into another rat-a-tat conversation. It ended with his mom speaking English again. "Mar-ried, you two?" she asked, nodding at Petra. "You get mar-ried, if you in love. Is God's plan."

"Okay," said Ruby, making a face at Petra. "Go. Escape now. Go downstairs, okay? I'll find you later." He raised an eyebrow. *You can finish that blowjob*, he meant.

He nudged her off his lap and she fled the room. It was okay. She shouldn't freak out. All moms were like that, weren't they? Encouraging their kids to fall in love and marry? Except for her mom, who had decried love and marriage as the world's biggest crock of shit. Petra took the stairs down to the living room and then turned to go to the kitchen. Liam sat at the counter on his laptop, a notebook and briefcase beside him. When he saw her, he closed the notebook and slid it into his bag. He looked suave, dressed for work in a button-up shirt and tie.

"You're up early, aren't you?" he asked. "For a day off?" He was being a little too bright.

She crossed the room to join him. "Rubio says I dance in my sleep. I guess I kicked him and woke him up. He's upstairs talking with his mom."

"Can I get you some coffee? Something for breakfast?"

"Coffee sounds great. Thanks."

She resisted the urge to look at his computer screen when he rose to pour her a steaming cup from their super luxury coffee machine. Everything in their house was luxurious. She'd miss this place when she left it. If she ever left it.

"So..." she said, trying to sound casual. "What's the latest news on Scary Gary?"

He was silent for a moment. The only sound was the ting of her spoon against the china coffee cup. "It's not great news," he finally said. "But it's nothing we didn't expect. He's losing patience with the status quo. He's making more threats."

"What kind of threats?"

Again, Liam paused before he spoke. "Unpleasant threats. Just know that we're doing everything in our power to keep you two safe."

You two. "He's making threats against Ruby?"

"I would say he's mainly angry with Ruby. He blames all this on him."

Petra stared down into her cup, thinking of the smiling man upstairs talking to his mom, a woman who depended on him for her well-being and livelihood. She thought of his talent, all the joy he brought to the world of dance. Then she pictured his beautiful body broken, stabbed or shot, bleeding in the street. She squeezed her eyes shut against the image.

"Nothing's going to happen," Liam said, touching the back of her hand. "It'll be okay."

"But what if it's not? If anything happens to him because—because of me—"

"Petra—"

"I'm kind of in love with him," she burst out. She stared at Liam, shocked that she'd said it.

He made a soft sound. "We kind of suspected."

Petra looked down at her lap, twisting her fingers into knots. *In love.* It sounded so hackneyed. "I don't know if I love him," she said, backtracking. "I don't know what I feel. I can't figure out if we have a future, if we belong together."

She fell silent and considered the man beside her. Liam was soft-spoken, kind, obviously protective. He was the typical woman's idea of perfection: long gold-brown hair, gorgeous eyes, and a ridiculously hot body. On top of all that, he was rich as King Midas. This guy was paying her salary just so his friend could have a great partner onstage. This was the kind of man she ought to be falling for, not Fernando Rubio. Even so, she didn't feel the slightest attraction to Liam and her heart ached so badly for Rubio and...and what? *Damn it.*

She put her head in her hands and groaned. "He's my partner," she said. "We work together."

"I can see that throwing a wrench in things."

"My mother..." Oh, this again. When was she going to stop obsessing about her mother's mistakes? "When my mother hooked up with her partner, it ended up in a big shitload of suck."

He made another faint sound, of doubt or perhaps denial. "It ended up with you, didn't it? I don't think you're a big shitload of suck."

She was going to start crying in a minute, if he didn't stop using that voice. "Everything is so screwed up," she said, and then she did start crying. "If he gets hurt— If Paulsen attacks him or k-kills him—"

"Nothing's going to happen to him."

"Maybe I should stop dancing. Retire early and move somewhere and just...just live in some cottage by the sea."

He studied her. "Is that what you want to do? Retire?"

More tears slipped out, not that they helped anything. She swiped them away. "I don't want to retire, but I don't want Ruby to get hurt either. I would stop dancing if it would keep him safe. If it would just— just make all this end and go away."

"If you do that, Paulsen wins," Liam pointed out. "And you've lost everything that makes you happy in life. I don't think you should retire or go back to New York. Give the system time to work. Paulsen's threats will expedite things, but it still has to move through the international legal system. It's slow. I'm sorry."

"No, please. Don't be sorry. I know you're doing everything you can." She forced herself to stop crying. This guy was busting his ass to help her, putting time in every day. The least she could do was keep her shit together. "I can't tell you how much I appreciate all you're doing. I don't know how I can ever thank you."

"You can keep dancing. That would be thanks enough."

She forced a smile, and found as she met Liam's gaze that it was genuine. His eyes flicked over her shoulder and she turned to see Rubio standing at the bottom of the stairs. He gestured to her, the merest flick of a finger, but it communicated exactly what he wanted it to communicate. *I want.* Liam, Paulsen, everything was forgotten except for the command of that beckoning finger.

I want. I want you. I want you, here, now.

She looked back at Liam, who winked and nodded in Ruby's direction. "Go on. Have fun, you crazy kids. But Ash is sleeping, so try not to make too much noise."

* * * * *

Petra sat at dinner the following night, with Ruby, and Liam and Ashleigh, and a contemplative Mem. She couldn't stop feeling contemplative herself. *You get mar-ried, if you in love. Is God's plan.*

Was it in the plan? Did you have to marry someone you loved? Or was it enough to dance with them, and make art, and enjoy the special moments while they lasted? What was more important to her? The increasing devotion she felt for Rubio, or her career?

She glanced at him over her wine glass. He smiled back at her. It wasn't his bedroom smile, the sadistic smile that made her quake inside, or his stage smile, which was always a bit fake. It was his happy, natural smile that made him look so charming.

Conversation dropped off by the end of the meal. Liam was uncharacteristically quiet, and Mem lingered even though it was his habit to leave the table once he finished. Ashleigh groaned, easing back in her chair. "I ate too much. This baby doesn't give me enough space."

She was in her last trimester now. Petra eyed her rounded stomach as Mem and Liam made sympathetic sounds. Liam looked at Petra and then back at Ashleigh.

Ash held his gaze a moment, then turned to pat her on the shoulder. "Want to head up to the roof with me for some fresh air?"

Hm. Okay.

Petra nodded and went to pull on a light coat. She got the feeling she was being purposely herded away, but she loved the Wilder's rooftop garden, with its pergolas and benches, and its unimpeded view of the stars. She followed her friend to the elevator tucked into the back of a room adjoining the dining room. Ash fanned herself as the doors closed.

"I'm so hot these days, even though it's cold out." She ran a hand over the rise of her stomach. "The baby's like a heating blanket. Oh, I love this," she said, touching the sleeve of Petra's fitted blue coat. "Did you get it back in New York? I miss being able to fit into normal clothes." She kept up a steady stream of banter until they were up on the roof, relaxing on cushioned chairs. Ash slung an arm over her head, staring at the night sky.

"The cool air feels good," she said with a sigh. "Thanks for keeping me company."

Petra gave her friend a sideways glance. "I guess they're talking about Paulsen down there?"

For a moment, she looked like she might try to come up with a lie, but then she shrugged. "Probably. Yes. They're in court with him this week."

"With Paulsen? Don't I have to be there for that?"

Ashleigh picked at the edge of her cushion. "I don't think so. It's best if you aren't there. It will only feed his obsession. Liam doesn't tell me everything, but I know they've collected a boatload of evidence to prove he's a threat to you. Emails, letters, photos. The lawyers will take care of it."

Petra crossed her arms tightly over her chest. A boatload of evidence, of which she'd seen nothing. "We just talked yesterday," she said, "and Liam didn't bring up anything about Paulsen and going to court."

"He doesn't want to burden you with it. I think he also doesn't want to get your hopes up that this court date will solve anything." She reached out to touch Petra's hand. "Try not to be annoyed with him. He's very protective, especially to women. Well, he's protective to everyone, but when it comes to women and children, he gets kind of nuts."

"That's sweet," said Petra. "He must make you feel very safe."

Ashleigh laughed. "Sometimes. But other times, like down in the play room, I don't feel safe at all."

"You mean, in a good way?" Petra clarified.

"Oh yeah. A very good way. We have a lot of fun down there."

Petra was extremely curious about Ash and Liam's thing. They seemed so connected, so in love, even though they were completely different on the surface. For starters, Liam was a big, muscular man, even bigger than Rubio, while Ashleigh was pale and petite. Liam was brainy and social while Ash was more fluttery and shy. She knew they hung out down in the play room all the time, even in Ash's pregnant state. "So, were you already into that BDSM stuff when you met Liam?" she asked.

"Oh God, no." Ashleigh covered her face and peeked at her from behind her fingers. "I was traumatized when I realized that was his 'thing.' I ended up at one of his Saturday night parties by mistake and..." She paused. "Let's just say it was eye-opening. Me and Liam had some hard times starting out, a lot of secrets we had to pry out of each other, but it makes all this sweeter, you know? I trust him with everything. My heart, my love, my life. And BDSM is really fun with someone you trust, with someone protective. I mean, you would know. Rubio's really careful, isn't he? He plays like he dances. He pushes his partners' boundaries but always keeps them safe."

Petra nodded. "He's great to play with."

For long minutes the two women relaxed side by side, listening to the nighttime city noise, then Ash massaged her rounded bump. "Be nice, baby girl."

"She's kicking you?"

"Yeah. Liam says she's going to be a dancer." Both of them laughed at that. "I complain all the time," Ashleigh said, "but I love being pregnant. I think Liam loves it less. He's been insufferable, hovering and worrying about me. In a way, your problems are a blessing, because tracking Paulsen provides some other outlet for his nervous energy. Not that I'm happy you're being stalked."

"Oh, I know."

"It's just..." She bit her lip before she spoke again. "This pregnancy has been really hard for him, and it seems to be getting harder the closer we come to the end."

"The baby's due in February?"

"Yeah, just a couple more months. I mean, Liam has his reasons for all this anxiety. Has Rubio told you anything about Liam's past?"

"Not really."

"You're probably too young to remember this, but did you ever hear that story about the welfare mom in L.A. who got postpartum depression and shot all her kids? Well, not all her kids. All but one." Ash squeezed her hands together, then smoothed them over her belly. "All but Liam. He was twelve at the time."

Petra stared at her in shock. Liam? Calm, polished, well-spoken Liam? "Oh my God," she breathed.

"Yeah. So you can imagine he has some anxieties about this pregnancy, and being responsible for such a vulnerable, fragile baby. He's still resisting it, in some way."

"What do you mean, resisting?"

"I mean, he's supportive. He does everything I ask. He's spoiled me rotten through this whole pregnancy but...I don't know. I don't get the feeling he's excited about the baby. Like, genuinely excited. It's more like an act he's putting on to make me happy." She turned away from Petra, staring off into the distance. "Maybe I shouldn't have pushed the baby thing."

"Oh, Ash. He'll come around. I can't imagine someone like Liam being a distant father. As soon as he holds that little girl in his arms, he'll fall head over heels in love. My mother was miserable and angry throughout her entire pregnancy, but she says the moment she held me in her arms, everything changed. Babies are magic like that."

Ashleigh pressed her fingers into the corners of her eyes.

"Go ahead," said Petra. "You can cry in front of me. I cried in front of Liam yesterday. We seem to be cool like that."

Ashleigh giggled and wiped at a stray tear. "I don't want to cry though. I want to be happy. I know he'll be a good father. He'll be a responsible father if only to support me. But if he can't be close to the baby... Oh, God, how will the baby feel, if she thinks her father doesn't love her?"

Petra drew her knees up, hugging them to her chest. "I know how she'll feel. She'll try really hard to be perfect. She'll try to earn his love by being as amazing and wonderful as possible..." She gave Ash a crooked smile. "I have some experience in this area."

"Oh, I'm sorry. I forgot about the Grigolyuk thing."

"I don't think Liam could ever be as cold as my father. I know he couldn't, but even if he was, I turned out okay. Mostly. I think."

Ashleigh smiled and squeezed her hand. "You turned out great. You're an amazing person, with or without your father. Grigolyuk is an ass. His art has always been all about technique, no heart. Didn't it make it awkward for you two, whenever you crossed paths in the business?"

Petra shrugged. "We never crossed paths. I think I was nine or ten years old when I realized he was actively avoiding me. If I knew he'd be at a performance or class, I'd try my damndest to get an invitation, and he wouldn't show up. Or he'd show up and leave as soon as he realized I was there."

"Oh, God. I can't imagine."

"It made my mother furious. It seemed like she spent her whole life furious and unhappy, all because of my dad. I guess that's why I've been so conflicted about Rubio, about starting up a relationship with him."

Ashleigh gave her a puzzled look. "What does Rubio have to do with your dad?"

"Everyone calls him this generation's Grigolyuk."

"Yeah, in sex appeal and talent, but..." Ash made a face. "Rubio's no Grigolyuk. He has a heart like a steel trap. Once you're in there, you're never getting out. The day he found out I wasn't going to dance with him anymore, he came storming over here and lit into me. Literally bitched me out and made me cry. The next day he sent flowers with this note...my God. Talk about crying. It was about the good times we'd had together, and our best moments on stage, and how he knew I'd be the best mother in the history of the world—and I know he wrote it because his handwriting's awful and he writes just the way he speaks." She was blinking back tears again. "He thought I wouldn't be his friend anymore. Like that would have been possible. I'll keep that note until I die. I was glad for him when you came along. I like you two together. You're a good fit."

"Do you ever miss ballet?" Petra asked.

"Of course I miss it," Ash said with a shrug. "But back when I was dancing, I wanted all the things I have now. So when I miss the dancing, I remind myself how much I wanted love, and home, and family, and then the sadness goes away. Sometimes when I see you dancing with Rubio I miss ballet so desperately I almost start bawling, but then Liam takes my hand, or the baby moves inside me, and I know I wouldn't trade my life for anything."

Ashleigh's expression glowed with love, so much that Petra felt a sharp pang of envy. "You and Liam are so great. So amazing. I'm glad we became friends."

The two women hugged and then Ashleigh drew back, fanning herself. "It doesn't feel like the week before Christmas, does it? It's warm out here."

Petra laughed and hugged her coat closer. "It's not warm. I think that's your pregnancy talking."

"Hey, are you and Ruby going to stick around for the holidays?"

"If you'll have us. I don't have anywhere else to go, and he can't leave because he's performing."

"We don't do a huge Christmas, but it will be fun to spend it together. And we don't fuss with presents or anything. Mem and Liam have always kept things very zen."

Petra's eyes went wide. "You guys don't do presents? But you could buy anything you want."

"We already have everything we want," she said, wrinkling her nose. "That's the problem. Although..." Her voice trailed off as she glanced shyly at Petra. "There's something I've always wanted to get Liam for a present. But you'd have to help me. I think Rubio might like it too."

"What is it?"

Ash put her hands over her mouth like she couldn't believe what she was about to say, which piqued Petra's curiosity even more.

"Tell me! What?"

"Promise me you won't go along with it only because you feel you owe me or Liam something."

She shook her head impatiently. "I won't. Just spill it."

Ashleigh started whispering in her ear. Oh. Wow. It wasn't anything she would have considered before she met Rubio...but now... The more Ashleigh whispered to her, the hotter and more curious she felt. A kinky, one-time foursome: her, Ashleigh, Liam, and Rubio. She was right about one thing—Rubio would love it. And if Ashleigh was willing to share her husband, Petra couldn't mind sharing a guy she wasn't even in a relationship with.

"Okay, I'll give it a whirl," Petra agreed with a burst of nervous laughter. "I can't say I won't chicken out between now and Christmas, but I'll try it. Yes." She laughed again. "For the moment, I'm in."

Chapter Fifteen: Present

Rubio always liked spending Christmas at Liam's. It was low-key, laid back, and usually involved good food and wine. There wasn't any pressure to come up with presents or a bunch of holiday cheer, although Ashleigh and Petra had promised them a present after dinner.

Ashleigh used to get him lots of presents when they danced together, silly stuffed animals and chocolate bars she knew he wouldn't eat. Petra never gave him anything, but then she was so concerned with preserving a distance between them. No, not a distance...just a caution. She was a very cautious girl.

He looked at her over the rim of his wine glass. Since this was Liam's wine, he was sure it was some spectacular vintage that cost hundreds of dollars a bottle, but it all tasted the same to him. At Christmas he felt uneasy as much as he felt happy. He knew his family was cared for back in Brazil, but he couldn't forget bleak Christmas mornings as a child. There were always fights about money and presents—or lack of them. There were always fights about him. *Dancing is for girls*, his father used to scream in his drunken rages. *You're turning my son into a fucking girl.*

Ruby felt a hand on his arm. Petra had come around the table to him and he hadn't even noticed. She crawled into his lap, stroking his face. "You look tired. Don't forget, you still have a present coming."

"I'm not tired," he said, staring down the bodice of her low-cut black dress. "You look pretty today. I like your necklace. Is silly, but..."

"It's not silly. I love it." She touched the sleek silver chain at her neck, with its gleaming engraved tag. *Rubio's Pet*, it said. *Return if lost.*

It was more of a collar than a necklace. As much as he enjoyed the BDSM lifestyle, he'd never wanted to put a collar on a girl, not until now. He wasn't sure what Petra thought of it. She said she loved it but there had been some gravity in her eyes when she lifted it from the fancy bag. Maybe a pet tag seemed like too much "commitment." It was only a joke, a play on her name.

Well, mostly.

"It looks good on you," he said. "And you can take off the tag if you want to wear it, you know, without everyone knowing how kinky you are." With those words, he cupped her tight, round ass and squeezed it. That was the other nice thing about Christmas dinner with the Wilders— groping wasn't frowned on at the table. He glanced over at Liam and Ashleigh to find them giving one another amorous looks.

"I think it's time to go set up that present," said Ashleigh, turning to Petra. "Ready to head downstairs?"

"It's in the play room?" Liam's brows arched up.

"Yes, it's in the play room," said his wife. "But we'll need five minutes or so to get it ready, so don't come down before then."

Petra grinned as she followed her friend from the room. Rubio turned to Liam with a speculative look. "Do you know what it is?"

"Haven't the slightest idea. Ash and Petra have been sneaky and giggly about it all week. Even Mem doesn't know."

"Where is Mem anyway?"

"With a lady friend," Liam said. "Mem has ladies, you know. A whole harem."

"Like you, back in the day." Ruby drained the last of his wine, feeling the liquid relax and warm him. He glanced sideways at his friend. "Is nice for you, isn't it? Having a family life? Good friends, good food? Pretty wife with a big pregnant belly?"

Liam smiled. "Yeah. I'd say it's okay."

"Is not so fun to live alone. I was thinking about asking Petra to move in with me. You know, when things calm down. What do you think?"

156

For a moment, Liam looked shocked, but then he changed his expression to something more neutral. "Have you two talked about it? Do you think she'd want to move in with you?"

He shrugged. "I don't know. Probably not. Maybe is a bad idea."

Liam looked at him a long time. "You're dying, huh? You're so in love with her."

He thought about trying to protest, to play it off as a joke, but Liam knew. Liam always knew stuff like that. "I don't know what love is all about," Ruby said, and that was the truth. "I just want her closer to me. Not because of Paulsen and all that. I mean, that's part of it, but..." He shifted in his chair, scratching a hand down the side of his face. "Mostly I want to sleep with her at night, and wake up with her in the morning, and eat breakfast with her at my table."

Liam nodded slowly. "Yeah. That's love, all right. Then comes interior decorating and babies. It's okay," he said, when Ruby frowned. "It's natural."

"No, not natural. Not for me and Petra. We have career responsibilities. People take pictures of us and make up silly stories, and it upsets her. The more I want her, the more she pushes me away. She thinks I'll destroy her." He thought a moment, with a sinking feeling in his stomach. "Maybe I will."

Liam grimaced. "You know what I think? I think both of you are stressing way too hard over this relationship-versus-career thing. It's Christmas Eve, my friend, and life is short. Ask her to move in if you want. Maybe she'll say yes. Maybe she'll move out again in a week or maybe she'll stay for life. Maybe she'll say no. But you should be happier, both of you. Love shouldn't be so hard."

"I know that," he said. "That's why I think maybe we're not in love."

Liam rolled his eyes. "Whatever. Ready to head downstairs? I gotta find out what this super secret gift is. I'm guessing some awesome new equipment she ordered on the sly."

"If it is, I get to use it first."

"It's my play room."

"My partner isn't pregnant."

"Ha. That hasn't slowed her down. I get to use whatever it is first."

They argued back and forth all the way down the stairs, even though Rubio knew Liam would win. When the men arrived downstairs, the play room was dark except for some candles illuminating the raised bed in the corner. And in the middle of the bed—two beautiful, seductive women in each other's arms.

"Holy fuck," Liam breathed.

Ruby went still, struck speechless. Petra lounged against the satin sheets in a sheer black bra and skimpy g-string, with her new silver collar around her neck. Ashleigh wore a wisp of a negligee that framed her round belly. The women had applied matching dark lipstick and teased their hair into crowns of luscious waves, one black as night and the other blonde as the sun. They regarded the two men with teasing, provocative smiles. Ashleigh's hand strayed over Petra's hip in a leisurely exploration as Petra reached out to stroke Ash's breasts above the swell of her bump. It was every secret-horny-perverse-fantasy centerfold come to life, there in front of them, in living color.

Merry Christmas, Rubio thought. *Merry wonderful Christmas. Please let them make out. Please let them kiss and lick and tease each other.* How beautiful they looked together, aroused and at ease in their girl-girl embrace. *Please*, he thought, his cock going rigid against the fabric of his jeans. This was the best present ever.

Ashleigh moved her hand lower to cup and stroke Petra's pussy through the scrap of her g-string. With a sigh of pleasure, Petra turned to her and they began to kiss. They were tentative at first, then bolder. Then they started kissing with outright abandon, all arms and hands and soft, smooth bodies pressing together, and tongues. They were kissing with *tongues*.

"This isn't a dream, is it?" Ruby asked his friend. "Is really happening, right?"

"Jesus fucking Christ," Liam growled. Then both men were in motion, racing to see who could get naked first.

* * * * *

Making out with a girl wasn't at all like making out with a guy, thought Petra, but it was still pretty hot.

She didn't know if it was hot because Ashleigh was so sweet and nervous, or because she knew just where to touch her, or if it was hot because of the sounds the guys were making as they yanked off their clothes. She had a feeling it was all three.

For a while the men just stood on either side of the bed and watched them. Their proximity and intent stares incited Petra to put on a show—

she was a performer after all, and so was Ashleigh before she retired. What started as exploratory kisses soon transformed into honest-to-goodness making out, and it wasn't from any prompting by the guys. She was fascinated by the soft, smooth feel of Ash's skin, and excited by the way she could make her shiver if she stroked her clit just the right way.

"Oh my God," she heard Liam murmur every so often. When she twisted a finger in the tiny triangle covering Ashleigh's pussy and drew the silk up between her labia, Rubio let out a breath and said something in Portuguese that sounded very, very dirty.

"Does that feel good?" Liam asked, sitting beside his wife on the bed. "Is Petra making you feel good, baby?"

"Yes, Sir," Ash said against Petra's cheek. "She's making me feel really good."

Petra slid her fingers down inside Ash's panties. Her friend's pussy felt so hot and wet. Petra touched her the way she did when she masturbated, slipping and sliding over her clit, rubbing it in circles. They hadn't planned much beyond the idea of making out for the guys' pleasure. Now the mental part of it was fading away, replaced by pure physical urges and sensations. When she felt Rubio ease onto the bed behind her and reach between her legs, Petra arched her hips back against him. His cock was rock solid, poking between her thighs. She heard the ripping of a condom wrapper, and then he tugged aside her flimsy panties and pressed himself inside.

"Sexy, horny girl," he sighed. "Why don't I fuck you while you play with your friend?"

"Yes, Sir. That sounds wonderful."

Meanwhile, Liam was busy taking off his wife's panties. His warm hand covered Petra's, guiding her fingers through Ashleigh's slick folds. He was as perfectly made as Rubio. Now, lying in bed with these two men, it hit home how strong and masculine they both were. Ashleigh caught her gaze and she could tell her friend was thinking the same thing. Making out with each other was exciting, but so was the opportunity to enjoy twice the virility, twice the dominance.

Petra moved back against Rubio, moaning as he eased in and out of her. Two sets of fingers stroked her waist, her thighs, and then her breasts, caressing and pinching her nipples. At some point her bra and panties disappeared, whisked off and away.

"Can I touch your girl?" Ruby asked Liam.

Liam drew his hand back. "Oops. Were we supposed to ask first?"

Rubio chuckled and reached for Ashleigh as Liam's fingers clamped on Petra's nipples again. She shuddered at the hot, aching pain. "Oh...ow," she said. "That hurts."

"What do you think happens when you tease two sadists?" asked Ruby.

"I haven't been able to play with Ashleigh's nipples in a while, with the pregnancy and everything," said Liam. "So I'm really enjoying myself."

Petra winced as Liam's fingers tightened. She and Ash exchanged looks. What had started as a girl-girl makeout session was quickly turning into something a bit more intense. "Petra likes when you hurt her," said Ruby. He stroked her face and nudged it closer to Ashleigh's. "Kiss some more, pretty girls. I like when you kiss."

Petra locked lips with her friend, squirming at the pain of the nipple torture, but loving it too. Ruby had taught her to find pleasure in pain, or maybe she'd had the craving inside her all along. Ashleigh stroked her clit and Petra returned the favor. The sweet, wet contact felt great, but it wasn't enough for either of them.

Liam got up from the bed. "We need toys. More toys."

Ruby withdrew from her, took off the condom, and crossed to the wall of implements and gear to consult with Liam. The girls watched as they grabbed all kinds of stuff...butt plugs, clamps, whips and straps. "Holy shit," Ashleigh said. "I didn't realize we'd get them so wound up. And with me being pregnant, I think a lot of the hard stuff is gonna fall on your shoulders."

Petra let out a deep breath. "Good thing I like the hard stuff, huh?"

The men returned with their gear after a short conference. Rubio turned her on her back and flicked at her nipples with sharp, fleeting teases. He had a pair of gold clover clamps in his hand. "Spread your legs," he ordered, while he pinched her nipples to an even tauter point. By this time, Petra knew not to question. She spread her legs wide. A moment later Liam guided Ash down between Petra's thighs.

"Kiss her sweet pussy," he said to his wife. "See if you can make her come."

Petra felt the simultaneous pain of nipple clamps biting into her tender skin, and the pleasurable wetness of Ash's tongue on her clit. "Oh, Jesus." Then Ashleigh jerked as Liam flicked her ass with a thin whip. She could imagine how painful it was, but Ashleigh never stopped licking her pussy.

"You want the plug?" Rubio asked.

Petra looked up at him, but he was talking to Liam. "Not you," he said to Petra, slapping her flank as he handed the toy over to the other man. "You don't get a plug for preparation. When I fuck your ass, I want it to be tight and painful. I want to force my way in. You like that, don't you? You like to feel like a punished little slut."

She moaned. She did like it when he made her do things she didn't want. "Please don't hurt me too bad," she said, even though she meant *hurt me as much as you think I can take.*

Ruby's lips turned up in a half-grin. "If you're a good girl, I'll give you some lube first. A tiny bit."

Liam was lubing up a delicate stainless butt plug. He tossed the bottle to Rubio and slapped his wife's ass. "Raise up for me."

Ashleigh moaned against Petra's thigh as her husband eased the plug into her asshole. Petra reached down to stroke her friend's hair, to soothe her, only to have her hands caught by Rubio, cuffed, and fastened through the iron bars of the headboard. Her nipples ached from the clamps every time she arched or moved. Ashleigh's tongue worked harder, faster, as Liam hit her again with the whip. *Thwap. Thwap!*

"When Petra comes, the whip stops," said Liam with a menacing edge to his voice. "So make her feel as good as you can, baby."

Ashleigh's little squeaks and moans of pain were as arousing to Petra as her tongue. She strained against the cuffs, trying to come in order to spare her friend the continued pain of her husband's whip, but there was so much going on. Just as she was about to climax, Rubio yanked on the clamps, sending sharp pain shooting through her breasts. She felt the echo of it in her clenching pussy walls. If only she had his big cock inside her, anywhere, she'd come in a heartbeat. She whimpered on Ashleigh's behalf and then cried out as Ruby slid a hand beneath her.

She struggled to regain her elusive orgasm as he started working a lubed finger in and out of her ass. "I'm going to fuck you here," he whispered next to her ear. "I'm going to shove my fat cock right up there, and this is all the lube you're going to get."

"Oh, please..." She didn't know what she was begging for, exactly. Just generally to come, to be fucked, to be used and treated like Rubio's toy—and Liam's toy too. Ruby yanked on her nipples again and she bucked her hips up into Ashleigh's face. Finally, the torment and pleasure blended together to the sounds of the whip, and Petra cried out from the onslaught of her orgasm. At last, Liam put the implement down. "Good girl," he said to his wife.

"Thank you," Petra whispered.

"Oh, no. Thank you," said Ashleigh, looking up with a dazed, sub-spacey grin. Liam crawled onto the bed behind his wife, taking her hips in his hands. Ashleigh moaned as he entered her with one firm stroke. Petra watched their faces, so beautiful with arousal and longing. The sound of their coupling made her pussy throb with need. She looked up at her own lover, half mad from the ache of the nipple clamps.

"Open your mouth," he said.

He didn't have to ask twice. She opened her lips so he could nudge into her with his hot, thick length. He held her around the neck, his fingers wrapped in her "pet" collar, and drove in and out of her mouth, forcing her to take him farther in her throat than she thought she could. Occasionally he tweaked the clamps, and then drove even deeper when she opened her mouth to whine. When she started to choke, he shifted so his balls were at her mouth, and she lapped at those too like a good, horny girl. *Rubio's Pet. Return if lost.*

"The harder you get me," he said, "the more it's going to hurt when I put it in your ass."

"Oh, please, fuck me," she begged. She was so, so lost.

"Please put it in my ass," he corrected her. *"Please fuck my ass, Sir.* Say it."

"Please fuck my ass, Sir."

"You're a horny little slut, aren't you?"

She heard a giggle from Ashleigh, and Liam's low laughter, but Petra was too wrought up to care. Ruby turned her over and knelt behind her, between her legs. Her arms were still stretched above her, cuffed to the headboard so she was unable to move more than a few inches in either direction. Rubio lifted her onto her knees. "Arch your back," he ordered. "Make it pretty. Make it sexy."

She struggled to assume the position he wanted as he drove a finger in her lubed ass, then another. She shivered, knowing his whole cock would come next, and that it would stretch her and hurt terribly until her inner muscles accepted his girth. "Say it again," he ordered, tugging her collar. "I want to hear it one more time."

"Please fuck my ass, Sir."

She braced as he nestled his length between the cleft of her cheeks. She made a soft, plaintive whine. It was so hard to fit him in there. He pressed the head against her tight hole and she worked to open up, to admit him. "That's it," he said when he got the tip inside. "That's my beautiful girl."

Her whine rose to a cry with each ensuing inch of forward motion. By the time he was fully seated, she felt conquered. Her breasts stung against the pressure of the mattress and she writhed to feel relief, but that just excited him into deeper thrusting. She surrendered herself to the familiar pain/pleasure of anal intercourse, to the discomfort that made her feel so submissive and replete.

"Good girl," he said, pulling back and easing forward again. She squirmed, limp and willing beneath him. Yes, her nipples ached. Yes, she felt vulnerable with the pain in her ass, but it was a good kind of vulnerability. Liam handed the whip to Ruby and the men took turns striking her and Ashleigh while they fucked them. Not long after, Petra heard Ashleigh gasp and cry out in ecstasy.

Petra ached for her own orgasm. Rubio slid all the way in, stretching her, bucking his hips against her ass while he squeezed her thighs. He made beautiful animalistic sounds, occasionally spouting garbled syllables of Portuguese. If only he would touch her clit, just one touch. She would go off like a fucking firecracker.

Then someone was touching her. Small, delicate fingers traced down the side of her hips and brushed over Petra's pussy, parting the slick lips. Ashleigh fondled her clit to the accompaniment of Liam's low encouragement. Their eyes met and Ash smiled at her while Petra's eyes rolled back in her head. She didn't think she'd ever felt so controlled and manipulated, so basely sexual as she did in that moment. Rubio's arms braced on either side of her and she surrendered to a shuddering orgasm. Her asshole constricted around his thick cock as he buried himself all the way inside.

The climax wrung her out completely. She lay still in her bonds with Rubio slumped over her back, slowly drawing in breath and letting it out again. Ashleigh gave her pussy an affectionate pat and then turned away to enjoy her husband's kisses and endearments.

Petra watched furtively, fascinated. As much as she distrusted love, Ash and Liam seemed to have a really strong relationship. Ruby withdrew a moment later and went to wash in the nearby bathroom, then returned to uncuff her and remove the nipple clamps one by one, hanging them on the headboard alongside the small but potent whip.

"Go on." He gave her backside an affectionate slap. "Cuddle up with Ashleigh. Yes," he said as they moved into each other's arms. "So beautiful together. Such a beautiful gift."

It did feel beautiful, the feeling of closeness. Of sexual abandon and sexual release. The men lay behind them, forming a warm cocoon around their bodies. Ashleigh curled up beside her with a sigh. They looked into each other's eyes, letting their smiles communicate what they were too sex-dazed to say.

"Well," said Liam, kissing his wife's shoulder. "I guess we should let them rest for a while."

Petra turned back to look at Ruby. He nodded with a spreading smile. "Yes, we'll let them rest while we discuss round two. And three. And four."

Ashleigh made a faint hum of distress and took Petra's hand. "Oh, my. I'm afraid we've unleashed something."

"These kinds of gifts are supposed to last twenty-four hours," said Liam with a wink at Petra. "You both knew that, didn't you?" He looked at his phone, then back at the two women. "One hour down, twenty-three to go."

"Is he kidding?" Petra whispered to Ashleigh. "What is it with them and the timers?"

"Honestly, I don't know," she muttered back, as they dissolved into more laughter. Liam and Rubio sauntered off, heads together, toward the wall of ouchy toys. While they rested, Ashleigh traced a finger over the dangling tag on her pet collar. "This is so pretty. It looks beautiful on you."

Maybe it was the emotion of the moment, or excitement, or dread, but Petra felt her eyes mist with tears. "I didn't get him anything. You told me you guys didn't exchange presents."

"We don't." Ash lowered her voice to a bare whisper. "He doesn't do things like this. He's in love with you, Petra. Seriously, this collar might as well be an engagement ring."

Petra felt sudden, smothering panic. Chains of love, chains of engagement, chains of marriage. All of this was moving so fast. She was losing herself to her partner. She was just like her mother...

Ashleigh put her arms around her. "Are you okay? Don't worry about the present thing. Are you having fun?"

"Of course I'm having fun."

"This doesn't feel weird?"

"Well, it feels kind of weird, but good-weird, you know? Exciting. Crazy. Like, I'll never forget this night."

Ash stuck out her tongue and crossed her eyes. "You're talking about it like it's over. It's definitely not over. Well, not for you, anyway. For me..." She touched Petra's face, a light trace of a caress. "I know I planned this whole thing, and I want to keep going, but this pregnancy saps my energy so bad."

"It's okay for us to stop," Petra said at once, even though she felt a pang of disappointment. She glanced at the guys, who were fixing cuffs and chains to a towering bondage rack. "If it's too much for you—"

"It's too much for *me*," Ashleigh said. "But you'll be fine. Why don't you stay and play with them while I go up and rest?"

Petra gawked. "Me? Alone?"

Her friend winked at her. "I've done it before. I mostly survived."

Oh God, Ash had played with Liam and Rubio together. It was shocking and yet not shocking. They were so close, all of them, and had known one another for years before Petra came along. She wondered when it had happened, how often it had happened. She wondered if Ash had had sex with them at the same time, sandwiched between their virile bodies. The vision of it stole her breath, and sent aching heat to the nerve center between her legs. "But...Liam's your husband," Petra said. "You're married."

"And Rubio's your boyfriend," she replied in a matter-of-fact tone. "No, don't say he's not really your boyfriend. The point is, this is just for tonight, and it's fun and exciting like you said. I don't want to ruin the experience because I'm a tired, pregnant lady, you know?"

"You're tired?" Liam overheard their conversation as he returned with Rubio.

Ashleigh yawned and sat up. "Yeah, unfortunately. I know you and Ruby were planning more yumminess, but I'm beat."

Petra could see disappointment in their expressions too, but only for a moment. Liam was much more concerned for his wife. He sat beside her, running his hands over the curve of her belly. "Is everything all right? I tried not to go too hard. And the twenty-four hour thing—I was kidding."

"Don't worry," she said. "I just wear out more quickly than I used to. But you all can keep playing. I'm fine with it, if you want to." Ashleigh looked at Petra, her lips curving in amusement. "As long as Petra agrees. She's the one who'll have to deal with two cocks—er—

guys at once. Both of whom are renowned sadists. One of whom…" She paused, looking sideways at her spouse. "Has been very restrained for months, due to his pregnant wife and everything."

In that glance, Petra saw that Ash had intended to get "too tired" all along. The second part of her Christmas gift was to give her husband a whack—literally—at someone who wasn't too pregnant to handle the harder stuff. Wow.

Liam made a soft sound and embraced her, while Petra pondered if she could be so selfless in the same situation. The married couple talked with their heads together, protesting and affirming, gazing into each other's eyes. She supposed this was love…this generosity, this level of trust. Well, love with a little kinkiness thrown in.

"You're sure?" he asked when he released her.

"Yeah, I'm sure. We planned this whole thing for you guys. It shouldn't wrap up this early."

"Will you at least stay to watch the fun?"

Ash laughed and shook her head. "I'd be too tempted to join in when I shouldn't. It's bed for me and baby. Just remember everything that happens, so you can tell me about it tomorrow. I want explicit details."

Liam promised a "blow by blow" account, which made all of them chuckle. In the silence that followed, all eyes fell on Petra. "What do you think?" asked Ruby, taking her hand. "Are you up for another round?"

Petra met Ashleigh's eyes. If she'd seen any jealousy there, any doubt, she would have said no and gone upstairs with her friend, but all she saw was an encouraging grin. They'd done this before, so it was no big deal to them, only to her. It was a chance to play, to blow off some steam, especially for Liam, who needed it.

Was there even a question? She'd never have this chance again.

"I'm game," she said, a warm flush flooding her cheeks. She felt sorry that Ashleigh was too pregnant to enjoy the rest of the proceedings, but having the undivided attention of two large, horny, dominant men was too tempting a prospect to pass up.

Chapter Sixteen:
Un-Pented

Liam went to deliver Ash upstairs, leaving Rubio and Petra alone. He sprawled next to her in the bed. "You're feeling brave, no?" he asked.

She immediately looked less brave, and he regretted his words. "Will be fun," he promised. "Liam is safe. A good Dominant."

"With a lot of pent-up frustrations, it sounds like."

"But you know, when things come un-pented, it can be a mine-blowing experience."

Petra made a face. "I don't think un-pented is a word. And it's *mind*-blowing, not mine-blowing. Mine-blowing makes me think of blasted-off limbs, which isn't shoring up my confidence about what you guys have in mind—"

He kissed her to silence her, because she was nervous, and he didn't want her to be nervous. He wasn't nervous and he wasn't jealous to share Petra. Well, maybe a little jealous, but it was Liam after all, who was deep in love with someone else. He and Liam had shared tons of women, back when his friend was single. Those women had been playthings. Even Ashleigh had been a plaything to Ruby, a novelty, since he didn't really understand her then. But Petra...

"You're sure about this?" he whispered against her cheek. "If you don't like it, if you want to stop in the middle, you can safeword. That's always a choice."

"I know."

"You trust Liam? He's very careful. But I promise I'll watch out for you too."

She gave him a teasing smile. "Is that supposed to make me feel better? Your idea of watching out for me is making sure my nipple clamps are tight enough not to fall off."

"Well, is important," he protested. "No one wants nipple clamps flying all over the play room."

"No," Petra agreed. "No one wants that."

She excused herself to the bathroom and Ruby waited, wondering if Liam would stay upstairs with Ashleigh after all. It would be okay if he did. Ruby could still play with Petra, and they'd have fun and pleasure, and satisfy each other, but a third person gave more possibilities. And poor Liam, not able to play hard scenes with his wife...

A moment later, he heard Liam's footsteps on the staircase. No, he wouldn't be jealous, because if Ashleigh could share her partner, so could he.

Petra came out of the bathroom just as Liam reached the landing. The three of them looked at each other as if to say, *what now?*

"Come," Ruby said to Petra, assuming control. "Come kneel by me."

He put her halfway between him and Liam, her eyes right at the level of their hardening cocks. When she bowed her head, blushing, he tipped it back up again. "No looking down. Pay attention and be a good girl for us. Listen for directions. You understand?"

"Yes, Sir," she said, going all soft and spacey. He knew she loved it when he used his extra-bossy voice. Liam studied his pretty Petra, who knelt so still and gracefully. After a moment, he touched the top of her hair.

"She's so much like Ash. Her body, I mean."

"Well, they're both ballet dancers," said Ruby.

"This hair though. It's as light as Ashleigh's is dark."

Ruby considered a moment. "She's a lot like Ashleigh. Maybe Pet can take a little more pain. She likes to be tough."

"That's good to know," Liam murmured, moving a hand down to her shoulder.

On purpose, they discussed her like she wasn't there. Dominance was a fun game; there were so many ways to play it. Liam's thumb traced along the delicate line of her clavicle. Ruby could see her shiver and tense her legs.

"I think she's turned on," Ruby said. He put a finger under her chin to capture her attention. "You want to be hurt, yes? To be used for our pleasure? You want that?"

She swallowed hard and nodded. "Yes, Sir. I'm yours."

He flicked a nod at Liam. "And his, too."

"And his," she agreed. "Yes, Sir."

"Very pretty," Liam said. "Well trained."

Ruby rolled his eyes. "Not always. We'll see how it goes. Up," he said to Petra. When she got to her feet, he led her over to the bondage rack he and Liam had prepared earlier. They'd gotten cuffs for two women, but one could offer plenty of satisfaction.

"More room to spread out now," said Liam. "We can spread her wide open."

"I was thinking the same thing," Ruby said, positioning her so she faced the structure. "I'll go get the bar."

* * * * *

Petra could barely breathe, she was so scared and excited. They were good at this double-teaming thing, that was for sure. Liam spread out her arms and fastened the cuffs in a detached, businesslike way that said, *I can do what I want to you.* Now Rubio was nudging her legs apart and fixing her ankles to a bar that would keep her spread open as long as the two men wanted it.

"Make sure they're secure," Liam said as Ruby tightened the last buckle. "We don't want her to be able to get away."

Oh God.

Two men. Two bodies, four hands, two monster-sized cocks. She'd already gotten an eyeful of those as she knelt before them. Eventually those cocks would grow fully hard, and then... She couldn't think about that, how one woman managed with two cocks coming at her. Ashleigh had survived it, at some point. So could she.

But first there would be impact and pain. Petra braced for craziness as the two men conversed behind her, discussing various tools, who would use what, and when. She blocked out their voices because she preferred not to know. Better to drift along, wanting, waiting, receiving, suffering, processing the pain and the adrenaline as it came.

When Rubio returned to her, she leaned back into him, pressing against his warmth. He wove fingers into her hair and pulled her head back, kissing her deeply.

"Ready, girl?"

"I think so."

"Close your eyes, okay? I want you to keep them closed."

Oh God.

"Yes, Sir."

Nothing was scarier than submitting with her eyes closed, which was probably why he made her do it. As soon as she complied, she expected an onslaught of pain, but first there was caressing, stroking, soothing. She was pretty sure Liam was on her left and Ruby on her right, but both their hands were all over her, so she couldn't keep track of who was who. She didn't know for sure who pinched her nipples, or who cupped and squeezed her ass. She'd think for sure it was Ruby, but then something would be off and she'd think, *no*... Someone's fingers dipped into her pussy and it freaked her out that she didn't know who it was. Whoever it was, they took their time exploring her sensitive center, parting her labia and teasing her deftly, making her gasp and tremble in her bonds.

"She's wet," said Liam with a low chuckle. Liam then. Another hand parted her ass cheeks and she flinched, drawing away as far as the cuffs would allow.

"No," Ruby chided. "Be good. We own this body right now."

"Yes, Sir." Petra knew it was true, but that didn't make the loss of control any easier. Her body was theirs, her breasts and her pussy and her ass cheeks and the little hole currently being probed by Ruby's finger.

She sighed as he withdrew. A moment later his hand tightened at her waist, and he pressed two fingers in there, all the way inside. Ruby had fucked her ass less than an hour ago but already, again, it hurt to be breached there. Not sharp, injuring hurt, but hurt that turned her on and opened her up. Her sphincter tensed around his fingers and she ached for more, for pain and torment to go with the invasion of her body. He withdrew and she could sense Liam move closer, taking his place.

It was Liam who gave her the first taste of impact, a warm-up spanking with a rubber paddle. In between sharp, light smacks, he groped her pussy, and then squeezed her ass cheeks with a firm, unforgiving grip. She tried not to cry out. It wasn't time for that yet, but she struggled, making the cuff chains rattle. The grating metal sound made everything seem worse, made her feel she was in a terrifying predicament, although, rationally, she knew she could safeword anytime. It was more fun to feel scared and traumatized.

Rubio returned, and they started using floggers, still light, still warming up. They laid strokes up and down her back, then down to her buttocks and the backs of her thighs. Both of them worked in tandem, covering her body in heated tingles, taking breaks when the other one wanted to play. Floggers were thuddy and they sounded scary, but they didn't hurt as much as the thinner implements did. It occurred to Petra that a long warm up like this meant they were planning to play hard with her. Well, that was the whole point, she reminded herself. For Liam to unleash his pent-up sadistic urges.

The floggers finally ceased. Petra stretched her arms and legs as well as she could in her restrained-and-spread position. There was more discussion, this time in soft tones she couldn't hear. Their voices rose after a moment. "I'll hold her for you, you hold her for me. Why not?"

"Because she can be a baby, that's why not. Is better if she's restrained."

"Maybe it's time to make her grow up a little."

A pause.

Then, from Liam: "If we have to, we chase her. Right?"

Petra squeezed her eyes shut tighter. Holy hell. What were they planning? Rubio came to her and started working on the wrist cuffs. "You can open your eyes, girl. We're letting you go for a moment." His lips quirked up in a half-smile. "But not really letting you go. Okay?"

"Yes, Sir."

"Oh, Jesus, that sounds hot. Quick, suck me." He urged her downward and she had to bend from the waist because Liam was still undoing the spreader bar. When her ankles were free she sank to her knees and sucked Ruby avidly, aroused by the flogging and spanking. "That's good," he said with a sigh. "Stick your ass out for me, pretty girl. Arch your back, that's right."

She rearranged herself, straining to maintain the position he wanted. Then, *crack*! A sizzling stroke lit up her ass cheeks. She looked behind her to see Liam wielding a long, narrow leather strap.

"No, forward," said Ruby, hooking a finger in her silver collar. "Ass out."

She did as she was told—reluctantly—but she couldn't help crying out as the strap connected again, and again. Ruby held her collar so she couldn't turn, couldn't do anything but service him as ordered. She sucked harder, faster, as if that might mitigate the pain coming from behind. After a while, Liam started alternating the blows between her ass and the sensitive skin at the top of her thighs. The strokes came harder, faster, with excruciating accuracy, until she pulled away from Ruby and collapsed with a cry.

She waited for a reprimand, but she was only nudged back into position. "Your turn," Ruby said to his friend.

Liam rolled on a red, cherry-flavored condom. Petra knelt before him in dread, not dread because it was Liam, but dread because Ruby had taken the strap and the position behind her. She looked up at Liam, finding no sympathy, only a steady gaze. "Maybe a little something to get her started," he said to Ruby over her head.

With a gasp, she opened her mouth, taking him deep at the same time the strap burned across her ass. His cock was big, like Ruby's, a challenge to deep throat. She gagged and cried, tears running down her face as the strap kept falling. *Just suck him, Petra.* There was a cosmic comfort, a release in just focusing on what she was supposed to do. She was giving the sloppiest, messiest blowjob ever, punctuated with pleas and whining, but Liam made her continue, and, from the look on his face, was enjoying it quite a bit.

Finally, he pulled away. "I don't want to come yet. She's not done yet."

Not done yet? Petra shuddered, wondering what "done" meant.

Ruby gestured to some nearby equipment. "Let's bend her over the horse."

"Good idea," said Liam. "We'll crop her like a recalcitrant filly."

"Like a—what?"

"Nothing. Who's going first?"

Rubio went first. Petra knew how much he loved riding crops, and how good he was at flicking her all over the place until she was begging to escape. He started hard, with a volley of punishing strokes. When she couldn't stay bent over, when she started kicking, Liam went around to the front of her and captured her hands, and stretched her arms in front of her so she couldn't twist away. Ruby continued the cropping, placing red-hot bites all over her ass and legs. She wanted this, she loved it, but it hurt *so much*... "Please," she begged, staring up at Liam and trying to pull away from him. "Please!"

"Please, harder?" asked Liam, tightening his grip. "Hey, man, she wants it harder."

Ruby grinned. "Maybe you should take over then."

"Okay, you hold her. She's getting kind of feisty. Maybe some clamps? I'll get the whip. And the cane."

"The cane?" Petra cried.

"She's never been caned," said Ruby as Petra straightened and regarded both men in fear. Clamps? Whip? Cane? How long was this session going to last? She was already aching hot, with a scarlet ass and thighs, and they were ramping up to ouchier things. Rubio nudged her back down over the horse, taking the clamps when Liam brought them.

"Please, no," she begged as he knelt in front of her. "Please, no more clamps."

"She doesn't want the clamps," Ruby said to Liam.

"That's funny," his friend replied. "It's kind of like she thinks she has a choice."

"Yeah. Could you give me a hand?"

Liam lifted her and held her back against his chest. His cock pressed against her ass cheeks as he gripped her arms hard at the small of her back. She took quick, frantic breaths as Ruby approached with the first clover clip. *Oh, God, mother of God. That fucking hurts.* Liam's grip tightened as she struggled; she wasn't going anywhere. He licked the side of her ear, his long hair brushing over her shoulders. "It's not so bad," he whispered. "You *need* this."

Tears gathered in her eyes, because it was true. She hadn't always needed this but *now*, now that she'd experienced how much pleasure she got from enduring pain, she did need it. She gritted her teeth as the other clamp closed on her sensitive nipple. Ruby gave the chain a playful tug.

"Lean her down."

She groaned as Liam pressed her forward. This chain was heavier than normal, weighted. As she bent over the horse, gravity did sadism's work, tightening the grip.

So, so, so, *so* much pain, and it was only the beginning. She cried out as the first whip stroke fell, and struggled to get away. Rubio came closer and secured her with his arm around her waist. "Don't fight it so hard," he said. "Be a good girl."

"But...but..."

Another stroke fell, a line of fire right at the apex of her thighs. Then another. Tears flowed down her face, her voice one long wail. "I can't," she cried. "I can't take it."

"Use your safeword then," Ruby said calmly.

She bit her lip, sobbing through another stroke. The chain swung from her breasts, a constant ache in her nipples that exacerbated the pain of the whip. Before, she'd been excited-scared. Now she was *holy-shit*-scared. How much would they give her? She was already nearing the limits of what she could take.

"Cane now," said Ruby.

"No! Please," she begged.

"Just try it," he said, tightening his grip on her. "You might like it. He'll start slow."

"You should do it," said Liam, "if it's her first time."

"No, you. Me and Pet will have plenty of time for canes later. Won't we, baby?"

Oh Jesus. Petra hadn't forgotten about the Plexiglas cane under his bed. She went limp over the sawhorse, her way of psyching herself up for more pain. *I can do this. I can survive this. It's not my body, it's theirs. I'm their toy, their instrument to play with. I have to let go of everything, including my will…*

She felt the teasing caress of a slender cane, then Liam's fingers probing her pussy, filling her until she squeaked. "She's still wet," he announced. "Wetter than ever."

She whimpered. Whimpers, squeaks, wails. It was as if she was losing her power of speech along with her will. "I'm scared," she managed to say.

"You're a good girl," Liam replied. "And so beautiful, submitting this way."

Her reward for her submissive "beauty?" A sizzling cane stroke across her already aching cheeks. Ruby was right; Liam hadn't lit into her full strength. It hurt, but not unbearably.

Still, it *hurt*.

As she suspected, the next one was harder. The one after, a bit harder yet, so she was yowling and struggling against Rubio's grasp. Her lover stroked her back. "You're being so brave, good girl. You're almost there."

Almost where? Almost "done," as they'd said? She hoped so, because she couldn't take much more. Ruby shifted and she felt the clamps released, with the accompanying bursts of pain. Liam thwacked her again, a dull, quiet sound, but a resulting line of agony. Again. And again. It was too much. She couldn't take any more.

"Let her go," said Liam, just as the safeword rose to her lips.

Ruby stepped away and Petra did the first thing she could think of, which was to scramble over the top of the horse and run away from them, away from more sadistic ideas, and more implements, and more pain. Ruby caught her first, then Liam was on the other side of her, both of them holding her close. She sobbed as their palms pressed and caressed her. Gentle fingernails traced welts from ass cheek to ass cheek.

"No broken skin," Liam said. "She came through all right."

"Okay, good girl," Ruby said, soothing her.

"You're so strong and brave," said Liam in her other ear. "That was hard, wasn't it?"

"Yes, Sir." She broke down in a fresh torrent of tears.

"Poor baby." Ruby wiped her cheeks. "Is okay to cry."

They pressed closer, two strong, muscular bodies, their cocks hot and hard against her skin. Her blood raced with fear and longing, her nerves alive with shameful lust. She wanted them, *needed* them to fuck her senseless as the grand finale, but she couldn't ask, not from the depths of subspace. "Is it...is it over?" she asked instead, a quiver in her voice.

"Do you want it to be over?"

She looked at Liam, then at Rubio, wondering how they couldn't hear the frenzied pleading in her brain. One of them squeezed her hot, sore ass. Again, she didn't know who. She didn't care. She thought she'd die without them holding her.

"Do you want to go?" Ruby asked. "If you want to go now, you can."

"Go where?"

"Wherever. Somewhere safe from us."

She didn't want to be safe. That was the last thing in the world she wanted. "If I go, will you..." Her breath stuttered in her throat as Ruby's fingertips traced the underside of her breasts. "Will you chase me and drag me back?"

Liam laughed, the deep sound bouncing off the soundproof walls. "Ruby, you've gotta marry this one. I'm serious."

Ruby shoved him. "Quiet. Shut up." He looked back at her. "Do you want us to chase you? Not let you get away?"

She nodded shakily, then shook her head. "I guess. I don't know. I don't know what I want."

"I think we know what you want," said Liam, his grip tightening around her waist. Her heart raced, her whole body trembling with adrenaline. Rubio took her hands, trapping them in his, and she started to struggle. Not because she wanted to get away, but because she wanted them to *make* her do this, because they were big and strong and there were two of them and only one of her. Liam chuckled under his breath. *I'm glad you're having fun*, she thought wildly. *Now do it. Throw me down and...*

Rape me. She couldn't think the words, because she knew rape was wrong, but that was what she wanted. She wanted no control, no measure of consent. *Take me. Just take me.* The harder she fought, the harder they worked together to subdue her. When they got her on the cold, varnished floor, Ruby pinned her with his body. He kissed her roughly, pulling her hair until she arched her back in agony. "No," she said. "No, stop!"

He ignored her, as she'd hoped he would. He manhandled her onto her stomach and pressed her shoulders to the ground. "Get your ass up," he ordered. She heard a rustle and the slick sound of a condom going on. Her sore ass cheeks were pulled apart. "Here," Ruby said. "Use a lot."

She tried to crawl forward, away from them, but they grabbed her ankles and yanked her back. Cool lube drizzled into the cleft of her ass. Fingers pushed it into her asshole, pistoning in and out.

"Stop! Please," she begged, squirming away with renewed energy. The fingers stopped fucking her.

Rubio murmured, "She means yes. Only stop for *Romeo*."

"*Romeo*? That's your safeword?" Liam laughed.

"Yes," Ruby snapped. "It works for us, okay?"

Petra tried again to crawl away while they were sniping back and forth, but two sets of hands gripped her before she got very far. "Slippery little slut," Rubio said, slapping her ass. "She almost got away," he said to Liam.

He palmed his lubed-up erection. "She's not going anywhere once I get this inside her."

Liam took her shoulders and wrenched her legs open with his knees, and thrust deep into her pussy. She tried to fight but there was so much of him—not just his massive cock, but his massive bulk and the massive hands holding her down. He fucked her with hard, steady strokes, moving in a rhythm that hit all her favorite spots, while Ruby watched, an appreciative voyeur.

"Her pussy feels good, huh?"

"Oh, God." Liam's breathless exhalation was apparently all he had to say on the matter.

Ruby pumped his shaft a few times, palming his balls and sidling closer. Liam pulled her up, so she tottered on her knees with only his cock centering her balance.

"Open your mouth for Ruby, Petra."

It was an order, rough and curt. Liam had never spoken to her with anything less than perfect courtesy before now, which made this all the more exciting. Ruby took the back of her head and guided his cock into her mouth.

She sucked him, choking, gagging, gripping his thighs for balance as Liam continued to pound her from behind. She wasn't trying to get away anymore, only trying to survive the onslaught. *You wanted this, Petra. You wanted to be taken hard and rough.*

And this was the kind of stuff Liam couldn't do with Ashleigh at the moment, so she was glad she could give it to him. In a way she was offering it up for her friend. *Here you go, Ash. It's okay, I'll probably recuperate in a day or two. Your husband's a fucking sex maniac, by the way.*

Ruby drew her from her thoughts with a tug on her collar. Liam pulled out of her pussy, leaving her juices dripping down her slutty leg. It couldn't be over, could it? No, not yet. Ruby was rolling on a condom, pulling carefully on the tip. "Safe, yeah?" he said to her with a fleeting smile. He dropped to the floor and held his cock upright, signaling Petra to climb on top.

She crouched over Rubio with a little centering nudge from Liam, then sank down, until he was buried to the hilt in her pussy. She groaned, tensing her muscles, milking the long, strong length of him. Being fucked by Liam was nice, but Rubio owned her in this. Bought, captured, enslaved. She was his cock slave, pure and simple. Ruby held her thighs and prevented her from moving in any direction except the direction he liked.

They never did it this way, with her on top. Because he was her top, she supposed. Tops belonged on top, or at least they usually did. Not that she felt very dominant at the moment. Before she had much time to think about it, she felt Liam move behind her. He took her hands and trapped them up by her shoulder blades, forcing her breasts out.

When she turned her head, distracted, Ruby took her nipples in a jaw-clenching pinch. "Ow, ow, ow, *ow*," she whined, reeling back, but Liam had her arms in some kind of ju-jitsu ninja lock and she couldn't go very far.

"Uh-oh," Liam said. "She doesn't like that."

Ruby squeezed tighter. "Come here, baby. Lean down."

He tugged her by her nipples until she collapsed on him, cringing from the pain. Her pussy clamped around his cock, so hard she might have orgasmed if there wasn't so much else going on. Her knees slipped on the smooth floor, her pussy riding Ruby's thrusts. Then he went still and let go of her nipples, and moved his hands to her hips. "Okay," he said. "Put it in her."

Put what in her? She felt the head of Liam's cock against her asshole and she thought, *oh no. Oh wow. That's not going to fit.* She struggled in earnest then, shaking her head, pulling at her wrists where Liam held them, but he held tight. Ruby's hands tightened on her waist.

"Let him do it. You'll like it, both your holes filled."

"It won't fit," she said.

"Won't it?" Liam eased the head in, shifting, playing with the angle. "We've managed it before. Although, not with someone as small as you."

Not comforting, Liam Wilder!

All the lube they'd smeared on her crack came in handy as Liam wedged his erection into her little hole. It was so tight, so bizarrely cramped and unnatural. Liam had to work his way forward, prying her open inch by terrifying inch.

"Petra, look at me," Ruby said as she panted through the penetration.

She gazed down at him, afraid to breathe, afraid to move.

"He won't hurt you," he whispered, squeezing her hips. "It's going to feel so good."

"It's too tight. He's too big. It hurts."

"You like to be hurt."

Damn him, it was true. "Oh, God," she cried as Liam pushed deeper. At some unseen signal, Ruby withdrew, lifting her, so she felt both of them moving inside her, one in, one out. The feeling of fullness was shocking, scary. Amazing.

Liam withdrew as Ruby surged in again. *Ohhh...* Now that her ass had grown accustomed to Liam's thick tool, inklings of pleasure began to unfold. With his free hand, Liam reached around to flick and tug her nipples, pressing his hips against her backside. Then he drew out and Rubio drove deep into her sopping pussy. Yes, she was wetter than she'd ever been. Yes, this was the raunchiest thing she'd ever done.

At first the rhythm was slow and steady, a team effort. They were careful, helping her, manipulating her, and protecting her from harm. But once she got into it, all of them let go. She started moving her hips in rhythm to their thrusts, arching her ass so Liam could bury himself inside her, then clenching her pussy to make Ruby bark with pleasure. After a while, Liam released her hands.

"Lace them at the back of your neck," he said. "Keep them out of the way while we fuck you."

She obeyed, letting them hold her, manipulate her, pinch her, scratch her, pull her hair as they moved her back and forth. Her pelvis ached with peaking arousal as they worked both her holes. "Oh, please," she begged. "Please let me come. I'm gonna come."

"You can only come with both of us inside you," Ruby said. "When you're filled up with both our cocks."

Liam pressed against her from behind, bracing his arms on the floor, while Ruby tugged at her nipples, squeezing them until she cried out. She felt trapped between them, conquered and impaled, at the mercy of their masculine will.

"She's so tight," Liam said. "Holy shit." He made a sound like he was dying. Petra could sympathize. This felt so carnal, so deeply elemental, their cocks driving into her as she ground her hips. Liam paused to finger her clit, tapping it, teasing it. She sucked in a breath and reached down to guide his fingers.

"No," he snapped. "Where do your hands belong?"

With a sob, she made fists and returned them to the back of her neck, wishing to God she could rub herself to orgasm.

"Do you want him to touch you again?" Ruby asked.

"Yes, please, I want him to touch me," she said with a hysterical note in her voice.

"Ask nice," he said with a jolting thrust. "Maybe he will."

Petra racked her brain for nice words, but all she could come up with was *please, do it, now.* "Um, uh. Please... Liam, sir, please..."

"*Please play with my pussy while you fuck my ass.* Try that," Ruby said.

"Please play with my pussy while you fuck my ass," she repeated eagerly, bucking on their alternating cocks. "Please."

Liam made a soft growl of a sound. "How about, *Please play with my pussy while you destroy my asshole.* Try that."

"Hm, good idea," said Ruby appreciatively.

"Please..." Petra couldn't remember anything he'd said. She just wanted to *come.* "Please...fuck me...destroy me...blow me up with a mine...whatever!"

Liam grimaced at Ruby. "I think we broke her brain, man. Sorry."

Ruby grinned back. "At least her pussy is still working."

"Please," Petra said, squeezing on both of them, teasing her nerves into a frenzy. She was so close to completion, to blessed release. "Oh, God, *please.*"

Liam drove deep in her ass, palming her clit at the same time. She jerked against his hand, needing more. He was teasing her on purpose, only giving her so much. If she moved her hips, she could get a bit more sensation. At her sinuous movements, the men each groaned in turn. Ruby's hands tightened on her hips, then he let go with one hand and licked his thumb, and slid it across her clit in a direct blast of sensation. Now both of them were touching her, teasing her, exploring her wet folds. She threw her head back, banging it against Liam's chest.

"Please, please, don't stop..." Her whole body felt poised to explode.

"Come on, baby," Ruby said. "Show us how much you like being fucked."

They both drove inside her, so thick, so deep. Her arousal sparked and expanded into something more, a blue-bright flame that broke wide and set her on fire. Her mouth fell open as her body contracted around their cocks, with wave after wave of delicious pleasure. Liam grabbed her from behind, hugging her tight as his own orgasm exploded. A moment later, Ruby's hands trembled against her skin as he bit out expletives in a mixture of English and Portuguese.

Oh, God. Thank God. She wouldn't have survived another minute. Her pussy and ass contracted intermittently for several long moments in the aftermath, each tiny pulse met with hoarse masculine approval. None of them moved beyond the basic needs of resting and breathing. For five minutes, maybe, they laid that way in the middle of the play room floor, with Petra sprawled over Ruby, and Liam hugging her on his knees from behind. She started to drowse, it felt so comfortable. All the energy in her body seemed to have flown in the wrenching explosion of her orgasm.

Finally, Liam shifted and said softly, "Still alive? Neither of you are moving."

"I died," said Rubio. "Look after Pet for me, okay?"

Liam squeezed her shoulders. "Can I get you anything, Petra? Some water? A blanket?"

"I need a shower," she whispered. "But I don't think I can walk."

Liam eased out of her and helped her totter to her feet, then Ruby swept her up and carried her to the bathroom. The Italian marble shower was big enough for three, and they slipped and slid together, soaping and rinsing each other in a mist of steam. When they got out, the men toweled Petra dry, checking out her welts and bruises. She didn't speak much during the inspection, only answered their questions and drifted on the feeling of their fingertips against her skin. What was there to say? *That was the raunchiest, hottest fuck-fest ever.* She'd come like a banshee with two cocks inside her, one of which belonged to her best friend's husband.

After that, they collapsed in the bed together, relaxing by the soft light of the play room's LED candles. Ruby took her speechless catatonia as a compliment to his virility, which it was. "Poor, tired Petra," he said, brushing her hair back. "Did you really have fun?"

"I had twenty-five Christmases worth of fun." She rested her head on his arm as he drew her closer. "Thank you for the unforgettable night." She turned to Liam, who was flicking through messages on his phone. "You, too, you crazy sadist. Thanks."

He smiled. "It was my pleasure, literally. From beginning to end."

"Can you remember all of it, to tell Ashleigh?" asked Ruby.

"She's going to love it. The end part especially. She's such a perv."

"Poor Ashleigh," Petra said. "She missed out on all the fun."

"It's not like we can't do it again." Liam thought a moment. "We can make it an annual tradition. Mark your calendars. December twenty-fourth."

Petra and Ruby exchanged a look. An annual tradition? Sure, if they were still together in a year. They'd be dancing together, certainly...but the rest? Ruby looked away before she did, before she could do the math of how close they'd become if they were still a couple a year from now.

Liam looked back at his phone, then went still, pausing in the middle of scratching his chest. "Jesus fucking Christ."

"What is it?" asked Ruby.

"Scary Gary has officially left the country as of ten o'clock this evening, with legal restrictions against coming back."

Petra stared at him, blinking, trying to process his words. "He's gone? Paulsen's gone?"

"According to my people, he's flying over the Atlantic Ocean right now."

"You're sure?" Ruby craned his neck to read Liam's phone. "You're sure he left?"

"My guys saw him get on the plane. He's gone." His smile widened. "Congrats, Petra. And Merry Christmas."

"Oh my God," Petra burst out. "Oh my God. Oh my God!" She hugged Liam and Ruby at the same time, in one big, jubilant embrace. "Oh my God. Thank you so much, Liam. This is all thanks to you, to your hard work."

"Yes, thanks," Rubio echoed with a huge smile. "Now we can sleep easier."

Petra turned into Ruby's arms and hugged him tight. No matter how panicked she felt about their increasing closeness, she still cared for him deeply. "I was so worried for you," she said. "I was so afraid he'd hurt you. I couldn't have lived with the guilt."

"Baby girl," he whispered. He grabbed a handful of her hair and breathed it in, nuzzling against her neck. "You don't have to worry anymore. The fucker's on an airplane. He's gone."

She felt high with happiness and relief, all her exhaustion fallen away into euphoria. "I can hardly believe it."

"Believe it," he said, tracing her silver collar. He leaned to kiss her, a deep, hard, kiss that reclaimed her as his own.

Chapter Seventeen: Freedom

Paulsen was gone. No more slipping into cars after work or looking over her shoulder to be sure she wasn't followed. No more waking up at night, frightened she'd heard a sound in the dark. No more nightmares, hopefully.

Paulsen hadn't given up, of course not. Liam warned that her stalker would probably grow angrier, but he could be angry an ocean away from her. Thanks to Liam's efforts he wasn't allowed back in the UK, and Petra had no immediate plans to leave London, so everything was okay.

A couple days after Christmas, she moved back into her old place, even though Rubio asked her to move in with him. "We've been living together for weeks," he said when she balked. But sleeping beside him in Ash and Liam's forest bed was different, less threatening. It was like sleeping together at a hotel. Moving into his loft was a completely different thing.

So she waffled. She said she'd consider it later, after the New Years Gala. She threw herself into rehearsals, pushing Rubio to practice the balcony *pas de deux* over and over, even though, by now, the scene had become their calling card. "We done this one million times," he groused, but she insisted they keep rehearsing. Avoidance? Probably. Sometimes in practice he stared at her neck, and she knew what he was thinking. But

Juliet didn't wear a collar in the balcony scene, so Petra left it at Rubio's place, where she still seemed to end up every night.

Gala night arrived in a flash, a mere week after their sexy Christmas Eve foursome. It was a big, annual fundraising party for City Ballet, and Petra and Rubio were a huge part of it. It was their responsibility to impress the donors and help Yves raise money. Liam and Ash were there too, dressed to the nines. Try as she might, Petra still couldn't meet Liam's gaze without a flush spreading across her cheeks.

Fortunately, there wasn't any drama or jealousy after the fact. Petra and Ashleigh were closer than ever. They circulated arm in arm at the gala, talking to people they knew, smiling and laughing. Ashleigh pulled her over to some chairs after a while. With the pregnancy, she was getting heavy on her feet.

"I heard you and Rubio are starting rehearsals for *Waking Kiss*," she said as she eased her shoes off.

Waking Kiss was the first ballet Rubio had choreographed, and it had been inspired by Ashleigh. To this day, only Ash and Rubio had performed it at City Ballet. Petra wrinkled her nose at her friend. "Is it going to feel weird that I'm doing it? You know? Your ballet?"

"It's not my ballet, hon. It's Rubio's. And no, it won't feel weird. You two will be beautiful in it, even more beautiful than—" She cut off mid-sentence, stopping Petra with a jerk. "Don't look. I mean, don't turn around or anything. Your dad is here."

Petra almost turned, but then she didn't. *If he sees me here, he'll leave.* But he had to assume she'd be here. She was the star principal of London City Ballet. Her face was on all the signage and invitations for the event. She looked furtively in the direction Ashleigh indicated. Her father stood in the midst of a group of theater heavy-hitters. Everyone paid court to him, including Yves Thibault. Petr Grigolyuk looked the same as always. Tall, handsome, aristocratic in his tuxedo. He looked so much like her. It was humiliating that he wouldn't cop to being her dad.

The same old feelings of shame and worthlessness washed over her. *He'd want to be your dad if you were a cooler person. If you were prettier, more interesting, more talented.* "I hate him," she said under her breath. But she kept watching, reluctantly fascinated. She hadn't been in the same room with him in years now, and certainly not for this long.

"I hate him too," said Ashleigh in solidarity. "He's starting to lose his hair."

Petr looked up then, right at her. Immediately his eyes flicked to Ashleigh at her side. He smiled at Ash and turned away. Her friend scowled at the back of his head. "Fuckwad. Total dick. You should walk over there and throw a drink in his face."

"No. Yves would probably fire me. Anyway, if he can't stoop to acknowledge my existence, I won't acknowledge his."

"It's going to be hard not to acknowledge your existence when you and Rubio take the stage in ten minutes or so."

"He won't watch," said Petra, even though she felt a pang of nervousness. What if her father did watch? Would he admire her dancing? Would he feel proud? Maybe if she danced well enough, he'd come over and say, *I'm sorry. Please forgive me. I don't know why I ignored you all these years.*

She screwed her eyes shut, fighting the fantasy. She hated that she still clung to that hope after all this time, after all the heartbreak and rejection. Grigolyuk didn't care about her. He would never love her. She didn't have a father and that had to be okay.

Ash touched her arm. "How about if I go throw a drink at him on your behalf? Yves can't fire me anymore."

"Where's Rubio?" Petra whispered through a numbing haze of pain. She needed Rubio. She needed to get ready to dance. "Here Ash, take this for me?" She shoved her wine glass into her friend's hand just as Liam came to join them.

"You okay?" He patted her shoulder in sympathy. "Yves didn't know he'd be here. He sent me to be sure you're all right."

"I'm perfectly fine," Petra said with more spirit than she felt.

Ash made a face. "If that pompous ass crashed this party, they should kick him out. I'll happily assist the effort."

"I don't think Yves can kick him out," he said. "Ballet royalty is ballet royalty. Just remember," he said, pointing at Petra, "he's not the only legend here."

He gave her a smile meant to encourage, to fortify. She loved both her friends for their unwavering support. Liam was right—Grigolyuk wasn't the only one here with talent and power. She was going to dance the hell out of the balcony *pas de deux* with Rubio, and her father could choke on it, or walk out if he wanted. She refused to give a fuck anymore.

"I better head backstage," she said, lifting her chin.

"*Merde*, hon." Ashleigh gave her a hug, being careful with her makeup and her delicate, flowing costume. "Have fun. You two do *Romeo and Juliet* better than anyone."

God, Petra hoped so. This had to be their very best performance, even if it was just a showcase event. She found Rubio in his dressing room, still doing his makeup. "Where were you?" she asked. "I've been out there all by myself."

He turned at her sharp tone. "You need my help to walk around and drink champagne? You didn't have to go out there before the show."

"And you didn't have to hide back here. You're the lead principal. You should have been out there working the room."

He put on a few finishing swipes of shading and straightened, adjusting his gray satin tunic. "And you should watch the way you snap at me, or I'll spank your naughty ass when we go back to my place."

She turned away from him, irritated that he'd try to play with her at a time like this. "I'm not in the mood for that crap right now. We're supposed to go dance."

He blinked at her, once, twice. "What happened to you? What's wrong? Is Paulsen back?"

"No. How would he be back?"

"What then?"

"It's my dad. He's out there."

As soon as she spit out the words, a little of her agitation bled away. Rubio unruffled too, his pinched features transforming into an expression of understanding. "Oh, no. What did he say to you?" he asked, taking her hand. "If he talked bad to you, I'll punch him in the face."

"He didn't talk bad to me. He wouldn't even look at me. I don't care though. I'm just annoyed that he's here." Ruby tilted her chin until he caught her gaze, but she pulled away from him. She didn't want his soul-searching, not tonight. She looked pointedly at the clock. "We're supposed to go on at ten-thirty. Are you ready?"

"Do I look ready?" He bent to brush a whisper of a kiss across her lips. He was ever mindful of her makeup, ever mindful of everything. He really was the world's best partner and she shouldn't have taken her irritation out on him.

"I'm sorry," she said against his cheek. "I'm sorry I was snappy with you."

"You can make it up to me later. You come sleep over tonight, yes?"

Petra didn't answer. She wasn't sure. Seeing her father had brought up a bunch of prickly, angsty feelings, and for some reason they were transferring to Rubio. She was annoyed with his confidence and sexual innuendos, his assumption she'd be there in his bed wearing his pretty silver pet collar whenever he wanted. As she stood at the balcony as Juliet, watching for Romeo's entrance, she imagined a future gala, where Rubio stood like a king, like her father, worshipped and revered in his fancy tuxedo.

Where would she be? At his side? Or at home, aging and forgotten, bitterly reminiscing about her ephemeral career?

She ran down to throw herself into Romeo's arms. She had to concentrate and stop obsessing about her commitment issues. The ballet came first. The first few moments of the *pas de deux* were okay, if tense. But then things started to go wrong.

"Stop," Rubio hissed through his smile. "Don't think of him." He held her gaze as he swung her around in a lift. "Dance with me."

She tried to push her dad out of her mind, but the more she did, the more she imagined him out in the audience, scrutinizing her every step. Her body fought the movements so she lagged behind the music. She was heavy for Ruby to lift because she wasn't working with him the way she was supposed to. He made a warning sound after one excruciating sequence.

"Do it," he said under his breath. "Dance, damn you."

Petra tried…but everything was fucking up. To the audience, their performance probably looked normal, if not stellar. She wasn't tripping or forgetting steps, she was just out of tune with her body and out of tune with him. Ruby tried to compensate. He stopped sniping at her and put all his efforts into making her look better than she did.

She was furious with herself but she couldn't snap out of her tailspin. The music flowed on, nightmarish to her ears. She wanted this *pas de deux* to end. She wanted to take off her costume and makeup and go home to hide under the covers until tomorrow.

But she couldn't. She was Petra Hewitt and this was her job. Rubio put his arms around her as Romeo, gazing into her eyes. She was supposed to love him. She was supposed to be transported by her love for him, so what had gone wrong? Juliet could love, so why couldn't she?

What the fuck was wrong with her?

The moment she and Ruby moved into the next series of lifts, she knew something had gone terminally bad, so bad it wasn't fixable. His hand slipped and she flopped onto his shoulder. He grabbed a handful of her dress and righted her, but it was too late to make it look good. They'd totally botched the lift. All the patrons would assume he was drunk, or she was on drugs, and gossip about it behind their crystal champagne flutes. Her face burned and her ankles wobbled through the last humiliating steps. Finally, it was over.

She would have fled the stage if Ruby hadn't grabbed her hand in an iron grasp. "*Reverence*," he said. "Do it."

She was losing it. She bowed her head and sank into a curtsy, not wanting anyone to see her face. She couldn't look out at the audience. She didn't want to know if her father had stayed to watch, if he'd seen her egregious mistake—because it was her mistake, not Ruby's, that made him fumble that lift. Anyone who was a dancer would have known it.

After a painfully polite bout of applause, they swept off the stage. "Happy now?" she asked, pulling away from him just inside the wings. "You dropped me in front of everyone."

"Be quiet. They'll hear you." He tugged her arm, guiding her back into the deeper recesses of the stage. "What *was* that?" he asked when they were alone. "Did that make you proud, that performance? Proud for your dad?"

She burst into tears. "No, it didn't make me proud. It sucked. I told you we had to practice more, but you didn't want to—"

"Oh, no," he said, cutting her off. "Don't put this on me. None of that was my fault."

"I was nervous. You weren't out there with me earlier, when I saw my father. You should have been with me." Even as she said the words, she recognized her hypocrisy. She constantly held him at arm's length, but then lit into him when he wasn't there.

He took her arm and held her against him, and wiped at her tears. "Okay, is enough now. Pull yourself together. We have to go out there, you know, even if you just danced Juliet like a fucking mess. Your father will not say nothing. If he does—"

"He won't," she yelled. "Don't you get it? He doesn't talk to me, he doesn't give a fuck about me. He never will."

"Then why are you so upset?" he yelled back. "Why do you care? What is going on in your crazy head? Why did you dance so bad, and embarrass both of us?"

"I didn't mean to." She wrapped her arms around her waist, hating this moment, hating this blow-up between them. Hating herself for being the one to blame. "I suck, okay? I guess that's the problem. I'm a total fuck up and I can't do this anymore."

"You don't suck," he said. "Calm down, okay? You had a bad night. It happens."

"No, I mean, I can't do this thing...with you...and dance... I can't handle it all anymore."

He sobered, narrowing his eyes. "What do you mean?"

"What do you think I mean?" She said it meanly, spitefully, so she wouldn't start crying again. "I mean that I just want to dance. I just want..." She put her hands to her head, rubbing her temples. "I need some space, okay? Ever since you gave me that stupid necklace or collar or whatever—"

"Stupid? Oh, very nice. You call my gift stupid?"

"I'm not a dog! I'm not your pet. I'm a dancer. I'm Petra Hewitt. I don't belong to you, okay?"

He took her arm and backed her against the concrete wall. She could feel his groin tightening against the front of her. "What are you talking about?" he said against her ear. When she struggled, he held her tighter, pinning her with his chest and hips. "Does not matter who belongs to who. You want me, I want you. That's all that matters."

"No."

"No? It doesn't matter?"

"No, I don't want you. Not anymore. I told you, I just want to dance. I need a break."

"You don't take a break from desire, Petra." She flinched as he forced a kiss on her, taking bold possession of her lips. She pushed him back and moved to leave, but he caught her from behind, pulling her against his chest. "I don't understand this," he whispered. "You don't like me anymore? You don't want me? That's not what you screamed last night while you were coming."

"Yes, you make me come. So what? I can buy a fucking vibrator to do the same thing." Now that was a lie. There was no vibrator on the planet that would live up to Rubio's lovemaking, but at least a vibrator wouldn't distract her and torment her, and drop her onstage in front of her father.

"You're angry right now," he said with a sigh. The more she struggled, the more his arms tightened around her. "I understand you're angry. You're embarrassed, whatever. If you want space, you can have it for a while. I'll be here. We'll still dance together, yes?"

She nodded slowly after a moment. "Of course. We're partners. That's all I want, to dance."

"Okay. We'll dance." He finally let her go. She ducked away from him, brushing the wrinkles out of her costume. He looked shell-shocked, sucker-punched, which ripped at her heart. This would be the hardest part, re-establishing the boundaries between them, but it had to be done.

"Are you angry?" she asked. "Do you hate me?"

He gave a short, bitter laugh. "I don't hate you, no. But stop crying. We have to go out and work. You have to hold your head high and show your father what a beautiful, strong person you are. Everyone will forget the lift. Half are too drunk to notice anyway," he added, waving a hand.

There was no way Petra could walk back out into that theater and face everyone. Face her father. It wasn't physically possible for her tonight. "You go ahead," she said. "I have to fix my makeup. I'll be out soon."

He watched her a long moment, and then he nodded. "Okay." He sighed, one of his long, dramatic sighs, and slipped past her, back toward the stage. As he passed he caressed her arm, a soft, light touch. It felt like a goodbye, even though she knew she'd see him tomorrow in rehearsal.

In her heart, it was a goodbye.

* * * * *

Petra asked him for space, and he gave it to her. Now Rubio had so much space in his life he was going crazy. Space in his bed, space in his heart. Space in his loft with his goddamn window looking out on the goddamn city that held no attraction for him anymore.

He could leave if he wanted, negotiate a contract with some other company. He would miss Liam and Ashleigh, but he'd been in London forever, practically his entire career. He could leave and explore some other city, some other vistas. But no matter how far he went, he'd still be the same Fernando Rubio, a rough-edged asshole from the slums. He thought he was getting better with Petra, that he was maturing and becoming a better person, a lovable person, but she didn't want to make a life with him, so he must have been wrong.

Still, he wouldn't leave. In his heart of hearts, he knew that, just as he knew he'd never throw away her collar, even though he'd flung it in the trash can a hundred times. He wouldn't leave London if Petra was here, because she might need him. If she went back to New York, he'd go too. If she went to Moscow, Hong Kong, Timbuktu, it didn't matter. As long as Paulsen continued with his threats and harassing letters, Rubio would stick around. She'd gained another stalker—him.

Liam kept him updated about Paulsen, even though Ruby and Petra were no longer in a relationship, or sleeping together, or even talking together most days. They said only as much as they had to in order to work out the subtleties of *Waking Kiss*, the piece they were rehearsing as part of a love-themed collection of ballets.

Ironic.

Going along with the romance-oriented theme, the show was scheduled to premiere next week, on Valentine's Day. It grated to play lovers with Petra when she'd thrown his love back in his face. She was a heartless, cold, career-obsessed woman. He'd known that when he first met her. He knew it before he met her, for God's sake, and he'd pursued her anyway. He'd been a fool.

But heartless or not, he'd make her do justice to his ballet. He pushed her and challenged her and demanded one hundred percent of her, even in practices. She glared at him now, after his twentieth correction, her hands on her hips.

"Let me dance it," she said. "Let me interpret it my way. It's my role."

"It's my ballet," he retorted. "You do it my way. The way I told you to do it."

A few dancers drifted in to stretch and warm up for the next practice. Petra glanced over at them and lowered her voice.

"I don't take orders from you anymore."

"In here, you do," he said, making no effort to be quiet. "We go again. Do it right this time. No wild arms. Lyrical, like this."

He showed her what he wanted but she only scowled at him, pursing her lips. "Don't insult me. I wasn't doing wild arms."

"They looked wild to me. And I'm not insulting, I'm directing. If you'd take that crown off your head, princess, you'd dance better."

Petra bit her bottom lip hard. If the other dancers hadn't been there, she would have gone off on him. As it was, she nodded to the accompanist and proceeded to repeat the combination—ignoring every fucking thing he'd said.

He felt rage. She turned to look at him over her shoulder, dismissing his opinion. Dismissing him. Without thinking, he strode over and yanked her arms into the correct position. "Do it right, damn you. Like this."

She slapped his hands away. "Don't ever jerk my arms like that."

"If you won't do what I say, what choice do I have?" He turned to the gawking dancers sitting against the wall. "Get out. All of you get out. Next rehearsal is not for five minutes." A few of them moved, but not enough to suit him. "Get out!" he yelled in a breaking voice.

Even the accompanist jumped up, making a beeline for the door. Petra turned to leave too, but he grabbed her hand to stop her, hauling her over toward the mirror. "Not you. You don't go anywhere."

"Are you finished?" she asked, turning on him. "Are you done scolding and disrespecting me in front of everyone? Do you think you could give me just the tiniest bit of artistic license to interpret your ballet?"

She was talking too fast for him to understand, but it didn't matter. He only answered one thing to her these days. "No."

She ground her pointe shoe into the floor with a vicious twist and then turned to leave again.

"No," he repeated. "You do it the way I like or you don't go."

"Oh, really? Are you being serious right now?" She looked as beautiful as ever with her green eyes flashing and wisps of her blonde hair escaping her bun.

"We premiere this fucking show in five days, Petra," he said, his voice hard. "I don't have time for this bullshit."

"It's not bullshit. I'm trying to make it my own. I'm not doing the Ashleigh Keaton version."

"Why not? She danced as good as you. Better, in this," he added just to hurt her. It wasn't true. Petra did his ballet beautifully, but somehow, she wasn't there for him emotionally. She wasn't dancing love. She was dancing distance. Anger. Disgust.

"I've left you alone," he said quietly. "I did what you asked. Why do you hate me so much?"

He thought he saw her flinch a little. "I don't hate you."

"You hate me. You hate my work. You hate my ballet."

She turned away but he didn't let her go. He pulled her closer and leaned into the curve of her neck. Oh God, the smell of her hair. "Petra," he groaned. "I miss you so much. Why won't you come back to me?"

He felt her shiver. "I can't. I've explained why a thousand times."

"I still don't understand." He smoothed his fingers over her hair. "I don't understand nothing. I'm too stupid." His fingers skimmed lower, over her shoulders and down to her hips. The closeness of her body haunted him every second of every day. He pressed his cock against her as it stirred to life. "I'm stupid and selfish but I know how I feel about you. I don't care about other women any more. I don't look at them. I only think about you." He smoothed his hands over her practice tutu, then lifted it up out of the way to press his palm between her legs. He could feel her heat like he felt his own heart racing. "I know we belong together. You know it too."

"Stop." She pushed his hand away. "Stop it. The others are waiting outside. Someone will see."

He would have stopped if he thought she meant it, if she wasn't melting into him like a lost, frightened child. "I don't give a fuck if they see." He caught her hand and twisted it up behind her back, so she fell forward against his chest.

She made a soft, scared sound. "They'll see. Let me go."

"Why? Am I too dirty for you? Too nasty?" He ground his hips against her in rough anger. "I'm not good enough for you, yes? Well, too bad. I don't want to let you go. I care about you, Petra, I love you. What the fuck do you think about that? So what if somebody sees us? Does the world come to an end?"

She tipped her face up, pleading with him. "I told you from the beginning, I'm not going to be my mother. I'm not giving up all of this for you."

Enough. He'd had enough of that explanation. He let go of her and threw out his arms. "I don't want you to give up anything. I never asked you to give up one thing, not one. This is about you and your fucking father, not about me. You care so much about him, what he does, what he thinks. He doesn't give a shit about you. Me, I love you. I'd do anything to be with you, and this is what I get."

He could see his words hit home. She lashed out, her voice trembling in anger. "You keep saying you love me, but you don't. You just like to fuck me. I know you don't love me."

"*I know you don't love me*," he mocked in a high pitched voice. "You don't tell me how I feel, okay? Because you don't know. You're a very confused person, Petra Hewitt. You don't know what love means."

"That is quite enough."

They both turned at the sharp voice of the theater director. Yves Thibault stood across the room, his arms crossed over his chest.

"This is not a discussion for the rehearsal room," he said. "Every dancer outside can hear what you're saying to each other."

"I didn't say nothing that isn't true," Rubio spat, glaring at Petra. "She won't follow direction. We can't dance anymore, not like this."

Yves' eyebrows shot up. "You are contractually obligated to dance with her. The spring season premieres in less than a week."

"She won't dance *Waking Kiss* the way I like."

Petra spoke over him. "He won't consider any of my suggestions. He's being a hardass just to frustrate me."

"And you're ignoring my suggestions to frustrate me," he said. "It goes both ways."

Yves held up a hand. "You two are the face of this company, the artists the other dancers look to for leadership. This squabbling and yelling cannot continue. It's not professional behavior and I won't have it at City Ballet."

Petra's rejection was bad enough. Now he was being lectured like a naughty kid. Him, The Great Rubio. Had he fallen so far? Was it even worth it anymore? He stared down at the lines in the well-worn parquet floor. "Fuck being professional," he muttered, stalking to the side of the room for his dance bag. "Do it without me. Do everything without me, however you like. I'm going home."

Chapter Eighteen:
All Your Fault

As always, the tabloids worked fast. *Brutal Ballet Break-up*, blared the papers the next morning, with some months-old stock photo of her and Rubio looking annoyed. Petra wished she knew which shitty little corps dancer was supplementing their salary by selling stories to the press. Maybe the theater's PR department circulated the stories to increase ticket sales. There was a last minute surge as curtain time neared, as people purchased tickets to watch the feuding dancers perform together. They'd be disappointed when The Great Rubio didn't appear as her partner.

No one could find Rubio, and no one could rustle him up on the phone. Not Yves, not Liam or Ashleigh, not Petra herself. The *Love Stories* premiere couldn't be rescheduled, so Yves tapped Edward to partner her instead. Edward hadn't danced *Waking Kiss* before but professed to know "most of the steps." If he got lost, she'd have to coach him along under her breath during the performance. Fun times.

She wondered how long Rubio would stay away from the theater, how long before he answered his phone. She wondered which of them would crack and leave City Ballet first. It ought to be her, since she was barely settled into London, but if she went back to New York, Paulsen could get to her again. She'd have to go somewhere else, somewhere far, far away. Australia. Maybe Romania. Japan?

Maybe Iceland. Did they have any professional ballet companies? Because her heart felt cold as ice. She struggled to dance through the chills freezing her body. She felt a tightness in her throat that wasn't illness, but the lack of her familiar partner. Everyone watched as she moved through City Ballet's halls, judging her, condemning her with their eyes.

"Oh, sorry," said Edward as they missed a connection. He shied away from her, like she might slap him or something. Was she that much of a bitch? She and Edward did the best they could to get the ballet worked into shape for the premiere, but he was no Rubio, not even close. She needed a good cry but there were no tears in her, no emotion except strangling self-hatred. She put on her game face, a brittle mask of resignation, but inside she felt lost.

Then, premiere night, at seven, Rubio showed up. She heard it secondhand, from a stage manager, that Mr. Rubio was in his dressing room putting on his costume and preparing to perform.

"Perform with me?" she asked.

The woman gave her a nervous smile. "I would assume so."

Petra refused to seek him out. Such drama, disappearing for days and then showing up for stage call. Yves ought to tell him he couldn't perform, but of course he wouldn't. She looked down at her pale blue costume, smoothing the voluminous tulle skirt. As much as she liked *Waking Kiss*, she wasn't looking forward to performing tonight. What the hell had happened to them? There was a time when dancing with Rubio had been the highlight of her day.

You happened, Petra. This is all your fault.

Their ballet was last in the program, so she hid in her dressing room until the last possible moment, and then reported to the wings with a sense of dread. She warmed up in the corner, not looking around to see if he was there. It was sad to dance like this, with so much dysfunction between them. *Dysfunction that's your fault.*

Her phone vibrated in her dance bag and she reached for it, flicking to the text.

Sorry not there. In labor. Valentine's baby, which only makes sense.

Petra stared at the message. Oh God, Ashleigh was having her baby, and yes, it made sense she would have it this day of all days, a day devoted to love. She hurriedly texted back. *So excited. Best wishes for a wonderful delivery.*

Then Ash texted, *Merde to you both.*

So Ashleigh knew Rubio was here. She looked over her shoulder to find him staring at her from the wings. He wasn't smiling. She put away her phone, shed her leg warmers, and walked over. "Nice of you to show up."

He didn't answer, just looked somewhere over her shoulder.

"Ash texted me," she added. "The baby's coming."

His lips tightened ever so slightly. "I know. I just came from there. From the hospital."

Petra digested that revelation. Rubio was closer to Ashleigh than he'd ever be to her. This ballet was about the transformative power of love, but really it was about him and Ashleigh and the friendship they'd struck up five years ago. She pushed down pangs of jealousy, because she had no right to be jealous. "How were things going there?" she asked.

He shrugged. "Okay. Ash was screaming lots, but now she had..." He made jabbing motions at the base of his back. "Pain shot. She's better now. Excited for the *bebê*." He tipped up into a perfect handstand. "She said I had to come. She said to come dance, so I'm here."

Petra let out a sharp breath. "No one knew where you were. You should have told someone you were coming tonight. Edward practiced for hours—"

"I wasn't coming tonight," he snapped as he righted himself. "But now I'm here. And when it's over I'll leave, okay? Professional only, from now on." He swept a dispassionate look down the length of her body and up again. She felt like he'd slapped her.

"Yes, fine," she said, turning away.

He gave a bitter laugh. "Is okay with you?" He laughed again and then they didn't exchange another word until they walked out behind the curtain to assume their opening poses. In the dim light she could feel him more than see him. She could smell the familiar scent of him like a remembered dream.

Waking Kiss wasn't a sad ballet, but it was wistful. As the curtain rose and the music began, Petra found herself in tune with the mood of the piece. She was wistful for old times, for Rubio's smiles and laughter, for his sensual demands. *I want...*

He didn't smile at her now, but he didn't frown. Instead he studied her, gazing at her with a focus he hadn't used in rehearsal. Perhaps he was entertaining his own thoughts and memories of her, or more likely Ashleigh, who'd given life to this ballet just as she was giving birth to

Liam's baby. As they danced through the steps, Petra came to a disturbing revelation. She had no life in her at all.

She could dance, but she couldn't love. She was too scared, too selfish. She was a dancing robot, just as Rubio had told her at the start.

She didn't want to be a robot. She dug deep and reached out to him emotionally, with her body, with her movements and her expressions. Even with the tension between them, Rubio gave it back to her, supporting every choice along the way. He wasn't selfish. He was generous and attentive and because she was stupid, she'd lost everything she could have had.

When they got to the part where they'd argued over the placement of her arms, she chose to do it his way. His eyes met hers while the violins wailed, and for a moment there was tenderness between them, even adoration. *I love you*, she thought. "So beautiful," he murmured beside her ear. "Thank you."

The ballet was over too soon. They took their bows and a stagehand brought out a massive bouquet of roses. Rubio took them and placed them in her arms. They weren't from Ruby; it was just the usual opening night pageantry. When she tried to smile at him, her face went all wobbly so she did another deep curtsy instead. She turned to the audience, to acknowledge their gracious standing ovation, and that was when she saw her father in the front row.

He was standing too. It would have looked churlish if he hadn't. Her eyes skipped away from his and back to Rubio's chiseled profile. A tautness in his jaw belied the brightness of his theatrical smile. The scent of the roses wafted to Petra's nose. They were red for love. Red for rubies.

He turned to her as soon as the curtain fell. "Was good," he said. "Thank you."

Company members watched them from the wings. If they were hoping for another fight, they weren't going to get it. "It was good," she agreed. "It's a beautiful ballet. You should be proud to have your name on it."

He looked pleased at her praise. He reached down and ran a finger over the curve of a rose petal. It struck her as highly sexual, because he'd pleasured her so many times with that light touch. He didn't mean it sexually though. He was maintaining a rigid, detached demeanor with her. *Professional only, from now on.*

She didn't like it. She was a miserable, conflicted wreck. "What are you doing tonight?" she blurted out.

"Going home," he said. *By myself* was clearly communicated in his tone.

"You're not going back to the hospital to see Ash and Liam?"

"No. They need privacy. Tomorrow I'll go, maybe. Take the baby a gift."

I'll go with you, she wanted to say. *Let's go together*. His expression dared her to say it and she chickened out. "I'm going to check if she sent any more texts," Petra said, heading offstage.

Rubio followed with a snort. "She's a little busy to be texting."

She checked her phone. Nothing. Well, Rubio was right. She was probably preoccupied at the moment. "Maybe Liam texted you."

He grabbed his stuff and headed out to the hallway. "My phone's in my dressing room."

He didn't invite her to accompany him but she went anyway. The halls were bustling, buzzing with the excitement of a premiere performance. She ducked around a group of dancers to keep up with Rubio and barreled face first into the hard planes of someone's back.

"I'm sorry." She held up a hand in apology before she realized who she'd bumped into. Petr Grigolyuk stared down at her over the point of his distinguished Russian nose. The entire corridor fell into hushed silence, and Petra herself couldn't summon a word. She'd never been this close to him, not in her life. His complexion was pale like hers, marred by finely etched wrinkles. His eyes were her eyes, down to the color of his lashes and the gold flecks in his irises. His lips slanted in a small frown.

Then, without a word or the least reaction, he turned his back on her and resumed his conversation with Yves and Gennady, the show's director.

Blood rushed in Petra's ears. If anything, the silence in the corridor deepened, broken only by the words of her father's conversation. She took a breath in and out, processing the hurt, the cruel rejection. Even now, face to face, he couldn't offer a simple hello. He couldn't smile or deign to congratulate her on her performance. He'd looked at her as if she was something sticking to the bottom of his shoe. She hated him, but more than that, she feared him, feared his power to make her hurt. She felt pummeled to dust, reduced to ashes.

She moved to flee but Rubio's fingers closed around her wrist. His voice rang out in the hushed corridor.

"Hey, Grigolyuk. I never realized what an asshole you are."

Yves glanced around at the pockets of gawking dancers. "That will do, Mr. Rubio. Perhaps you should go to your dressing room."

Rubio ignored him, his eyes fixed on her dad's. "Perhaps you should say hello to your beautiful daughter," he said in a dangerous lilt. He nudged her forward, his arm at her back preventing her from shrinking away.

Grigolyuk gave her another dismissive glance. "This is not my daughter. I don't have a daughter."

Yves was pale behind his glasses and Gennady looked like he wanted to disappear into the wall. Rubio made a low sound of derision. "If you believe that, you're even stupider than I thought."

"Ruby," she whispered, beyond the bounds of humiliation. "Forget it. It's okay."

"No, it's not okay. He's your father. Everyone knows it. You look exactly alike." He turned to Grigolyuk, his eyes glittering black and hard. "Look at her," he said, pulling Petra closer. "She's your own flesh and blood. She worked hard all her life to gain your attention. One smile. What would it cost you? She's standing here, right in front of you, so beautiful and talented. What the fuck is the matter with you?"

Yves made a warning sound to silence Ruby, then, like everyone else in the corridor, turned to Grigolyuk for his response. Her father looked around for somewhere to go but Ruby had him boxed in on one side and Gennady was standing firm on the other. The rest of the company formed a circle of accusation around him.

Petr Grigolyuk didn't seem to care. "You are not my daughter," he said to Petra, "but it was a good performance." He managed the barest hint of a smile before he turned back to Rubio. "Happy now?"

Ruby muttered a vicious epithet in Portuguese and launched himself at her dad. Yves pushed him back, putting himself between Ruby and Grigolyuk. "Petra, take him out of here," he ordered. "Take him home before he gets himself in trouble."

"Rubio. Ruby. *Fernando*," she pleaded when she couldn't get his attention. She turned his face down to hers, the bouquet of roses still clutched in her arm. "Please," she said. "It's enough."

She stroked a hand down his cheek to calm him. The dancers parted like the Red Sea as Yves steered Petr Grigolyuk down the hall and away. Rubio's chest rose and fell beneath his gray-blue silk tunic.

His expression looked as savage as his heart was pure.

* * * * *

Rubio's leg bounced next to Petra's in the backseat of the car. It was partly leftover anger from the confrontation with her father, and partly nervous energy that Petra was coming to his place.

He didn't want her to go home by herself. Petr Grigolyuk had reached into her chest and ripped her heart out in front of the entire company and Ruby didn't want her to be alone. "No sex," he promised. "We'll be professional."

He was coming to hate the word "professional," especially since he couldn't seem to master the art of it. Professionals didn't throw tantrums and they certainly didn't throw punches, even when the biggest asshole in history was tormenting someone dear to his soul.

I love you, he wanted to say to her. *I still love you. I never stopped.* "Hey, you think your asshole father will press charges on me?" he asked instead.

"I think Yves stepped between you two before it became an all-out assault. But if he does press charges, Liam will help you, don't you think?"

Ruby checked his phone again. "No more texts from the hospital. I hope everything is okay."

"I'm sure she's fine. Maybe they're already holding their little girl."

It made a pretty picture in his head, Ashleigh and Liam holding their baby. "Maybe we can visit tomorrow."

"Maybe," said Petra.

The car eased up to the curb of his building. Rubio got out first and looked around the immediate area, a habit left over from the Paulsen days. Then he bent down and helped Petra out, holding the roses until she could shoulder her bag. He didn't want to assume anything, but maybe she'd spend the whole night. It would be enough for him to hold her close, to breathe in the scent of her sugar-vanilla hair. Maybe she'd let him do more. Maybe she'd let him touch her and torment her and make love to every beautiful inch of her the way he did in his dreams every night. Then in the morning they could visit the hospital together, see the baby and maybe go out for lunch...

No. He couldn't assume anything where Petra was concerned. "Be careful," he said, guiding her over the lip of the elevator. "Someday I'll get that fixed."

She chuckled nervously. "Your elevator's broken?"

"No, is fine. I think the floor is broken. Old buildings," he explained with a shrug.

She laughed again and he took heart at the sound. She was behaving more like the old Petra, the soft, melting one he'd come to love. He stared at her nape as they glided up the eight floors to his place. When it stopped, he opened the door and led her out. He flicked on the lights and reached out a hand.

"Give me the roses," he said. "I'll put them in some water."

Instead, Petra dropped the whole bunch on the floor. He followed her frozen gaze to the couch, where Gary Paulsen sat with a gun trained on the middle of Ruby's chest.

"Don't make a sound," the burly man said to Petra. "Don't move, don't scream. Don't try anything or your boyfriend eats a bullet." His fingers tightened on the gun, a muscle ticking in his jaw as he stood. "And don't look at me that way, you little bitch. Spare me the drama. This is all your fault."

Chapter Nineteen:
So Close

Ruby stood still, gauging the man's willingness to use the weapon. Petra's voice rang out in the silence.

"How are you here? You're not supposed to be in England. There's a restraining order."

Paulsen snickered, a chilling sound. "I have a lot of money, Petra. I can circumvent just about any obstacle. I can buy my way onto airplanes and into private residences pretty easily." He nodded at Ruby. "I thought he'd be showing up alone, but it will be better this way."

"What will be better this way?" Ruby asked, not sure he wanted to hear the answer.

Paulsen narrowed his eyes. "You shut up. I have nothing to say to you. As for you..." His cold gaze fixed on Petra. "I'd like you to explain the meaning behind all your games. I've tried and tried to talk to you. It's taken a lot of my time and energy. I've tried to warn you about him but you don't listen. You never listen." His lips twisted and his voice rose with increasing rage. "I wrote you a thousand letters, called you again and again. Why the fuck didn't you answer me?"

"Because I don't know who you are," she replied, her voice matching his in intensity. "Because you're a psycho. Because I don't want you in my life!"

Ruby was torn between admiration for Petra's pluck and fear that she was acting kind of insane. It took a lot of balls to yell at a psychopath.

"Get out of here," she demanded. "Stop pointing that gun at him."

Paulsen vaulted off the couch, stalked toward Ruby, and shoved the cold muzzle against his forehead. "What's that, Petra?"

She stared at the weapon, then at Rubio. *What now?* Ruby hated that she was so scared. He hated having a gun at his head but he hated Petra's panic worse. He tried to calm her with his gaze. He didn't dare speak.

Paulsen tapped the muzzle against his forehead, once, twice, and then backed up a few inches with a smug smile. "I think you should talk to me a little more respectfully. What do you think?"

Petra made a sick, choked sound. "Please, don't. Please don't shoot him. I'll talk to you."

Ruby was afraid, yes, but he wasn't terrified. He was from the worst neighborhood in Rio. He knew about guns. He looked closer at the firearm still pointed at his head, studying the weapon that might end his life. It was a smallish semi-automatic, probably illegal in origin. He wondered if Paulsen knew how to shoot it or just how to wave it around. He wondered if it was fully loaded and how many rounds it held.

He caught Petra's gaze. *Talk to him.* He thought the words really hard, trying to communicate telepathically. *Keep him talking until I can figure out some plan to save us. But don't make him angry enough to kill you too.*

"Are you looking at him? Really?" Paulsen snapped at Petra. "I told you time and time again that he was a bad person. He uses women. He used you and you let him. I saw you in the papers, in the photos. I saw you having fights. You know he's an asshole, don't you?"

Nod, Rubio thought. *Nod your head and agree with whatever he says.* If only Paulsen didn't have the gun. If it was him and the creep, he could kill him with his fists and the sheer force of his rage. He'd kill him without a second thought, only for the terror Petra was feeling right now.

"Please let him go," Petra begged. "It wasn't him. It was me. I was the one who chased after him." *No, Petra! Bad girl!* "I didn't answer your letters because—"

"You didn't answer my letters because he wouldn't let you," said Paulsen. "Tell the truth. He's bad for you, Petra. I have to kill him."

"You'll get in trouble if you do that. You'll go to jail." Tears squeezed from her eyes. "Please, what do you want? Do you want me to come back to New York? Do you want to be with me?"

Paulsen's face transformed at her words. "Yes. That's what I want."

"I'll do that. But you have to let him go first. If you kill him...that...that will scare me too bad. I don't know if I'd be able to love you after that."

Ruby watched Paulsen as he thought this over. His fingers opened and closed on the handle of the gun. "Are you lying to me?" He shut his eyes a moment and opened them, blinking. *Next time,* thought Ruby. *Next time he does that, I'll take him.* "Are you lying to me?" he asked again.

"I'm not lying."

Paulsen turned and looked at Rubio like he was looking at something inanimate. A tree. A shoe rack. "If I don't kill him, he'll come after you."

"He won't. I told you, I'm the one who wanted him. I didn't realize..." Her voice trailed off. "I didn't realize until now how much you loved me. Now that I know, I want to be with you. Let's go now. Let's go to New York and be together. I can meet your friends and your family, and we can go out to dinner together, and go to shows and parties..."

"I don't like to be around people," Paulsen said grimly.

"Then we can stay home. There are so many things we can do together. At home. Alone."

Ruby had to give her credit. She didn't choke on the words. She said them softly, seductively. She was purposely keeping her eyes locked on his. He couldn't imagine what this tense flirtation was costing her, but it was working. Paulsen was looking at Petra more than him. *Please keep going. Keep it up, baby. Don't stop.*

"You said I was a psycho," he said. "You screamed it at me."

"I know. That was before I understood how strongly you felt about me."

"But..." He worked his lips nervously. Ruby was almost certain his arms were getting tired. "How do you feel about me?"

Talk, little girl. Tell lies, one after the other. Keep talking as long as you can.

Petra took a soft, dramatic breath, like she was carefully considering her answer. "At first you scared me. You came on so strong. I never had anyone talk to me the way you talk to me. I've never had anyone try so hard to get close to me. Honestly, I didn't understand what you wanted. I didn't understand how deep your feelings were."

"They're deep, Petra. I promise you."

"I know that now."

"Say my name," he said. "Say my name, the way I say yours."

She took another breath. "Gary. Let's go to New York, Gary. We'll live together, just you and me. We'll spend our days and nights doing whatever you want. *Whatever* you want," she emphasized. "If you want to make love to me..." Her voice broke off. *Come on, Petra, please. They're just words. Keep talking. Make it filthy.* Paulsen's eyes were practically glazing over.

"I would love to make love to you," she said. "All day and all night. There's nothing I won't do in the bedroom. Do you like sex, Gary?"

He stared at her. "Yes, I love sex."

"Being a dancer and everything..." She bit her lip, a perfectly seductive affectation. "I can do all kinds of positions, and I have a lot of stamina. I could suck your cock for hours if you wanted me to. Whatever you like. I promise, I'll make it so good for you."

Paulsen had forgotten Rubio was even there. He had to act before he remembered again. Ruby launched himself forward, grabbing the hand holding the gun. With his other hand he slugged Paulsen full force in the face. The attack was part ballet grace, part pissed-off kid who'd been beaten up one too many times for being poor, and scruffy, and a faggot ballet dancer. Paulsen doubled over, blood streaming from his nose. Before Ruby could get the gun from him he was upright again. Ruby wrestled him sideways so the gun was pointed away from her, toward the window. "Go, Petra, run," he shouted. "Go get help."

Paulsen fired off a volley of shots. Bullet holes riddled the wide glass window. Cracks spread in concentric circles with a shattering sound. Another shot went wild, into the kitchen, then one into the sofa. Where was Petra?

"I'll kill you," screamed Paulsen, struggling to point the gun at him, but Rubio was stronger. The next bullet hit the center of the window and the entire glass wall of his loft shattered with a deafening crash. He heard Petra's scream and another gunshot, a dead click. The gun was out of bullets. Paulsen flung it away and grasped Ruby by the shoulders, pushing him down and dragging him toward the maw of the shattered window. Ruby dug in his feet but his shoes slid across the glass littering the floor.

"No! Stop!" Petra shrieked, pulling at Ruby from behind. She tried to wrench Paulsen off him, but Ruby pushed her back. He was large enough to fight Paulsen, but the guy could fling Petra from the window like a rag doll.

"Stay away," he yelled at her. "Stay away from the window."

She was screaming, screeching curses and prayers and intermittently crying out "Help!" but Rubio was silent, focused on the jagged-glass line that separated his loft floor from the open air and the eight-story drop to the street below. It was one thing to struggle with Paulsen's fat bulk on his feet, but another to grapple with the man on a glass-strewn floor. He bit Paulsen and got kicked in the face for it. They wrestled, each of them struggling for the upper hand. The edge was five feet away. Four.

"Ruby! Ruby, oh God." Petra's hysterical screams might alert a neighbor, but what would they do? Come over to the edge and try to help him? And by the time the police came...

He fought harder against Paulsen's lunatic energy, his grasping fists. He tried to kick him in the balls but missed. Each strike, each kick was a precarious loss of control.

"Push him," Paulsen barked. "Help me push him out, Petra. Then he'll leave us alone. Then you'll love me."

"I'll never love you," she shrieked. "I hate you. I'll always hate you. Let him go."

"Help me throw him out," he pleaded, ignoring her words. "You'll never be safe as long as he's around."

Ruby's fist connected with his face, but Paulsen trapped his hand and latched onto it with brutal force.

"Stop it." Petra surged forward, kicking at Paulsen's head. Rubio wanted to scream at her for putting her own safety at risk, but he was using all his waning energy just to survive. Rubio was strong, but he was a sleek, streamlined dancer. Paulsen was a brute lump. Petra kicked Paulsen hard in his doughy stomach. He jerked back, drawing both of them closer to the edge.

"Petra." Ruby found some adrenalized pocket of strength to shout at her. "Go get help, damn you." He didn't really expect her to find help in time. He just wanted her out of danger. If he had to go out the window, he didn't want to see her falling down after him. He didn't want that to be his last vision before he died. "Go, Petra," he begged. "Please go."

"No, I'm not leaving you."

He groaned as a shard of glass dug into his side. Bad, bad girl. He'd never been one for training obedience into his subs. Too late now. He felt Petra's weight on his back, as if she could sit on him and hold him, but then the weight was gone. She was gone. Thank God. *Petra, go. Please stay safe.* He wasn't sure he was going to survive this. All in all, he'd had a good life. But Petra...he regretted leaving Petra. He loved her so, so much.

In the midst of his maudlin thoughts, a Plexiglas cane whistled past his eyes and slashed full force into Paulsen's face. The man screamed, covering the bleeding weal across his eyes. She hit him again across the cheek and he reared back, pulling Ruby with him. Rubio braced with everything he had inside, braced against the bitter edge of life and death and fought to escape him.

"Hit his hand, baby," Ruby whispered, because he didn't have the energy to yell. "Hit it hard."

She struck Paulsen's wrist with vicious force and his fingers jerked open. Ruby was free, scooting away from the window's edge. He shoved Petra toward the couch, back to safety, then picked up the cane. When Paulsen came at him, he slashed him across the chest with all his strength. Paulsen reeled back with a wail of pain and tilted over the edge. He grabbed for Ruby, but this time he couldn't reach him. He clawed at thin air, once, twice, with his great grasping hands, and then he was gone.

There was a moment of shock, and silence. "Petra." Ruby spun around and tried to stand up, but he couldn't. His side ached with a dull pain. "Petra, where are you?"

She flew to him, dragging him away from the window, as far away as she could. Now that the life-or-death struggle was over, he realized he was bleeding everywhere, from a thousand large and small cuts, but he was more worried about her. "Are you okay?" He touched her arms, her legs. She wasn't hurt. She was alive. He held her face in his hands, leaving trails of blood everywhere. "I'm sorry," he said, looking at his shredded palms. "I'm a mess."

"Oh, God. You need a hospital." She ran for her phone and dialed, shaking from head to toe. She was crying so hard she had to keep repeating herself to the person on the line. Ruby stared at the clear cane lying on the floor near the kitchen. He didn't think he could bring himself to use it ever again. All the roses from the performance were still scattered over by the door.

"He went out the window," she sobbed into the phone. It jolted Ruby. No, not him, Paulsen. Paulsen had gone out the window. "I think he's dead, and my partner is hurt." Her voice rose in panic. "There's so much blood. Please hurry."

"It's okay, baby," he said when she hung up. "Everything's going to be okay." He wanted to get up and hold her, and comfort her, but he was having a really hard time finding the energy to move. The world went hazy as she hurried over to him. "Don't cry, Petra. He's gone now. He can't scare you anymore." He patted her hair to soothe her as she sobbed into his chest.

"You scared me," she cried. "You scared me so bad."

"And you didn't listen to me," he reminded her in a reproachful whisper. "Bad girl, when you don't listen. Even if you saved my life."

* * * * *

Petra sat beside Mem on the couch in the private hospital room. Rubio slept in the bed, though he seemed far too large for the narrow, institutional mattress. They'd sedated him because he was so agitated, and because he had so many cuts, so many splinters of glass embedded in his skin. Each had to be picked out one by one, each wound covered in antibiotic cream and bandages. The only really deep cut was a gash on his side that took sixty stitches.

As for Petra, she had no physical injuries except a bruise on her leg, probably from the last time Ruby shoved her back. Emotionally, she was a lot worse off. She couldn't stop shaking, couldn't stop thinking about Paulsen and his grisly death. *It might have been Ruby's death*, she thought over and over. *Or yours.* The entire episode was burned in her brain, Paulsen's flailing arms, his fury, the look on his face as he lurched backward...

She'd texted Mem and Liam on the way to the hospital, and Mem had arrived first, holding her in the waiting room until her volcanic shudders eased. Liam came later, when Ashleigh and baby Alanna were settled and sleeping a few floors above them. He looked exhausted, his features tense with concern.

"Petra, how are you? Are you all right?" He crossed the room in two strides and pulled her into a smothering embrace. "I can't believe this happened. I can't believe that fucking lunatic got to you after all."

"It's not your fault," she said to calm him. "And I'm fine. Mostly fine. There's just...stuff I saw that I wish I could forget." She shivered, burying her face against his shoulder. "He put a gun against Ruby's head and I was so afraid he'd shoot him. I couldn't breathe. He—he tried to push Ruby out the window. He almost did."

"I'm so sorry." Liam rubbed her back as she trembled against him. "I'm so sorry about what happened. But everything will be okay. Ruby will be okay. And Paulsen..."

Is dead. Splattered on the sidewalk. She closed her mind to that thought as Liam released her and crossed to Ruby's bed, taking in his bandaged arms and hands.

"He's all cut up," she said in a quavery voice.

"Ruby will be fine. He'll be running around annoying everyone again within a week or two. He's a tough guy."

Liam's words triggered more flashbacks: Ruby grunting and grappling with Paulsen mere feet from the window, from the eight-story drop.

"Pictures. I need baby pictures," she begged. "Distract me, please. Show me your little girl."

They sat near the bed while Liam flicked through about a hundred photos he'd taken since Alanna's birth just before midnight. "Look at her hair," he said, the epitome of the proud father. "She's so beautiful. Her eyes look like Ashleigh's. She's so soft, like a...a cotton ball. A beautiful, sweet little cotton ball."

Petra glanced over at Mem, who stifled a smile. "She's even prettier than a cotton ball," she said. "And I love her name."

"It's Irish. God, she's just...oh, look at this one. It almost looks like she's smiling."

"It's good luck for a newborn to smile," said Mem. "She will surely be a blessed child."

Liam chuckled. "You can say it. She'll be a spoiled child. But that's okay."

The man was ecstatic, glowing from the inside. So much for Ashleigh's worries about a father's love. Petra felt a pang of sadness, that her father had never taken a hundred pictures of her, or called her a sweet little cotton ball. She had to make peace with it. She had to accept that she was fatherless and move on. At least she'd had her mother's love, which was more than some kids had. She had Rubio's love too, and she'd taken it for granted.

She swallowed down a choking sob. "No, I'm okay," she said quickly at Liam and Mem's concerned glances. "I just keep remembering how close...how close I came to losing him tonight."

Not just tonight. Forever. She'd almost given him up, the man who loved her more than life itself. He would have gone out that window to save her, she was sure of it. When she thought of how she'd treated him, how she'd pushed him away, the tears started up again, even harder than before.

Liam hugged her while Mem went for more tissues. "It's okay," Liam murmured. "Ruby's okay. I mean, he's gonna wake up a little cranky, but everything's going to be fine."

"No, I was awful to him," she sobbed. "I've been awful and cold from the start because of my stupid fears."

"Fears are never stupid," said Mem. "But they are sometimes unfounded."

"I'll never be able to make it up to him. All this stuff he went through since he met me... He almost *died*."

Liam made a soft sound. "He never lived before he met you. So, I don't know. Is almost dying as bad as never living in the first place?"

"*Mamãe?*" Rubio stirred, coming to wakefulness. "*Mamãe, você tá chorando?*"

The three of them hurried over to the bed. Ruby tried to turn over and groaned. "Don't move," Liam said, pushing him back. "You have a shitload of stitches."

"Where is Petra? Petra fell down?" His face twisted into a haggard mask of torment. "Oh God, I tried to save her."

"I'm here," she said, leaning close to him. "I'm right here. I'm okay."

"I think he's still sleeping," said Liam. "The sedatives."

"Don't wake him," advised Mem.

"He's half-awake though. He's scared." Liam touched his arm. "Petra's okay, Ruby. I promise, she's fine."

He shook his head. "She left me. She left me, Liam. She's gone."

"No, she's right here. She's the one touching your hair."

"Oh." He closed his eyes again and went still. "I thought it was my mother."

Petra pressed her lips to his cheek. "You can call your mom in a while. I'm here and I'm fine. It's okay to sleep now."

He seemed to do that for a few precious seconds, but then he came awake again, caught between consciousness and lingering sedation. "I don't want to sleep. Paulsen—"

"Is at the city morgue," said Liam. "He's not going to bother either of you anymore." He eased Ruby's head back on the pillow. "Relax so you don't hurt yourself."

"I think he stabbed me. *Filho da puta.* I have very bad pain in my side."

Petra covered her mouth, torn between crying and laughter. Rubio was most certainly alive, and his usual belligerent self. At the sound of her laughter his eyes finally focused on her. He blinked and reached out to touch her cheek. "Petra. Thank God. You didn't fall out the window?"

She shook her head, swallowing back tears. "I didn't fall out, no. I'm totally fine. How are you?"

"My side hurts. I'm not sure I can dance tonight. I'll try."

"You're not dancing tonight. You're going to need a break, but it's okay. Edward knows the part."

"Edward?" Ruby looked at Liam, his eyes clouding with confusion. "Why are you here? Everything's okay?"

The sedation seemed to be wreaking havoc on his ability to have a focused conversation. Liam soothed his friend. "Everything's fine. I'm here because Ash had the baby. They're sleeping upstairs."

Ruby grew agitated again. "No, no, I won't make a baby in Petra. I promised. I want her to be happy. I just want her to be happy. Tell Petra I won't make a baby."

"No, it's Ashleigh, not Petra—" Liam began.

Rubio clawed at the front of his friend's shirt. "I love her. But I'll pretend not to, if she wants. If she'll come back to me. Tell her I don't love her, okay?" He fell back, wincing. Liam glanced at Petra.

"I'll tell her, Ruby, but I don't know if she'll believe me."

"We'll just dance," he said, his voice getting slow and measured again. "Professional. Maybe someday she'll love me and then I'll marry her and put babies in her. But not until she wants."

Liam winked at her. "That sounds like a good plan. But you should rest now. We can talk later, when the sedatives wear off."

"Sedatives," he said, his body relaxing. "What is that?"

"It's kind of like truth serum," Liam answered. "But don't worry about it."

Petra stroked Rubio's glossy black hair. "*Mãe?*" he asked again.

"No, your mom's not here. It's Petra."

"Petra," he said, drawing out the 'r.' Liam and Mem left quietly, shutting the door behind them. Ruby reached up to cup her face, then grunted in pain. "*Merda*, my side. Come, please. Come closer." He put his hand on her neck, stroking her pulse. "You're alive. You're here."

"Yes, I'm here." She stared down at his sculpted features, at the hint of stubble coloring his cheeks. He was so beautiful even half asleep, drugged out on meds.

"Ohhhh," he said, taking a deep breath. "I'm so glad. I love the smell of you. Tonight... Petra...I was so scared. I didn't want to lose you."

She hunched beside the bed, stroking the worried lines from his face. "I didn't want to lose you either. I didn't want to lose my wonderful partner."

His expression softened. "Wonderful. You think I'm wonderful?"

"I know you are."

He gazed at her, his black eyes narrowing into sharper focus. If she had to guess, she'd say he was finally emerging from his sedative haze. "I had this dream," he said tentatively. "It was a terrible dream."

"Was it about Paulsen, and a gun, and glass all over your loft?"

"Yes," he breathed warily, looking around the hospital room.

She reached to touch his lips. "It wasn't a dream. I'm sorry."

"But you're okay?"

She nodded, her throat too tight to speak. Now that he was awake, now that he was fully there, she could have died from the concern in his eyes.

"You saved me," he said after a long moment. "You saved my life. You beat him off with my cane."

"Yes. Thank God you told me about it." She traced the line of his jaw, lingering over a little mole by his chin. "Paulsen died, Ruby. He fell out your window."

"I know." He swallowed hard. "I pushed him, right? But I had to."

"That's what the police said, that it was self defense. They came and took my report while you were under sedation. Liam was here, and Mem."

"Under what?" he asked, wrinkling his brow.

"Under sedation. They made you sleep while you had surgery to stitch up your cuts. Are you comfortable? Do you hurt?"

"As long as you're here, I don't hurt too bad."

She closed her eyes and pressed her cheek to his. She felt the same way. It would be a while before she got over the events of the past night, but his nearness gave her comfort. For a long time she bent near him, touching his hair, breathing in his familiar scent. "I can't lean down anymore," she finally sighed, straightening. "My back."

"Then come in bed with me."

"I don't know if the hospital allows that," she said, eyeing the narrow mattress. "And you're hurt."

He made a dismissive sound and inched over. "You weigh what? A hundred pounds? There's room for you."

She climbed up next to him, being careful not to jostle the stitches on his injured side. It had been a long time since she lay beside him in bed. Too long. From the expression on his face he was thinking the same thing.

"Hey, you know what?" she said. "Ashleigh had her baby. It's a beautiful little girl. They named her Alanna."

"Alanna," he repeated thickly. "That's pretty." He gave her a sideways glance. "I feel tired. Am I talking funny?"

"You always talk funny, but I love you anyway."

He used the tip of a finger to lift her face, and traced her lower lip. "I love you too, Petra. So much." He shook his head. "No, I mean, I don't love you. I mean, I love you only as professionals. As friends. Whatever you want, to make you happy."

She pressed her forehead to his. "It would make me happy for us to be together. To be in love, really in love. The thing is, I love you like crazy, in every possible way, so I don't think we can stick to the professional thing anymore."

He stared at her, the tiny worry lines returning to his brow. "Is this real? Or a dream?"

She giggled through the emotion choking her voice. "It's real, I promise. I...I've done a lot of thinking in the last twenty-four hours. About you, about Paulsen and my father." She took Ruby's hand and held it in her lap. "I thought about all of you, and I realized that Paulsen wanted me too much, and my father never wanted me enough, but you always wanted me the perfect amount. You're kind and wonderful and perfect in so many ways."

"I'm not perfect. I'm rough and I'm stupid and my English is not so good—"

"You're perfect," she said, silencing him with a finger. "And I'm in love with you. Not just professional, not just at work. Not just friends. I'm desperately, whole-heartedly in love with you and I hope you can forgive me for being confused for so long."

"You love me?" he asked, like his English decoding skills might be failing him.

"I love you," she repeated. "I love you a billion times."

"A billion times." He grinned, drawing the "billion" out into three long syllables. "Then I forgive you, yes. And I didn't mean what I said earlier about not loving you."

"I know."

He sighed and laced his fingers into her hair. He kissed her, tenderly at first, then with a deeper passion, the release of all his previous restraint. She wanted the passion, all of it. She wanted him to be himself, no matter how rough and perverted he was, because she loved his kindness and warmth, and his staunchly protective nature.

"Don't fall," he said in the middle of his kiss, wrapping a bandaged arm around her. "Is a little bed."

She wouldn't fall, not with him looking after her. Petra thought she loved his protective nature most of all.

Chapter Twenty:
Perfect

Liam and Mem helped move Ruby's things into Petra's apartment, and his furniture into storage. His loft wasn't exactly habitable. He'd fix it up and sell it eventually, because he couldn't live there anymore. He'd really liked his concrete loft, but he couldn't bear to live near that window. For weeks afterward he couldn't be near any windows.

But Petra's place was okay. She was there with him, so even up off the ground a few stories, he felt safe. He loved spending his days with her, sleeping, eating, going to the theater, making love and playing BDSM games, and kissing her whenever and wherever he wanted. There was no hiding anymore. All through the summer tour and into the autumn season, they flirted openly during rehearsals and held hands in the halls. They made out in their dressing rooms, kissed during curtain calls, and fucked sometimes after performances, aroused by the synergy of their partnership. The tabloids ran stories on their romance for a few months and then lost interest and moved on.

But Rubio never lost interest. He waited for boredom, for the itch to sleep with other women, but it never came. He understood now about Liam and Ashleigh, the way love had changed them, because he felt very changed. All his life he'd slept around, jumping from bed to bed, looking at women as temporary and disposable. That old life seemed empty and depressing now. He was much happier with Petra.

She was so different now too, so much softer and relaxed now that Paulsen wasn't stalking her. She'd also let go of her issues with her dad. "All the bad men out of my life," she'd said. "Out of my life for good." Yves promised to bar Grigolyuk from the backstage areas if not the theater audience, and he held firm on that. Perhaps someday Petra and her father would negotiate a peace, but Ruby wasn't holding his breath. He tried hard to fill that hole where her father should have been, with love and fun times, and understanding.

Because *Jesus Cristo*, he loved filling Petra's holes.

"Come on," he said, leading her down the steps to Liam's play room. They had an open invitation to come over and use it, especially since the Wilders were so busy with little Alanna, who at eight months was learning how to crawl. Rubio was sure Ash and Liam would get back into it eventually, but for now the play room was all theirs. He stripped Petra by the door, running his hands over her lithe body. He held up her silver collar with the dangling pet tag and fastened it around her neck. "Ah, *safada*," he crooned. "My naughty girl. I'm going to hurt you today."

"Today?" she said, pressing against him. "You hurt me every time."

"Because you like it," he said with a smile. He led her over to the horse by the far wall, the one they'd played on at the first party, when she showed up in the long black wig. "Stand there." He pointed to a spot beside it and then bent to adjust a bar near the bottom. "I'm raising it up a bit so your feet can't touch the floor. That first night..." He made a face. "I was too soft on you."

"That was too soft? I was freaking out the entire time."

"Because you were a scaredy vanilla girl. I was super nice to you, you know," he said, nodding.

"I do know. We play a lot harder now. So, when did you realize I was a vanilla newbie?" she asked. "Halfway through the scene?"

He scoffed as he moved to adjust the horse on the other side. "I knew from the start." He gave a wild laugh, remembering. "You were shaking all over. Everything. Your lips, your body, your voice. I could see you were scared to death and it turned me on so much, that you went through with it anyway." He straightened and turned to her. "Why did you do it? Why didn't you stop me?"

"I did stop you at the end. It got to be too much."

"How, too much? Too much turned on?" His voice dropped lower. "You were going to come, weren't you?"

She crossed her arms over her chest and looked embarrassed. Well, let her be embarrassed. She looked even prettier when a blush heightened the color of her cheeks. "No, no," he scolded. "Put your arms down." He moved to her, uncrossing them and pinning them at her side. "Don't cover yourself. Let me look at you, beautiful girl."

He stroked her breasts and pinched and flicked her nipples until they stood at attention. "Let's do everything the same from that night," he said, gazing into her eyes. "Let's see if you remember."

"I had clothes on that night. A bra and panties."

"Everything the same but that," he said, leading her over to the horse. "Up with you."

She straddled the narrow padded top, balancing all her weight on the vee between her legs. She eased her pelvis back, trying to take some of the pressure off her pussy. "I could touch the floor that night too," she pointed out.

"Hush." He took her arm and tilted her forward, purposely drawing her off balance. She clenched her legs and moaned as her clit contacted the horse. "You like that?" he asked. "Does it hurt your pussy?"

"It's—it's uncomfortable. A little."

"You want me to let you sit back again?"

"Yes, please."

"Okay. For now, only." He went for some cuffs and fixed them on Petra's wrists. This time, instead of raising her arms over her head, he cuffed them at the small of her back. He could see by her eyes she was already halfway down into sub space. Having your pussy mashed against an unforgiving surface and your hands cuffed probably had that effect.

He went for some rope and wound it through the cuffs and up through the carabiner. She gave a small sound of protest as he tightened the slack. With her arms raised behind her, she was forced forward by the pressure on her shoulders.

"You said you'd let me sit back," she said forlornly.

"I did, for a minute or two." He pinched her nipples, tugging both of them in a firm grip. "You be a good girl and do whatever I want. I'm in charge here. Yes?"

"Yes," she said, squirming in the bondage.

"Yes, what?"

"Yes, Sir."

He smiled and walked around her, tracing his fingers down the arching curve of her back. "Is better like this. Easier for me to get at your ass." She made a whining sound that had him heading straight for his trunk of sex toys. He pulled out a thick glass plug and plenty of lube. She eyed him as he approached.

"I know for a fact you didn't use that the first night."

"Okay." He changed direction, returned to his trunk. "It's a gag for you. Too much complaining."

"No, please. I'll be good." Petra hated the gag. She said it was because she wanted to be able to talk to him and kiss him, but in reality he thought she hated to drool. He'd work on it with her, showing her all the sexy things about it, but today, he relented and returned to her side.

"No more chances, okay? One more protest, one more complaint, and the gag goes on. You understand?"

"Yes, Sir."

He lubed up the plug and spread her cheeks. It would be amusing, making her take the thick glass toy now that she wasn't allowed to complain about anything. He teased her first, pushing the tip in and out, whispering dirty, sexy things. When he pressed it deeper, she mashed her lips shut in the effort not to make a sound. Her body strained and she trembled, making stifled noises. So, so sexy. He clamped a hand over her mouth as the noises rose to a hum. When it was in, she sagged in relief.

"Good girl," he said, giving her a well-earned kiss. "Very quiet. How does that feel, having that big plug in your ass?"

She wiggled against the horse. "Your cock feels better."

Ha, the vixen. She wasn't getting his cock yet, not until her pretty ass was marked up a bit. He went for the same crop they'd used, and held it up before her eyes. "You remember this?"

"Yes, Sir."

He flicked her nipples with it. The poor thing was still trying not to cry out. "You can show me how much it hurts," he said. "I like that part. But no more whining not to have this, not to have that. Okay?"

"Yes, Sir. *Oww.*"

He brought the whippy part of the crop down on her left ass cheek. She jerked and then gasped as her pussy ground into the top of the horse. He'd barely tapped her the first time they played. Now he challenged her more, leaving red marks with every sharp strike. Her cries of pain filled his cock to bursting with pleasure. "Oh, the poor ass," he murmured. "The poor pussy. It hurts?"

"Yes, Sir." She drew in a deep breath. "But I'm not complaining."

He stopped to squeeze and fondle her breasts. "No, you're being a good girl, aren't you? Hmm..." He went back to his trunk for a pair of clover clamps. Honestly, he hadn't planned to torment her so much; it was just so arousing to see the changes in her. She was nothing at all like the uptight, shrinking girl he'd played with that first night. When he returned with the clamps her eyes went wide. She swallowed back any complaining words.

"I know, I know," he soothed, tugging on the first nipple. "I know we didn't use these either. What can I say? You're so beautiful when you're in pain." He closed the clamp, drinking in her rasping groan. "And then you come anyway, because deep inside, you love it." He attached the other clamp, jerking his cock as she shimmied around on the horse. He could see the slickness between her thighs, see the shine of it on the vinyl.

He went around the front of her and pulled her head back for a kiss. She was limp and loose, deliciously surrendered. "If you like it, show me," he said. "Arch your ass back. Offer it for the crop. I'll spank your ass until it's nice and red and then..." He walked back around behind her, admiring the way she'd obediently stuck her ass out. He pressed the plug a little deeper. "And then I'll ride you. Right here."

"Oh..." she said, twisting her hips. "Mmm."

She might as well be gagged, since all she could seem to manage were incoherent noises. But that was okay. He picked up the crop and started to whip her. Ass, hips, outer thighs. That first night, he'd cropped her inside her thighs, right beside her pussy, but he couldn't do it now, not in this position. He contented himself with cropping her ass a hot, uniform red. "You remember the safeword?" he asked when her tossing and turning grew more frantic.

She never safeworded. It was partly her stubbornness and partly that he knew how much she could take. Her cries rose in volume until he judged that she was finished, and then he gave her just a little more.

That "just a little more" was always the best part. When he tossed aside the crop she slumped forward, her legs tense and shaking, her back rising and falling with each breath. He noticed with pleasure that she still had her ass offered out, exactly as ordered. He eased out the plug and set it aside, and straddled the horse behind her, pumping his cock. When she rose to turn to him he pushed her forward again. "No, no. Be good."

Unlike her, his feet reached the ground just fine. He braced his legs and eased his cock into her asshole, one thrilling inch at a time. Her whole body was tense, struggling against the pain of her sore cheeks, and the clamps, and the pressure of the horse between her legs. He wouldn't make her endure it all much longer. Once he started fucking her, once he started tugging that chain between her breasts and driving her moans to screams, both of them would shudder into orgasm.

He grabbed her hips and pulled her back on his cock, forcing her to take every inch in her tight, tense hole. There was just enough lube from the plug to ease the way. Neither of them liked too much slickness—it had to hurt a little for Petra to get off. As for him, every second he spent in her ass was a fucking dream.

"Oh, baby," he sighed, bucking into her. "I love your asshole. It's so hot and tight. We didn't do this either, the first night, did we?"

"No, Sir," she moaned.

"But you wanted to. I bet you wanted this, you naughty slut. You wanted my fat cock in your ass?" He reached up and untied the knot from the carabiner, never stopping the jerking motion of his hips. When he released her arms he pulled her closer, pressing her down against the narrow horse. He could never get close enough to her. He always had to let her out of bondage at the end so he could grind on her, body to body, and squeeze her in his arms.

She yelped as he tugged on the chain between her breasts. He held it in one hand and slapped her thigh with the other. "You like that, huh? Or maybe not. You let me hurt you because I like it? Because you want to please me?"

"Yes, Sir," she said in a breathless, earnest voice. "Yes, Sir. I want to please you. Please..."

"Please what?"

"I'm going to come soon. Please, can I come?"

"I don't know. I want to fuck your ass a little longer. Maybe twenty minutes. An hour."

He laughed at her whimper. They both knew he'd never last that long. Not in one sustained bout, anyway. He took off the clamps one by one, driving deep inside her to the music of each tormented wail. Then he grasped her thighs and pressed his palm right over her clit. He held her close, squeezing her sore breasts. He wanted to be completely inside her, at one with her sensuality and beauty. She made him a new, better man and he'd love her forever for it.

He'd keep her forever...

"Come now," he whispered. "Come with me deep inside you."

She bucked back on his cock a few times, riding his hand, and then she went off. He could feel her orgasm, feel the squeeze and rhythm of her ecstasy. It set off his own pulsing climax, heightened by the feel of her in his arms.

"Holy fuck." He held her, wanting to stay buried inside her as long as possible. He breathed in her scent and basked in her closeness. When his fingers were able to work again, he unfastened her cuffs and rubbed her wrists. "Okay, good girl?"

She made some weak, fucked-out mewl that sounded pretty okay. He pulled out carefully, giving her ass one final pat. Then he lifted her, supporting her legs, and eased her up off the unforgiving horse. When he tried to set her down, she wobbled, so he picked her up again and carried her to a nearby bench.

Petra snuggled against his chest, drifting on the smell of him and the strength surrounding her. "That was nothing at all like the first time," she whispered against his neck.

He chuckled and held her closer. "It was better, no? At least this time you came."

Petra laughed with him, marveling at the way she used to be. She'd been so afraid, so closed off. So worried about her precious career, but ironically, she danced better now that she allowed herself to live and love on her own terms. She sat up and gazed into Rubio's eyes.

"I was lost back then." She smiled and tugged the tag on her collar. "Now I'm found."

"*Rubio's Pet.*" He nuzzled his cheek against her. When he drew back, he looked sober, almost sad. "I want to ask you something, but I don't want you to say no."

She sighed. "If it's about the peeing thing, I gave you my final answer. Not even in the shower."

"No, no." He covered her lips. "It's something else. Something important."

He was making her nervous. She traced over a small, light scar on his arm, one of many on his body that reminded her just how much he loved her. "Ask me. I'll try not to say no."

"You know, we've been together over a year now. I mean, over a year since we first met, and we've been through a lot together. We've had a lot of ups and downs. And you put up with all kinds of stuff from me and I think you love me."

"Of course I love you, you big pile of silliness."

"Not being silly," he said, easing her up. "I'm not being silly now. I want to ask you...if maybe...if...you know..."

"Please, just spit it out."

He rubbed a hand over his face. "I want to know if I got a ring and gave it to you, and asked you to marry me, would you say yes?" His face softened, a pleading note in his gaze. "I wanted to ask first, before I did it."

Petra stared at him. "So this is like...a pre-proposal? Are you asking me if you can ask me to marry you?"

"Sometimes I don't understand your English. But I think so. Yes. I want to ask you to marry me but I don't want you to say no. So if the answer is no, I won't ask."

Petra hid a smile behind her hand. He looked so serious. Was he really afraid she'd say no? But then, she'd fought the idea of love and relationships for so long. He must have taken her pause as indecision, because he launched into a persuasive spiel.

"We already live together, you know? And it's good. You make me happy, always. Even when we fight, an hour later I want to love you again because of your smile, and how you make me feel. And if you don't want to make babies, is okay. I don't care as long as I have you."

Now she was the one silencing him with a finger to his lips. "You don't have to talk me into it. The answer is yes. It's absolutely yes."

"Yes?" His expression brightened. "Yes, you'll marry me?"

"Of course I will. I feel like we're already married in our hearts." She pressed her palm against his chest. "Although, in my opinion, this is a really shoddy proposal."

"Is not the real one," he protested. "Just feeling things out."

"I see. Well, for the real one I think you should get some flowers, and romantic music, and maybe a ring."

He gave her a lopsided grin. "I was going to ask when I was fucking your ass over there."

Petra burst out laughing. "That would have been worse. But, maybe, oddly appropriate." Her laughter died away as she reached to caress his stubble-roughened cheek. "And when it comes to babies, we'll see what happens. Maybe we can have a little girl like Ash and Liam, and we'll call her Fernandina, and she'll look exactly like you."

"Oh, no," he muttered. "Perhaps some other name."

"And she'll be a great ballerina. Or not. Maybe we'll have a little boy. Maybe we can have both."

"I think you would make pretty babies," he said, toying with a lock of her hair. "Someday, if you want. No pressure. But how do you think they would look? I'm so dark, you're so light. Maybe our babies will be medium."

Petra had never wanted babies. That was never her dream until she thought about having a baby with Rubio, and then her feelings changed. He would make such a great dad, such a loving and sensitive parent. He loved Alanna and the baby adored Rubio, batting and squealing at him whenever he bounced her on his lap. Maybe they'd end up having "medium" kids, and maybe not, but she understood now that either way, there was a lot more to life than the spring and fall seasons and the summer tour. There was a lot more to life than class and technique and rehearsals.

She shifted on her sore bottom and looked into the eyes of the man she loved, the man who loved her the perfect amount. "Are you sure you want my babies?" she asked. "I've been told I have a tragically big forehead."

"Aw, Petra," he said, blushing pink beneath his bronze skin. "Your forehead is perfect. Really, I don't know who told you such a thing. Your forehead is the most beautiful forehead in the world."

Epilogue:
Twelve Years Later

Waiting parents lined the walls of the East London dance studio, their smiles reflected in the facing mirrors. If any of them noted the two ballet legends in their midst, they didn't make a fuss about it. Petra had been retired five years now, though Rubio still danced with City Ballet on occasion. Both of them taught workshops and acted as consultants at various ballet companies.

But not this one. This little company was ruled by Madame Doubrovska, an eccentric old lady who lived and breathed ballet, even in her mid-seventies. "Chins up, children," she chirped to the group of preschoolers as they took their places in front of the guests. They were mostly pink-tighted girls, but also a few boys in white shirts and navy tights, one of whom had jet black hair and shining dark eyes like his daddy.

Petra glowed with a mother's pride. It was Federico's first recital, a small affair held right in the dance studio. Ruby took her hand and squeezed it. "Look at him," he whispered. "Such turnout at four."

She shushed him, squeezing his hand back. Looking at her son, she had to agree. They hadn't pushed Federico toward dance, but he'd seen daddy dance enough times to want to emulate him. The children demonstrated simple ballet steps to the applause of their parents. Their awkward *pliés* and wobbly arabesques were touching. Petra remembered her early classes, when dance was all about her teacher's approving smiles and her soft, pink ballet shoes sliding across the floor.

The children did some gymnastics next, tumbles and cartwheels on multicolored mats. Petra didn't think she was being biased—Federico was strong and coordinated, and more graceful than the other kids. Dread battled with pride. Ballet was a hard life, although they'd enjoyed it. She looked over at her husband and saw the same conflict in his speculative smile.

When the gymnastics exhibition was done, they pushed the mats to the side and the teacher called smaller groups of children to dance short pieces. Five little girls hopped and swayed to an upbeat song, and then a young boy and girl performed a short balletic version of a nursery rhyme.

Then Federico came forward with two young ladies. He took his place between them and did a pose so Rubio-esque in quality that Petra gasped. As they began to move to the classical music, it became apparent that Federico was fonder of one of the girls than the other. When he focused his attention on her, the other girl protested that he wasn't doing the right steps. Madame Doubrovska tried to get them back on track, but by that point Federico had struck out on his own, moving boldly to the music.

"He's a rebel," Ruby whispered in her ear.

"He's a diva," she whispered back. "I wonder where he gets that."

She watched, fascinated, as her son swayed to the music, making dramatic gestures. He was aping his daddy, certainly, but he was feeling it inside too.

Oh God, they had another Rubio on their hands.

The music concluded with the dancers in three completely different parts of the room. Madame Doubrovska herded them together for a very pretty *reverence* to the laughter of the spectators. "Make nice bow, make nice curtsy," she said, clucking over the three of them like they'd done it exactly as she planned. Federico played to the crowd, bowing so low he almost fell over onto his knobby knees.

Later, when the program concluded, he came running over to them. He seemed energized by the applause, by performing in front of the intimate group. Rubio swept him into his arms. "You did very well," he said. "*Muito bem, rapazinho.*"

Petra stood on her tiptoes to kiss him on the cheek. "Mommy and Daddy are so proud."

"Did you see me dancing?" he asked. "Out there?"

He pointed to the studio floor, now crowded with families taking photos and hugging their tiny performers. In the middle, the snubbed little girl gave Federico the evil eye.

"I did see you," said Rubio, lowering his son back to the floor. "Did you follow the steps your teacher told you?"

"Kind of," he said, with a copy of his father's smile.

"I think you made your friend sad." Petra pointed to the pouting girl.

"I don't like her. I didn't want to dance with her."

Petra gave Ruby a speaking look. "Sometimes that happens. But you should still be nice."

"Yes, Rico," said Ruby with a sigh. "You have to be sweet to the girls. Go, tell her you're sorry." He led his son over to his classmate. Petra watched Federico murmur an apology and suppressed a giggle when the little girl scowled at him, twisting a white-blonde curl.

"Where have I seen that look before?" Rubio said to Petra under his breath.

She took his hand and gazed at him, taken back to a time they faced one another across a rehearsal studio, determined not to like each other. He was older now, his hair peppered with a smattering of gray, and the smile lines more prominent around his eyes. But he was as beautiful as ever, especially as a husband and a father.

And a dancer. He'd always be her partner, her other half in the ballet history books. Hewitt and Rubio were legendary, and perhaps Federico would be legendary too. It was early to tell. For now, he took his parents' hands and skipped between them down the corridor, occasionally leaping with joyful abandon into the air.

A Final Note

I hope you enjoyed this second book in my BDSM Ballet series. Rubio played a supporting role in the first book, *Waking Kiss*, as Liam and Ashleigh fell in love, and I knew early on he'd need his own story. It was tough finding a heroine who could stand up to such a strong character, but fortunately I found Petra. I began with the slap in rehearsal and followed through from there, and I loved how things worked out for them. Perhaps I'll write Federico's story one day.

Many thanks to my Brazilian friend Maryara for inspiring the character of Rubio and helping me with the Portuguese phrases in this book, and in *Waking Kiss*. Team Rubio forever!

Thanks also to my wonderfully supportive betas and editors: Audrey, Lina Sacher, Linzy Antoinette, Doris, and J. Luna Scuro. I appreciate all of you more than words can say.

Coming in 2014

Annabel's short story "The Neckcloth" will be included in the anthology *Best Bondage Erotica 2014*, edited by Rachel Kramer Bussel. Available NOW for preorder at Amazon.com!

Sign up for Annabel's Naughty Newsletter at annabeljoseph.com to learn more about upcoming releases and promotions.

About the Author

Annabel Joseph is a multi-published BDSM romance author. She writes mainly contemporary romance, although she has been known to dabble in the medieval and Regency eras. She is known for writing emotionally intense BDSM storylines, and strives to create characters that seem real--even flawed--so readers are better able to relate to them. Annabel also writes vanilla (non-BDSM) erotic romance under the pen name Molly Joseph.

Annabel loves to hear from her readers at annabeljosephnovels@gmail.com.